BLACK WATER CROSSING

A Novel

PETER H. LESTER

For the Next Generation,
Harper, Hudson, and Fox.
Like us, our ancestors were far from perfect.
But from time to time,
they did insert themselves into our history.

TABLE OF CONTENTS

List of Maps and Illustrations

INTRODUCTION

During the War of 1812, the Creek Nation had been divided. A faction, known as the Red Sticks, had opposed the United States, and allied themselves with Britain. At the same time, a separate group, the White Sticks, had sided with the fledgling country in the conflict. For their assistance, the United States government had promised compensation for losses of personal property and livestock – some of which had been inflicted by the Red Sticks on their Creek brothers.

It was out of this conflict and the Red Stick uprising that animosity toward the Creek Indians was fostered along the frontier, including the area that would become Covington, Georgia. These hostilities were foretold earlier in the year when a large meteor shower appeared which the Indians interpreted as a bad omen.

In 1813, Creeks under the leadership of Chief Red Eagle attacked Fort Mims in Tensaw, Alabama, in retaliation for the continued encroachment of white settlers on the Creek Nation. In response to this hostility, General Andrew Jackson recruited a militia and defeated the Creek at Talladega.

In 1817, James Monroe sent David Mitchell, a former governor of Georgia, to the Lower Creek Nation to act as Federal Agent to the Creek. During this time, Andrew Jackson pursued the Red Sticks into Florida, where they had sought refuge among the Seminole.

Much of what David Mitchell did while Federal Agent undermined the Creek Nation, and fostered animosity not only with settlers, but also within the Creek (Muscogee) and the Cherokee Nations.

In 1819, The United States acquired Florida, where many of the Creek Indians were seeking refuge. The territory was acquired from Spain via the John Quincy Adams Onis Treaty.

The story that follows is largely fictional. If you would like to understand more about what portions are true and what portions are fictional, I would direct you to the section in this book titled "Epilogue and Historical Notes."

This story, involving my great, great, great grandfather begins a decade later, in 1828.

STATE of GEORGIA - 1828

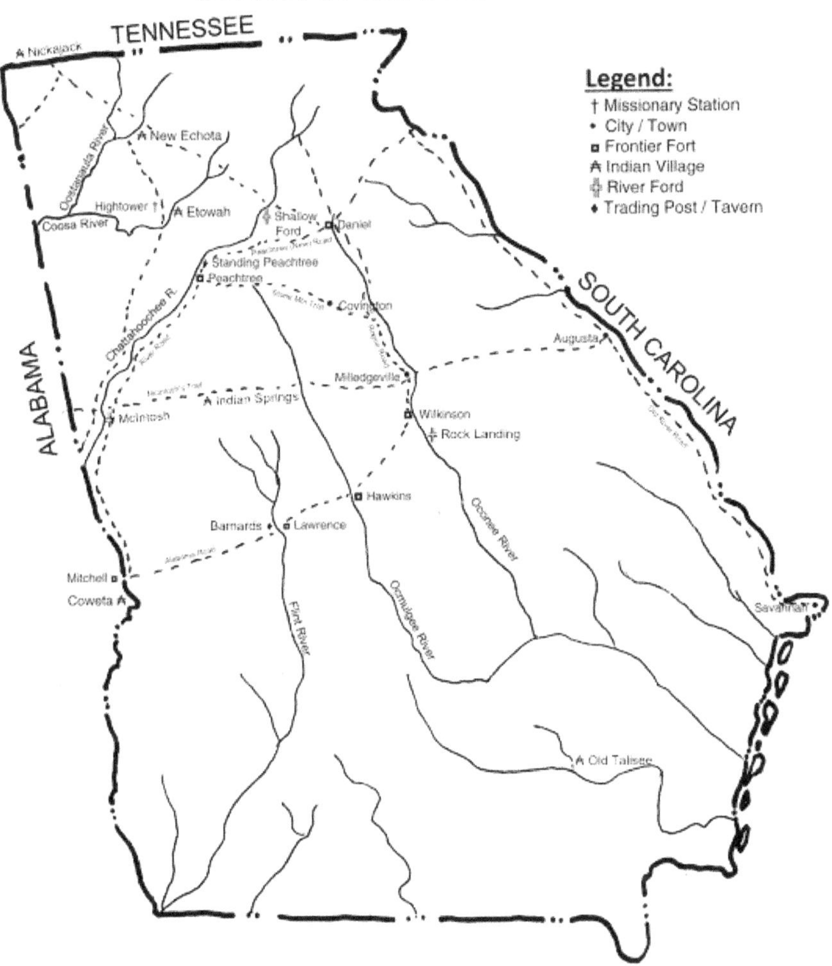

Map of Georgia – 1828

PART I

Covington, Georgia - 1828

The children had always been warned that they were not alone. When they played in the dense woods, cool streams and cultivated fields near the homestead, the first rule was "to have fun." The second was to "stay together." And the third was to "assume that others are always watching."

Richard Lester and his wife, Mary, had never told their children to be careful. They had agreed early in their marriage when they became parents that they did not want their children to live in fear of the woods or the people they shared them with. As a result, both sons and their daughter had a robust sense of adventure.

This day was slightly different than most. Their father had risen before dawn to make the journey to town, or what they considered town. The night before, their father had left instructions for the boys to repair the fence… Finally…before doing anything else. Like most young boys, the lads were easily distracted, and this task had gone ignored for several days.

The fence mending was in addition to their normal chores. Alice, the youngest of the three, would need to gather eggs from the hens and pull water for the day from the well. Because of her youth and the accompanying lack of strength and size, she would use the smaller of the two water buckets. As a result, the task of drawing water from the well, while simple, would take time. For her mother, this was good as it would occupy her daughter and keep her from being under foot.

Alice would also, most likely, be called to help her mother with cooking and cleaning as the day progressed. There was always butter to churn, herbs to pick, or, at the very least prune, and food stuffs to be stored. The boys, Paul and James, would need to feed the cows, goats, pigs, and the remaining workhorse, Danny. The family mule was largely left to forage for itself. Additionally, the cows would need to be milked. Once these daily chores were completed, all three children would spend some time working together planting beans under the sprigs of emerging corn.

Their father had taken the swifter, younger, and at times, ill-tempered horse, Banner. Mary referred to the horse as "a bit frisky," but then, Banner had only thrown the men of the household. Among the Lesters, Banner was widely regarded as a "lady's horse." He just seemed to know when a woman held his reins. Banner was at least three years old. By people who knew something about horses, Banner was considered "a prize." He was chestnut with a black mane and tail. Banner had a small white star in the middle of his long forehead. Because of his size, the previous owners had trained him as a jumper. For this reason, the horse was excellent at hunting. Richard had hopes of breeding him soon, but the family did not have a broodmare to pair him with. The horse had come to the family through a large estate that Richard had helped settle almost a year earlier.

Mary always dreaded the days when Richard was away. For most of their marriage this was a rare event, but recently, it seemed to be happening more often. When Richard was at home, nothing out of the ordinary seemed to take place. Bad things only happened when he was away. There were always sibling altercations, but nothing caught fire and no animal escaped an enclosure when Richard was home. When he was away, it was a sure harbinger that something eventful would take place.

Without their father around for guidance, the boys always seemed to get into mischief, and the excitement was too much for Alice to ignore. The children would disappear into the woods and come back with some tale, artifact, or worse still an animal or reptile that would require a conversation about keeping it. And, if it was a snake, salamander, turtle, or frog, all three would be covered with mud.

The boys had plans, and they did not include their sister. They rushed through feeding the pigs and goats. They milked the two cows and turned them out into the pasture. Danny, being old and tired from the previous days of ploughing, was easy enough… hay, water, the feed (a mixture of oats, corn, and molasses) could wait till later in the day. They rushed through the cornfield, and by then Alice, who was seven, had joined them.

The routine here was well-known by all the children. At this point, the corn was just over a foot tall. They were to poke three holes in the ground with their fingers near the base of each corn stalk and place a bean seed in each hole. The beans, when they emerged, would latch on to the corn.

In another week, they would be doing the same thing, but planting squash. The squash would act as ground cover and control the weeds. It was also the case that the deer and rabbits did not like the fast-growing squash, so this acted as a deterrent to them as well.

Paul appointed himself foreman, and being the oldest, there was only slight objection. Paul, having longer, stronger fingers, would poke the holes, James would place the seeds in the holes, and Alice would cover the seeds and pat down the soil.

With surprising speed and efficiency, the bean seeds were planted. It was late morning when the three headed to the house for a quick lunch of jam on bread, cheese, and apples.

Their mother was already working on dinner, which would include a pie for her husband.

It was unfortunate, but there were no additional chores for young Alice. If her brothers did not include her in their afternoon activities, Mary was certain she would get less done. After a quiet conference between the two boys, it was decided that their sister could join them.

"What are you two up to?" their mother asked.

"A few days ago, as dad finished ploughing the last few rows of corn, we noticed a hawk on the edge of the field. And he comes back every day. We are thinking we might be able to catch it with the mouse we caught in the barn yesterday," replied James.

"How do you plan to do that?"

"We are going to use some twine and tie the mouse to a stake. We are thinkin' the hawk will see the mouse and swoop in," continued James.

"We are going to use an old burlap feed sack to catch it," added Paul.

After a long stare and silence, Mary replied, "Well, water those new beans you just planted." She looked at the anxious boys. They were obviously thinking that their mother might call off their attempt to capture the hawk. "Your chores are all done?"

The children nodded.

"All right then, off you go." As they rose and headed out the door, Mary raised her voice slightly "And Richard Paul – watch your hands, that hawk is going to have claws like nothing you three know."

The use of his full name, "Richard Paul" was not lost in the ears of the oldest son nor the other two children. Paul knew they had all been warned.

The job of watering the beans they planted was done quickly, and well, despite the fact that the three children were ready to move on to their afternoon adventure.

Once the watering was completed, the three ran to the barn, grabbed twine, the small wooden cage built from twigs with the mouse, and a burlap sack that still smelled of sweet feed.

As they exited, Paul stopped for a moment. "Wait. We need something else." He went back into the barn and pulled several rags from a basket in the tack room.

The children walked across the newly ploughed field careful not to step on the emerging seedlings. There was a portion of the field that had yet to be planted. The boys discussed whether their father would plant cotton this year and could not agree. One of the tinkers in town had a new cotton gin, and at this point, it was only a matter of time until the Lesters turned at least a portion of their property over to the cash crop. It had taken every member of the family the entire fall and most of the winter to clear this new field of trees and grasses for the expanded field. As they crossed the field, the smell of freshly plowed earth was strong.

At the farthest edge of the field, after a short discussion, they selected a place they thought would be acceptable to the hawk, while also offering them cover from the trees and a hiding place from which they could spring to catch the unsuspecting raptor.

They placed the small wooden cage on the ground. It was at this point Alice realized what was in store for the mouse.

"Wait! Isn't there a way to do this without the mouse?" She asked.

"Oh. What do you suppose that hawk is going to fly down here for? A rock?" replied James.

"Well, you know, James, I am thinking we could tie this twine to Alice and stake her to the ground instead. That Hawk might like her!" added Paul.

After a quiet glare from Alice, the boys continued. They removed the mouse, being surprisingly gentle for handling something that was hawk-bait.

It was the tying of the twine that took the most time, as the mouse objected to the entire proceeding.

Finally, after a suitable stick was found in the woods, the three children drove the stick into the ground about three paces from the edge of the forest. They then took their burlap and rags and retreated into the brush near the edge of the field.

It was at this point that "the plan" seemed to unravel. Alice again objected to the mouse's fate. James and Paul both took turns quelling her concerns. Just as those concerns seemed to be abated, Alice decided she wanted to go home to be with her mother.

"James, you take her back. With all this noise and moving around, we are basically catching our own shadow, and that isn't even happening. This is worthless. Walk her back to mom."

"Why do I have to walk her back?" asked James.

"Because this whole thing was my idea" replied Paul, "and besides, I already have the rags wrapped around my hands and arms. And I know you don't want that ol' hawk taking your thumb off. Just do it."

Reluctantly, James headed off with Alice back across the field.

As Richard watched his two siblings head across the field, he fidgeted with the rags and wrapped them more tightly, as best he could, around his forearms and hands. He thought, "I really need James, this is not going to work." He did the best he could to wrap his arms so that they would be somewhat protected and then turned his attention to the mouse staked just a few paces from where he hid.

The mouse continued to move around, limited by the length of the twine. At times, the mouse would muzzle the twine, and Paul was often tempted to check the knot to make sure it was holding, but he refrained. He remained hidden by the low thicket of weeds and shrubs that had been encouraged to grow by the newfound sun where the field met the forest edge.

Moments later he could see James' head bobbing in the distance as he popped up over the horizon and into the opposite edge of the field. Paul was somewhat relieved to see that Alice was not in tow. He loved his sister, but there were times when she was both a distraction and unhelpful. This was one such time.

At that moment, from the opposite side of the field, he saw the hawk flying low to the ground., flapping briefly, then gliding with no effort to the edge of the field closest to Paul. As the hawk neared, Paul thought he heard the wind rushing through the brown and bronze feathers as the hawk sat back in mid-flight stretching its talons towards the mouse. The bird was beautiful.

As the red tail hawk hit the mouse, there was a squeak, and at that same moment, Paul leapt from the brush with the burlap.

The hawk, seeing Paul, sprang to leap back into the air, dropped the remains of the mouse, but was ensnared by the twine. The hawk crashed back to the freshly ploughed dirt.

All at once, there was a furious struggle of feathers, rag-covered hands, burlap, dust, and what was left of the mouse.

In this moment Paul was filled with fear, excitement, and confusion. He wanted the hawk. At the same time, he did not want to get hurt or injure the bird.

There was a flurry of confusion as Paul sought control of the hawk, and the hawk fought for its freedom. As the struggle continued, the hawk's talons became even more entangled in the twine. Realizing this, Paul gained confidence that the bird was not going to escape. He stood up and stepped back for a moment. While the bird flapped furiously, Paul took the burlap in both hands and waited for his moment. Finally, the hawk landed, both claws in the dirt and dust before the boy. Paul swiftly draped the burlap over the bird, securing the burlap using both his hands, knees, and feet.

Slowly, enveloped by the darkness provided by the burlap, the hawk seemed to struggle less – resigned, at least temporarily, to its fate.

As James approached all Paul could hear was "You got him! You got him!"

It was only then that Paul saw and felt the scratches on his hands, arms, and thighs.

"James, I think we may need another bag!"

What?" replied James.

"I am not sure we can get the hawk in this bag. The bag is the only thing keeping him from flying away!"

Just then, from the brush, a man stepped forward from the forest. It was a Creek Indian.

The man knelt beside Paul, and spoke fluently in English, "Let me. I will help."

He reached into a pouch slung around his neck that hung low to his waist and pulled out a rabbit. From the look of the wound, it was recently killed. With a knife the Indian carved off one of the legs.

As the boys watched, the man placed his hands on the burlap bag feeling the contours of the hawk.

The Indian looked at James. "Boy, kneel. Your brother has the bag, I need you to hold the hawk. You see here? This is the hawk's head. I think its beak is here." At that the burlap jerked quickly towards the man's finger. "Yes! It almost had my finger for lunch. That is its beak."

Both boys nodded agreement with wide eyes.

"I need you to place both hands firmly on my hands. They are on the hawk's shoulders. Be firm, but don't hurt him."

James' eyes were wide. "All right." He placed both hands on top of the Indians.

The Indian removed his hands slowly one at a time.

The boys smiled at each other. Paul had control of the burlap. James had control of the hawk.

The Indian peeled back one edge of the burlap revealing the hawk's head. He slowly placed a piece of the mouse in front of the hawk. Initially, the hawk was not interested. The hawk's head moved quickly up, down, right, and left. Its beak open, the boys could see the hawk's tongue and reveled in its sharp gaze.

The Indian moved the leg of rabbit he had offered closer to the large bird. He then covered the hawk's head with the edge of the burlap. The man sat down, and quickly removed the scarf around his neck. Taking a knife from his belt, he cut a small square and folded it into a triangle. Reaching into a bag slung over his shoulder, he removed a piece of curved bone that appeared to be a needle or a fishing hook. Using the bone and a short piece of thread he pulled from his own clothing, he sewed the triangle in several places to form a small hood.

The hawk, while it continued to struggle, also seemed to be, at the very least, calming down. Whether from the darkness or exhaustion from the struggle, there was less movement from under the burlap. At one point James removed one hand from the hawk's shoulder to check on the hawk. The struggle resumed for a moment until James could regain control of the bird.

The Indian smiled and said, "You will have plenty of time to look at him. Be patient."

After a few short minutes the Indian took the sewn triangle in one hand, the rabbit leg in the other and spoke. "Now you can find his head. Slowly."

James used his fingers to peel back the edge of the burlap. First the beak, then the piercing eyes of the hawk were revealed.

"Stop," said the Indian quietly. "Stop," he repeated with a whisper.

With his left hand, he showed the hawk the leg of rabbit, with the other he slowly placed the hood over the hawk's head. It was a slow but steady and purposeful motion.

"Done," he said and sat back.

The hawk had ceased trying to flee. It just cocked it head. Left. Right. Up. Down. It was as though the hawk believed its sight would be returned if it could position its head just so.

The boys looked at the Indian with amazement. Obviously, there was more to catching a hawk than they realized.

The Indian nodded. "You are Richard Lester's sons."

James replied. "Yes."

"I am Paul. This is James."

"Good. I am Joseph McIntosh."

It was only then that the boys took notice. Yes, his skin was dark, his hair was darker than their mother's. He wore a black coat with a red collar, a red and white checkered vest, and a white shirt. He carried a small pouch, a musket, and a short sword accented with a brass handle. The short knife he had used to carve the rabbit's leg had been returned to his belt, carried opposite from the sword. He wore an odd hat with several long feathers that could have easily come from their hawk or a larger bird.

"I would like to speak with your father."

Paul replied, "He is in Covington for the day. He will be back tonight."

"Well, I will return tomorrow or in a few days then." He paused looking at the boys, he then continued. "This hawk, you can train him to hunt. But it will take time for him to trust you. You must earn his trust. Feed him a leg once each day… squirrel, chipmunk, rat, mice… anything. Now, don't feed him too much. You want him to come to depend upon you for food. This will create trust between you and your hawk. You need the bird to trust you if you expect it to hunt for you. It will also eat some of the things your mother may throw away when she cleans a hen for cooking. Make sure it sees you when you feed it. If you want to make it happy, give it a heart every now and then. It will eat all the things you probably prefer not to eat." Joseph paused. Both boys were measuring him. "That hood, it would be better if it were made of leather. And also, when you tie the hawk down, use thin leather straps for that too. This twine will not work. That hawk peck through something like that and be gone. It is better to use leather. Don't forget to give it water too."

He sat for a moment longer. "You can remove the burlap, it is not going anywhere with that hood on its head."

The boys slowly and gently removed the burlap. Sitting back on their heels, they marveled at the bird.

The Indian looked at the boys, "It is young. Not yet one year old. See, it does not have its red tail feathers yet."

The boys nodded agreement, but again, that was more they did not know about hawks.

With that, he stood, smiled, and left as quickly as he had appeared.

By any standard in any era, Mary Lester would have been considered attractive. Although as she entered her thirties, even she had to admit life on the frontier was catching up. She had lost a tooth a year earlier, and when she looked in the mirror – that gap in her smile bothered her. Fortunately, it was not in the front of her mouth, so it was not noticeable to most. But she knew. And, because of this minor defect, she smiled a little less to hide the imperfection. Richard had noticed that her smiles were more infrequent and had tried to assuage the modesty this had instilled. But she remained self-conscious of the imperfection.

Like most of her family, the Sims, she was long limbed, slender, and strong.

Her husband had told everyone after their wedding that he was initially attracted to her by her hair, but when she turned and he saw her eyes for the first time, he was "troubled." He literally could not think of anything else. He had never seen such dark hair and striking eyes.

Truth was, Mary Minor Sims had choices when it came to would-be husbands. There were many young men as well as older men who had called on her. She had borne concerns initially that her father was going to press her to marry one of the older established farmers or merchants in the area. So many women died in childbirth that widowers often remarried quickly. Occasionally it was out of love. More often, it was a marriage of practicality or convenience – the men needed a wife to help raise children and manage the motherless home.

For quite some time, Mary had pleaded with her mother to convince her father to let her court someone closer to her own age. Over time, together, they had worn away at her father's resolve, and the women had prevailed.

It was about this time, in 1815, when Richard Henry Lester came into her life. At the time she was sixteen, and he was seventeen.

The Lester family was relatively new to Covington, Georgia, having moved to the area in 1802, when the fledgling town still had no name. The parents, German and Catherine, had become prominent in the community very quickly. German was a Methodist minister, teacher, and farmer. Catherine was a teacher as well, and the two had started an informal school for the area's children. Catherine had endeared herself to the women as a source of information from the outside world and was respected for being able to control a group of children that was typically known for being particularly uninterested in such things as numbers, letters, and verbs.

By 1814, the Lester family had woven themselves deeply into the lives of the farmers that relied on the small, thriving un-named town as a center of commerce. Mary had met the family's sister, Sarah. They had known each other through mutual friends, but being a few years younger, Mary did not feel particularly close to Sarah.

So, it was a bit of a surprise when Sarah invited the Sims family and Mary to her wedding. It was at this wedding to William Pettus where Mary first met the Lester men. Bryant and Fountain were the oldest of the brothers and they were both already married. Then there was Sarah, followed by Robert, Nancy, Richard, and Barksdale. Initially, as far as Mary was concerned, Richard was not the most notable of the Lester men. It had been Robert who introduced himself and had asked Mary to dance. Richard, at 17, had been the tall but quiet one. At just over six feet tall, he was slightly taller than the other Lesters. "Gangly" was the adjective most used to describe him.

It was late in the afternoon as Sarah was talking with her little brother when the initial introduction was finally made.

The Sims were about to leave, and Mary had wanted to wish Sarah and her new husband well before leaving. After pleasantries were exchanged, it was Sarah who broke the ice. She grabbed Mary's elbow as she turned to leave, looking at her brother she asked, "Richard, before Mary leaves, won't you dance with her just once?"

Later, Richard would recall that he was not sure he had even replied, but somehow, he found himself in the grass dancing with what had to be one of the prettiest women in the state, certainly the prettiest woman within a day's ride of where he stood.

Initially, Mr. Sims had been annoyed as he did not want to chase the setting sun returning to their home. But even he had to admit, there was something about the pairing. He knew Richard was intelligent. He was studying law and apprenticing under a local attorney. More importantly: it was what he was NOT known for.

In small communities on the frontier, everyone talked. And mostly, people talked about the altercations or social slights that had taken place. But, because of the isolation, everyone knew who they could call upon if or when trouble arose. The community could rely on the Lester family. This had been demonstrated time and time again. When there was an altercation between neighbors, the joy of a new birth, or the death of a family member, the Lester family was a wellspring of support. In this instance, as he watched the young man dance with his daughter, he was trying to recall a controversy that involved Richard Lester – and he could not.

For a young man who had grown up on the frontier of Georgia, Richard was well-educated. His mother and father had taught him to read at an early age. He had studied Latin, but to the frustration of his father, he had not been diligent in learning Greek. German Lester hoped he would go to Seminary, and German considered it an indictment on him personally that none of his boys had chosen to follow him in the ministry. At the same time, when Richard came forward and told his father that he had approached an attorney about an apprenticeship, he was pleased with that development.

Richard's life and career were both progressing nicely, but life got in the way. It was disconcerting to German when the attorney died after just over a year into Richard's apprenticeship. The mentor had caught a fever and never recovered – he was seemingly killed by a change in the seasons.

Richard stayed on in the attorney's office for a number of months following the death – settled a few matters, including the estates of others as well as the estate of his mentor. The wife was grateful, paid him well, and offered to give him a good reference to another attorney in nearby Decatur. Instead, Richard declined, keeping his future plans to himself. The clients he served had all been pleased with his work, but the positive words did not seem to move Richard to want to continue with his formal studies and the pursuit of a career in law.

German, as the young man's father, was confounded. His consternation seemed to be totally at odds with Richard's countenance on the matter. If he had a plan, he kept it peacefully to himself for several months.

Shortly after the work for his employer's wife was concluded, Richard walked in the front door of his parents' home and declared he would be a farmer. Because of his education and apprenticeship, he would be considered a "reader of the law." So, in addition to farming and helping his father at the local church, he could supplement his farm income with work for people in the community – which seemed to be growing. He could write wills, contracts, and in some instances settle disputes. In this last endeavor he was well respected, and despite his relative youth, even the older men in the Covington area deferred to him.

A generation earlier, both the Sims and Lesters had been slow to take up "The Cause." Being the most recent colony formed and bordering the Spanish Colonial efforts to the South, Georgia relied heavily on the protection of British troops. When settlers of what would become Covington added to that the tensions with both the Creek and Cherokee Indians, allegiance to "The Crown," certainly in the early stages of the Revolutionary War, seemed to be a necessity.

In the end, the dream of independence pulled both families into fighting on the side of the colonies.

The Sims had a larger farm, and they were converting the farm over to cotton. Like many of the other large landowners in the area, they had bought slaves. Slavery was not always allowed in Georgia. Initially, the colony had outlawed slavery – and, for many years, it was the only colony where slave ownership was illegal – as was the sale of rum, lawyers and being Catholic.

However, in 1742 the sale of rum was legalized, and slavery was also legalized nine years later.

German Lester did not oppose slavery, but he had not purchased slaves either. In truth, while they owned over 50 acres, they did not have much of a farm. They maintained a garden for their own personal use and a pasture for the few animals they owned. They did plant a few acres of corn, but most of their time was absorbed by the school and the church. And, as their children had grown and left the homestead, they had neither the time nor the need, much less the manpower to cultivate more. As a result, some of the land of the original 200-acre farm had been sold.

A small parcel, nearest the main road through town and the town itself, had been sold to a merchant, and now supported a thriving mercantile store. A larger parcel had been carved out and sold to a neighbor who had long desired the land owned by the Lesters.

Throughout his time as an apprentice in law, Richard had been persistent in his courtship of Mary. Following that initial introduction at his sister's wedding, he had made the long journey each weekend to her family's plantation. After a year of this weekly migration, they had become engaged.

Richard had arrived early in the afternoon and the two had taken a walk on the Sims' Plantation. After each of the young lovers had rambled briefly about what had transpired in their lives since their last meeting just the week before, Richard turned to her and proposed. Mary would never forget the words: "Mary. I think I am a cordial person, as are you. Maybe too much so for my own good. The truth is, there are probably a lot of people I could live with. I know that is true of you, too. You are beautiful and intelligent. But the truth is, I don't want someone I can simply live with – that is not enough. I have been searching for someone I cannot live without… That person is you."

In her heart, she felt the same way too.

Shortly after their engagement, the death of both Richard's mentor and his law career had brought a chill to the relationship. Mary was steadfast, but both of her parents had concerns. Throughout the courtship Mary's mother had been supportive and encouraging of Richard's attentions. Now, she wavered. This lack of support frustrated Mary.

Fortunately, in winding down the law practice, Richard had gained valuable experience and had accumulated a modest sum that enabled him to buy the farm that he hoped both he and Mary would call home. Richard bought the farm from another family who had decided to return to Savannah. That family had been awarded the farm through a land lottery in 1805 from land newly surrendered by the Creek Indians.

After an inspection of the farm, and coercion from both his wife and daughter, Mr. Sims consented to the marriage.

In the Spring of 1817, Mary and Richard married. And a little over a year into their marriage, Richard Paul was born. He had just turned 11. This was followed two years later by James, aged nine, and Alice who was six.

Richard and Mary had not bought slaves yet either, but they had discussed it. While their farm was more modest than the Sims, much of the Lester farm was still wooded. If they cleared more land to grow cotton or tobacco, the couple thought they would then purchase slaves like their neighbors.

When Richard purchased the 202-acre farm, a field for corn had already been cleared, as had a large, fenced pasture, but well over half of the farm remained wooded. The initial house consisted of a large room on the main floor and a loft. This had worked well for Mary and Richard until their third child was born. At that time, they added onto the house. With the help of Richard's brothers, the Sims, and several family friends, the addition was completed quickly. This addition extended the main floor and allowed the parents to have a room of their own. A second room for Alice was added just before her birth.

Due to the growing hostilities between the settlers, Creek, and Cherokee Indians, when the house was expanded, access to the larder was moved to the inside of the house and under the parents' room. While this was inconvenient at times, all of the children knew that this was where they were to hide. Richard, or if needed, Mary, would cover the door in the floor with a rug. It was hoped that a few carefully placed shoes and a slop jar on the rug would complete the disguise.

For further protection and hunting as well, the family had several guns. Richard did not consider himself to be a marksman, but he was good enough. At the same time, when the community gathered and contests were held, Richard knew better than to enter the contest because there were men in the area who were much, much better. It was often said "if King George and his redcoats had known the men of Covington could shoot the eyes out of a squirrel at 50 paces, they would have never so indignantly encouraged the revolution."

The family had two old muskets and two relatively new rifles that seemed to prove to Richard that his aim was better than he had always thought. Both muskets were standard flintlocks. One of the muskets was very worn and had been repaired so many times, it was difficult to tell what kind of gun it was. This gun was the one the boys used when they practiced shooting or went hunting with their father. The second was a Springfield musket that was newer and in better repair. This musket was hung over the hearth, its bag and ammunition hanging on a peg just to the right of the stone chimney.

The rifles were relatively new designs. One had been manufactured by the same Eli Whitney that had revolutionized the cotton industry. The rifling in the barrel made the projectiles spin. This spin allowed for greater accuracy. The Whitney was normally leaning lazily against the wall nearest the front door, but it was always loaded. The fourth was an even newer rifle. This gun was kept in the tack room or, if there was unrest in the area, next to the parents' bed. If Richard or the family left the farm, this gun went with them, and it was Mary who often inquired if Richard had packed the Hall rifle, particularly if he was traveling by himself.

While the family had never been threatened, out of precaution, all four guns were easy to retrieve, and most of them, save the musket over the hearth, were always loaded. All four guns required a piece of flint in the firing mechanism to create a spark that lit the gunpowder. Each gun also had a unique leather pouch that contained spare flints, cartridges or lead musket balls, a dry cotton cloth, and a small musket tool that could be used to make simple repairs.

The truth was, if a large group of men came to the farm wanting to create trouble, the family would likely not survive. However, if the family was threatened by two or three men, Richard and Mary were both confident that they had done everything they could to make sure their family was safe. All guns could be retrieved quickly, and none of them were considered decorative or ornaments for show.

Mary's father, Issac, had taught her how to fire a gun at an early age. And, before her marriage, her father had given her a Harpers Ferry flintlock pistol. Issac Sims had taken her hand and led her into a field near her childhood home. There, they had a nice lunch together and a brief and awkward conversation about her duties as a wife. As the conversation concluded, he had handed her a small wooden box that was over a foot long and ten inches wide. When she opened it, she was shocked to find the pistol.

Her father had laughed when she asked if the pistol was in any way "connected to her wifely duties."

"No, Daughter. Richard Lester will treat you well. I am certain of that." Then, Mr. Sims had taken the pistol from the box and taught her how to load and fire the weapon, which he made her do several times, until he was satisfied that she could do so with relative competency.

Before returning to their home for the afternoon, he had given her one last fatherly hug and kiss on the cheek and whispered, "… and if you do have any issues with Richard Lester, you know to come to me."

Mary would never feel the need to call upon her father's protection.

As one exited the Lester farmhouse, the barn was slightly to the left. The barn had six stalls, a room for tack and feed, and a separate room for tools. Halfway between the house and the barn was a well. Behind the house, several hundred paces down a gentle slope, ran a stream. While the family had lived there the stream had never been dry, although it certainly could slow to a trickle during the driest months of September and October. There was a "necessary" or outhouse, a generous chicken coop, a smokehouse, and a corn-crib. On either side of the house, the family had planted two cedar trees. A few of the chickens preferred to roost in these trees, but this made them easy prey for raccoons, opossums, and foxes. For this reason, the family preferred the chickens roost in the coop.

The sole decorative indulgence had been small plantings of daffodils in front of the home.

The family owned two horses, six pigs, a large number of egg-laying hens, four goats, two cows and one mule. The family kept the goats at the encouragement of Richard's brother, Fountain. Fountain maintained that the goats would eat "all of the things that the horses shouldn't." And this was largely true. The family found that the young goats had been easy prey to coyotes in the area. Richard had purchased small brass bells and tied these around the necks of the goats. As hoped, the sound of the bells perplexed the predators, and the family had not lost a goat for quite some time.

The hen population would grow through the spring and summer, and thin out during the fall and winter months as they harvested the hens that were no longer productive. The pig population was treated similarly, although in recent years, the younger sows had been particularly aggressive in eating their piglets. Fortunately for the family, one of the favorite sows had come through. As a result, the family had decided to harvest the "less motherly" pigs.

Close to the barn, the original owners had planted a small grove of fruit trees that, depending on the vagaries of the weather, bore fruit for the family: apples, peaches, and pears.

The primary crop to this point had been corn. The family mostly grew corn that supplied them with both food and feed for the animals. There was a smaller garden near the house that contained tomatoes, potatoes, and lettuce. In good years, the family could get at least two plantings of vegetables.

The woods around the house were a combination of pine trees and hardwoods, mostly poplar. In fact, most of the large beams in the house were poplar, presumably harvested from the woods that were now the cornfield.

The boys had worked hard one summer creating a small dam in the stream below the house. The dam was seemingly not substantial, but the result had been that a nice pool, enough to cover an adult's chest when sitting, had formed.

The stream was commonly called "Dried Indian Creek." This was not due to a lack of water, rather something much more sinister. Before Covington had been founded, the dried body of an Indian had been found tied to a tree – and this is how the stream had come by its name.

The children would routinely bathe in the pond but had never seen their mother do so.

The evening routine for the Lesters generally followed the same comfortable rhythm. They would eat. Afterwards, when Richard was at home, he would help clear the table and then get the children started on their studies. This consisted of numbers and reading. If time permitted, Richard and Alice would play the boys in chess or checkers. About an hour after sunset, the children would go to bed. During the winter, Richard would tend the fires, and then he and his wife would go to bed as well.

Mary and Richard both had gotten into the habit of waking around 1 AM. This gave them both time to read, pray, refresh the fire, or just ponder life and visit "the necessary." Several times each week, Mary would walk down to the creek to bathe. The boys were quite old, in their teens, when they learned of this. On the nights when her husband joined her, the bathing always seemed to take longer. After an hour or so, they would go back to bed for "second sleep," awaking easily before the sun was up. It was also during this interlude between first and second sleep that they made love.

On those nights, sleep did not always return immediately. When dawn came, lack of rest might be the burden of the next day, but this was accompanied with ample measures of peace and contentment.

As Winter waned into the early Spring of 1828, the couple had been married for almost 12 years and they were established in their own right.

It was still early morning when Richard Lester arrived in Covington.

While small, Covington was large enough to encourage commerce supporting two blacksmiths, three churches (the Methodist church being the church founded by German and his wife), a surprising number of mercantile stores (seven at last count) and several tinkers, who seemingly could repair anything, and for this they might accept livestock or other tradeable goods. There were several taverns that also rented rooms to travelers. While not located in town, the town fathers were proud of the new Wood and Grain Mill that had opened nearby on the Yellow River.

Richard was to meet two men at a tavern and write a contract for an exchange of land. Afterwards, he would go to the edge of town to see his mother and hopefully his father as well. As people were putting crops in, German Lester would most likely be doing the same unless he had to visit one of the members of their small church.

As Richard entered the town, he dismounted his horse and walked Banner to the first blacksmith shop he came to. The shop was owned by the town's best cartwright, and being on the edge of town, the proprietor was not constrained on either side for space. As such, wagons of various sizes and types were strewn about the property. Richard guessed that some were there to be repaired. Others were orphaned, destined to be gleaned from and used as a steady source of materials.

The blacksmith was a brutish man, and he treated the two slaves who toiled in the heat next to him harshly. Both men were heavily scarred with burns. Richard had seen the blacksmith scald one of his slaves with a hand iron. The burn was so bad that Richard was sure the slave's ability to work had been severely reduced for days.

Richard inquired if the cartwright could shod his horse while he was in town. Neither slave had stopped work to even look at Richard. The blacksmith replied that it would be at least a day before he could attend to Richard's horse.

The second blacksmith shop was just as busy, but at least he had shoes on hand, and Richard asked if he could buy the shoes, relating that he would shoe the horse himself later in the week. At this, the blacksmith frowned and replied, "I'll have it done for you by lunch. Just bring me back some food from your mother's and we will call the matter settled."

William Millar, the blacksmith, was a short man, but possibly the strongest man between Covington and the sea. He was solid as the trunk of an aged oak tree. He still had a Scottish accent that some found off-putting, but Richard found worldly and in a strange way comforting.

Walking through the mud across to the Tavern, Richard scraped his boots on the rough stone beside the door before entering. The two men he was to meet were already seated. As they were neighbors with no quarrel between them, the contract was a simple matter of capturing the details correctly, and as the two men could neither read nor write well, Richard's task was made simple.

Richard sat down as a sturdy woman approached carrying three pewter pints of ale. Richard knew the woman well. She and her husband owned the tavern. Richard found the woman friendly, but at the same time, when needed, she could assert herself with the force of a tornado. Richard had seen the woman single-handedly throw larger men out of the establishment into the mud streets of Covington.

Placing the pints down, she smiled briefly, promising to return with bread and boiled eggs.

One of the neighbors waited for her to get out of hearing range and leaned in towards the center of the table, "That woman is about as attractive as a well-dug grave."

The other man replied. "True. True. But she does know how to keep a man's cup full." With that, he picked up his pint, as did Richard, and the three pints clinked together loudly.

Richard settled into his chair and reached into his leather satchel removing a piece of blank parchment, a feather quill, and small sealed ink well. Removing the top of the well, he readied himself for the task at hand.

The two neighbors had both agreed on the land and the price to be exchanged before this meeting. And, both men trusted Richard to capture the details of the exchange accurately and impartially. The property description was relatively easy to describe and concluded with the phrase "meandering along a stream to a wagon wheel found." Such were the times and details.

Once completed, Richard handed the quill to both men, allowing them to make their marks on the agreement.

Having finalized the transaction, Richard left the tavern and headed towards his mother's home not just hoping, but knowing, she had enough to feed not just him, but also the blacksmith.

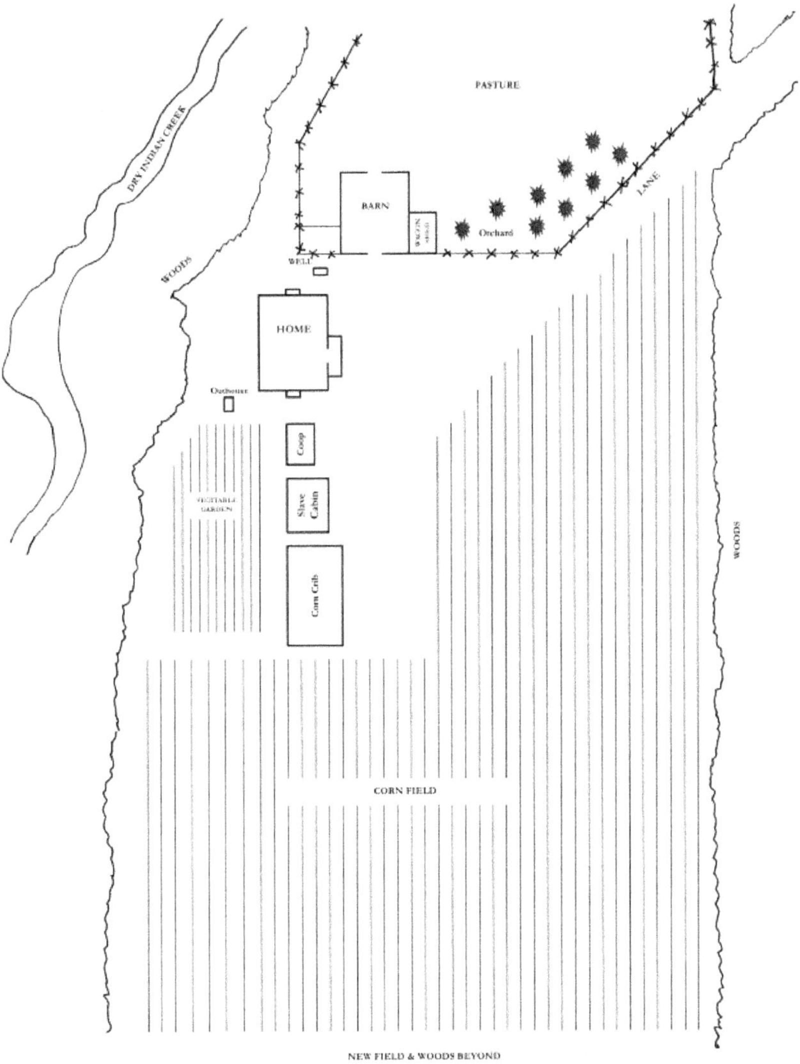

Lester Family Homestead – 1828

Richard walked into the house. It was surprisingly crowded but quiet. Normally, there would be a fire in the fireplace and his mother would be bustling about the kitchen. Instead, he walked into a room that was full of people, all of them faces that he recognized. His father rose, crossed the floor. His mother did not.

"Walk with me," German Lester said as he put his hand on Richard's shoulder.

They left the house through the door he had just entered and walked a few paces towards the large adjacent building that served as both a school and a church. Halfway between the two buildings, German Lester stopped. "It's your brother Fountain, and his wife." He paused. "They are both dead."

Richard stepped back. Everyone knew someone who had died. Death was not new. It was also not novel. But Fountain. He and his wife were both healthy and in the prime of their lives. They finally had two children. After years of trying, the blessings and responsibility of family had finally come.

"We do not have details yet, but it has been confirmed. They are dead."

After a brief silence, Richard asked, "What of Eugene and Betsy? How are the children?"

"Their neighbors are on their way with the bodies of your brother and his wife. Bryant will be bringing both children."

"Father, do you plan to raise them? They are six and five years old."

German nodded. "I think I must."

In that moment there was a hand on his back. He turned to see his mother.

What does a man say? What does a man say to his mother after he has just learned that she has lost a son? Richard, like his parents, was still in shock. He had lost a brother, one of the men he grew up admiring.

Catherine Lester, his mother, was a strong woman. But not today.

Richard hugged his mother and she started to cry.

That is the answer to the question, Richard thought to himself, you do not say anything.

After a few minutes, German touched his wife on the shoulder and said, "We must return to our guests."

Catherine sobbed, burying her face in her son's shoulder as she did so. "It is so kind of them to be here, but I really wish they would leave."

Richard suggested that his parents go to the church for a few minutes, and he would attend to the guests.

His parents agreed and they parted. Richard neared the family home and glanced over his shoulder at his parents as they entered the church. For the first time, they looked old to him. He paused for a moment to think, "When had it happened? At what point had he become stronger than the two people who raised him?"

He stepped into the main hall of the house. To his left, people stood around the long table in the kitchen that he knew well. It was the table he and his siblings had grown up gathered around for every meal. To his right, in his father's study, another group was gathered in deep, solemn conversation.

In a town the size of Covington, it did not take long for news like this to spread. Everyone had come with food. Some had even come with items. There was a quilt – he was sure it was new. And while his mother sewed, she never quilted. There was a basket of eggs, a barrel of something, Richard guessed grain.

Two men followed Richard into the house – it was the two men he had met earlier that morning in the tavern. They had come to apologize. They had heard of Fountain and his wife's death just after their meeting. The tavern owner walked in as well carrying bread and cheese.

Richard knew everyone in this room. Many had watched him grow up. Some had come to him for advice on various matters. After several minutes and light exchanges with everyone, Richard cleared his throat. "All of you are so kind. Frankly, I am overwhelmed. We really need to get word to my other brothers and sisters and decide how we are going to care for Fountain's children. Would you permit me to thank you all and ask you to come back tomorrow? I know my parents covet your prayers. And, tomorrow, they will be of a better mind to ask you for what is needed."

With that, everyone stood and left, shaking hands or hugging Richard as they left the house. Some lingered in the rutted road in front of the house before heading into town. In a short minute, it was quiet. The street was too. He was alone.

It was quite some time until Catherine and German returned to their own home.

It had taken time for the boys to decide how to carry their captive hawk from the field to their house. While just out of sight, the house was not far, but the distance could have been miles and miles. They had no plan as to how to carry a hawk back to the house. The conversation around how to best capture a hawk had so consumed and exhausted the minds of the two boys, neither had brought up the topic of what to do once the hawk was caught.

Fortunately, both had carried chickens before, and this was not new to them. Surely, carrying a hawk in such a way could work. They knew how to press the bird on both sides at the shoulder without damaging its wings.

They finally settled on pulling a healthy branch off a tree and wrapping it with the burlap bag. James selected a sturdy three-foot-long branch and held it while Paul lifted the hawk from the ground – careful to not damage any of the hawk's feathers or hurt its wings.

As Paul and James approached the house, they could smell the apple pie. What could make a day better than this?

Alice saw them approaching through the open door. She turned to her mother and yelled "They did it! They did it!" and she dashed out of the house.

Mary came to the doorway. She saw the hawk. She saw the blood on Paul's arms... She saw the hawk, and again looked at the blood. She saw the pride in their faces. She turned to get clean water and bandages.

The boys placed the hawk on the hitching post in front of the house as the hawk continued to cock its head in an effort to gain its bearings and regain its sight. They used more twine to tie the hawk's talons loosely to the hitch. While agitated, the hawk steadied itself on the post and settled.

After much coaxing, Mary finally persuaded Paul to come to the porch and let her see who had fared worse – the hawk having lost its freedom, or her son having damaged his arms.

After the second, "Richard Paul Lester, come here!" he obeyed.

Once cleaned of blood and dirt, his arms and hands really did not look too bad. Satisfied, she sat back. She gathered Alice in her lap and heard the story of how the hawk was captured.

The story went largely uninterrupted until they mentioned the Indian. It was then that questions came with motherly rapidity:

"What was his name?"

"Don't know. Joseph, I think."

"What tribe was he from?"

"Creek, but we really don't know. He did not say."

"What clan was he from?"

"We don't know."

"How did he know so much about hawks?"

"We don't know, but he did have two feathers in his hat. They had to be from an eagle 'cause they were huge!"

Mary stared at her two sons, assessing the exchange. Finally, she said, "Well, for being two intelligent, inquisitive boys, you two do not know much."

The boys looked at each other, then back at their mother and shrugged.

It was late in the day. The shadows cast by the loblolly pines were growing long.

"All right, you two, round up the livestock and put them in the barn for the night. And you better find a place for that hawk, or else he will be fox food. Alice, you, and I will scrub the table. Boys, when you're done, one of you will need to help me turn the table and get it ready for dinner. Better yet – Paul, you help me turn the table now. Then you can catch up with your brother."

Alice frowned, slightly annoyed that her mother did not think she was strong enough to help her flip the table. During the day, the family used one side of the table as a work surface. This surface was used as a butcher block, and even for light household repairs. But once the day's activities were done, the family would turn the table, revealing a clean, unblemished surface of which Mary was very proud, and this is what they used in the evening to eat, read, and write on.

Mary gazed at the late sky. She glanced up the lane that led away from her cabin. There was no sign of any traveler, much less her husband. She sighed. Twilight would approach soon. Mary reconciled herself to the fact that Richard would most likely spend the night in Covington and return in the morning. She would save a large piece of pie – the pie that was intended for him. They sat down for dinner.

After dinner, Mary lit a pewter courtship lamp and placed it on the table. She then placed a book between the boys. She did not have to tell them what to do. It was time to read. They would alternate reading a page of the story to their sister, while she cleaned the house and put items away and prepared for the next morning,

Before the boys had found their place from the previous night, Alice asked "Mom, what's a courtship lamp?"

The boys sighed. They all knew the story – Alice just wanted to hear it again.

"Now Alice, you know what that is," she began. "That is the lamp my mother and father used to light when men came to visit the house. When the oil burned out, and the flamed died, it was time for them to leave. At first, I was sure my father did not put much oil in the lamp when your daddy called on me. But as he got to know your father, my father would put a little more oil in the lamp so he could stay a little longer. And that is how we fell in love. We fell in love sitting around that lamp…. And one day, your father will have to fill that lamp with oil for the boys who call on you. It will be fun to watch his hands shake as he fills it with oil, don't you think?"

Alice nodded. The boys blandly blinked. Then, they began the nightly reading.

It was twilight in Covington before Richard remembered he needed to take food to the Blacksmith and retrieve Banner. He explained what he needed to his mother. She left the room and returned with a basket. Together they began to gather a large assortment of food from the items that had been brought by the family's friends. Once he was satisfied by the quantity and selection, he walked out of the house and down to the other end of town.

"William, I am so sorry… I…"

"No worries, Richard. I heard the news this morning when the rider came through from Fountain's family. I guess his children will be following," the blacksmith replied.

Richard nodded, "Yes, we are not sure when, but we are sure they will be here in the next day or so…. Soooo, you knew there would be food?"

William stopped wresting with the piece of iron in the long tongs in his left hand. He would be shutting down the furnace for the day soon. "Wherever there is death and Methodists, there is bound to be food. Just be thankful you're not Presbyterian like me – we would have to form a committee and you would still be waiting on the pot to boil."

"Well," Richard laughed, "You are probably right about that. Just don't tell the bishop. If you do, you may be doing your smithing for day-old food." Richard glanced at Banner, then at William, and extended a hand. "I cannot thank you enough. My horse's feet have been flying out left and right. I knew he needed tending, and I know you did a better job than I ever could. I hope there is enough food here for your troubles. And, if I can, I will drop off another basket the next time I pass."

"It's all well," replied William. "No need." He paused. "I did not know Fountain well. But what I knew of him, I liked. I am sorry."

With that, Richard mounted Banner, touched his brow with two fingers in an informal salute to William, and headed back up the street to his parents' home. Once there he walked his horse into the barn and removed his saddle, blanket, and bridle. He watered the horse and placed hay in the small trough. He turned and left, noticing that there was an extra horse in one of the spare stalls of the darkened barn as he walked out – closing the door behind him.

As he walked into the house, he was met by his oldest brother, Bryant. They hugged each other warmly. Bryant stood back, looking Richard over. "You look well."

"Well? You're kind. It's been a long day. When did you get here?

"Just a few minutes ago. I am sure the lather is still on my horse… I just can't believe it. Fountain." Bryant's voice trailed off.

As often is the case, the two oldest boys were close. They had left the home first, settling a half-day's ride away from Covington, but a stone's throw from each other. In a quiet moment, the brothers had confided to Richard that they wanted to be close enough to get back if they needed to, but far enough away to "live life without always being the preacher's sons."

Richard totally understood. At the same time, he had always been jealous of the two brothers and the way they could just disappear. They had done it when they were still young. They would grab two guns and two satchels and vanish together in the woods for days when they were still living at home before either had married. They would return with a story or two, and a few pelts.

After they had exchanged news on each of their families, the conversation turned to Eugene and Betsy, Fountain's two children.

Bryant said, "Well, my wife and one of my sons will be bringing them here in the morning…" the phrase lingered in the air. "We thought it best to get them away from there."

"What happened?"

"Their wagon turned over. Fountain, well, he died there. The wagon landed on top of him. JoAnne, she lingered for the better part of a day, but she died yesterday. I sent a rider with a note last night. He rode through the night. I wanted him to get here as the sun rose. I did not want you all hearing about this from some wanderer."

"We thank you for that" replied their father.

It was well into the night, and after a lengthy discussion, that the family agreed that Richard was best suited to raise Eugene and Betsy. Betsy, being close in age, had always enjoyed Alice's company. Eugene, being one year younger than James, would fit in with the boys.

It was resolved that at some point, the family would sell Fountain's farm, and the proceeds would be used to expand Richard's home. Any leftover proceeds would be held for Eugene and Betsy until they were old enough to spend it wisely.

Invariably thoughts turned to fond recollections of Fountain as a son, brother, and father. It was well past midnight when they turned in for the night – with the two brothers sharing a room, something they had not done for nearly 20 years.

Richard had just placed his head on the feather pillow as Bryant blew out the candle, the only source of light.

"Bryant, rest well. I will see you in the morning."

There was a long silence, before his brother spoke unexpectedly. "Richard, there is something you need to know."

Richard sat up and peered across the room into the darkness where he saw the silhouette of his brother still sitting on the edge of his bed. "What? What is it?"

"Fountain was shot," was the unwelcomed answer he heard from the darkness.

PART II

Richard and Bryant were both up early the next morning.

The two men had resolved to wait to tell their father of Fountain's murder until after the funeral. They would first tell their father, and then the three of them could decide how to break the news to their mother.

Richard needed to return home and prepare the family for Eugene and Betsy's arrival. They would return the following day for the funeral.

Bryant would wait for his wife, the bodies of his brother and sister-in-law, and the children; and then he would head to Richard's homestead. German and Catherine would organize the church and community to help in preparing the funeral for the following day. Letters would be dispatched to the siblings who lived further away: Robert, Nancy, and Barksdale, but given the distances, there was certainty that none of them would arrive in time for the funeral. Because several days had already passed and the couple's bodies had already begun to decompose, the burial would need to take place as soon as possible.

The day was warming quickly, Richard thought as he saddled Banner, placed his foot in the left stirrup, and hoisted himself up into his saddle.

For the first time in a long time, he checked the rifle he always carried but took for granted.

It was the Hall model rifle and Richard had owned the weapon for 10 years, purchasing the gun at Mary's insistence about a year into their marriage.

Like many of the rifles of its time, the gun depended upon the tried-and-true action of a flintlock trigger. The device held a piece of flint in a vice-like wedge. When the trigger was pulled, a spark was created which ignited the gunpowder behind the projectile.

The Hall rifle did possess several improvements that were innovative for its time. Its inventor, John Hall, had incorporated rifling in the barrel. Similar to the rifle produced by Eli Whitney, these grooves allowed the ball to spiral as it exited the barrel. This spiral resulted in a more accurate shot as the projectile pierced the air more cleanly. Of even greater importance, the gun allowed for the ammunition to be loaded in a breach in the casing. This meant that you did not have to load the gun through its muzzle by standing the gun on its butt, and that the gun could be loaded more quickly. Richard had bought the gun used, but it was still in excellent shape.

The boys woke early, eager to check on their hawk. Their mother was already busy in the kitchen area of their cabin, but it would be a few minutes before the breakfast of eggs, smoked ham, and biscuits was ready.

They walked to the barn, opened the door, and there was the red tail hawk, exactly where they had left it. But the hastily made cloth hood had been replaced with a neatly tied leather hood, and the twine was gone, too. It had been replaced by two thin leather straps, one tied neatly around each talon. And those were tied to the hitching post.

There were four hitching posts on the farm. Two were in front of the house spaced generously on either side of the front door to the home. A third was located just outside the barn's entrance, and a fourth inside the breezeway of the barn. This last hitch was where the boys had left the hawk. The person who had replaced the twine and cloth hood had come into the barn.

The two brothers stared at the hawk and the leather hood.

They looked at one another.

This was not the work of a 12 or 10-year-old. And they were relatively certain their mother had not done it. It did not cross their minds to even think of Alice. It had to be Joseph, the Indian from the day before. They walked back outside and quickly scanned the woods. They walked around the barn trying to discover some sign of who had come during the night.

Nothing.

Dissatisfied and curious, they set out to quickly complete their chores. A few minutes later, their mother came to the door and called, "Boys, come on in and eat your breakfast."

"James," Paul said, grabbing his brother by the arm, "it's probably best not to mention the leather hood to mom. It was a nice gesture, but she would be unsettled knowing someone had come into the barn last night." James nodded his agreement, and the boys ran inside the house.

Shortly after the children had finished breakfast, their father arrived. As Banner trotted down the dirt lane to his home, the only thing Richard Lester noticed was the unrepaired fence.

The boys were busy with the other chores, just not *The One Thing* their father had specifically requested. The only things keeping the other horse, Danny, the mule, and the cows from leaving was laziness, loyalty, habit, or fear. Maybe it was a combination of all those things.

Richard was tired of the boys ignoring his directions. He thought to himself, "now this was not laziness, fear, or loyalty – THIS was a habit and he needed to get them to stop. They were too easily distracted." He resolved in his head that he would deal with it. The normal "go cut a switch" was not working.

The truth was, Richard rarely spanked or punished his children. He and Mary both preferred explaining the "why" of something rather than an outburst of anger or a violent physical correction. At the same time, Richard was thinking that "some things should not need to be explained." The horses, cows, and even the mule, were important to the family. When they were let out in the grazing field, it was important to their well-being and the family's that the animals stay in that field.

Mary, having heard the horse approach, had come to the doorway, followed closely by Alice. The boys were of the age that they largely ignored his arrival. They would simply wave or nod. Alice still ran to greet him.

Jumping off the horse he lifted Alice, and hugged Mary. As he put Alice down, Mary stepped back to look at her husband. He stepped forward, placing his hand on the small of her back and the other to her cheek, reins still in hand. "I missed you."

"I missed you, too," Mary replied. He kissed her more deeply, lingering for a moment in the embrace. She felt his breath on her neck.

"Everything go well in Covington? How are your parents?" she asked as she stepped back. Before he could answer either question, she continued "… the boys have a surprise for you."

"Oh yeah, I have a surprise for them." Richard paused, "And for you as well."

"Let me take Banner to the boys and get them to brush him down and feed him. I will be back."

He turned, holding the reins, he led Banner toward the barn. As he entered the barn, Paul and James were standing next to their prize.

He had to admit, it was a beautiful hawk.

"Well, I heard you had been busy. This is what you were up to?" The boys nodded. He looked back at the hawk, and then the boys. He saw the bandages on Paul's arms. "Did the hawk do all that?"

"Yes sir," replied Paul. "It's not that bad. It doesn't really hurt."

Their father knelt for a closer look. "Goodness, this hood is nice. Where did you get it?" There was silence. He stood and looked at his two boys.

James straightened and replied, "We are not sure who did it, but we think the Indian did it. Joseph."

Seeing the concern on their father's face, Paul jumped in. "We caught the hawk and were trying to wrest it, when this man came out of the forest. He helped us and said he was looking for you, and that he would come by today or at least in a few days."

Richard stood, looked back at the house and then down at his two scavenger-sons. He sighed and said "Take Banner, brush him down, and stow his tack. Before you get into the rest of your chores, come on into the house. I have some family news."

With that, he handed the reins to James, who was standing closest to him, turned and left the barn.

Making his way to the house he entered and found the table set with eggs, bacon, biscuits, and a slice of apple pie that Mary had just toasted in a skillet.

"I thought I smelled apples." He looked at Alice. "Did you help your mother with this?" His little girl nodded and pulled herself on to the bench next to his chair.

The Lester home was nice, but modest. The main floor consisted of a room for the parents and a smaller adjacent room for Alice. Both rooms were just large enough for the beds and a small dresser for clothes. The rest of the main floor was devoted to the kitchen with a large walk-in cooking fireplace. The fireplace had an iron arm that could swing over the fire for boiling water and cooking stews. A large notch built low in the wall of the fireplace was used for cooking breads and pies, and sometimes used to keep things warm. At the other end of the room were several chairs, a tall press for clothing and linens, and a large chest. There was a second fireplace opposite from the cooking fireplace that was only used in the winter when additional heat was needed to warm the home. This had been the original fireplace before the house had been enlarged by the Lester family.

The boys slept in the loft above. The loft was accessed by a ladder that always seemed to be in the wrong place. The family had longed for steps for years, but they had never been built. The boys slept on separate feather and hay mattresses that were laid on the floor of the loft and had more space than needed. Monthly, the parents would journey to the loft and spend an afternoon collecting rocks, leaves, and various other "finds." On one such cleansing of the loft, they had found the skull of a large dog or wolf – which, while relished by the boys, because of its size, compelled a great deal of conversation both in the Lester household as well as the neighboring farms. Wolves had not been seen in the area for quite some time, and it was too large to be a fox or coyote.

The prize possession, however, was on the main floor in a corner next to the cooking fireplace. It was a mahogany cabinet that held some silver, pewter, and dishes too nice to use every day. This was called "The Company Chest" because the items in the chest were only used when company called on the family.

"So, tell me, how were your parents?"

Richard stared at his empty plate, picked it up and carried it to the washing pail. "Not well." He replied. With that, Mary turned revealing a look of concern. "Fountain and JoAnne died two days ago in a wagon accident. Bryant's wife and some neighbors are bringing the bodies to Covington, today along with Eugene and Betsy."

With that, Mary turned to Alice, who thankfully had been too busy to hear their conversation, and said, "Honey, can you go to the barn and help your brothers with the cows? Make sure they milk them well today and tell them I sent you."

Alice smiled, dashed into her room, and dropped her cloth doll on her bed and ran across the main room, and through the door heading fast for the barn, pleased that she had the authority to instruct her older brothers – a rarity for her.

"Oh my. I am so sorry."

A shadow came over her husband's face. "There is more. Fountain was shot. Bryant saw the wound. While it is true that the wagon overturned, the accident does not happen if Bryant is not shot." Richard paused.

Troubled, his wife asked, "Was JoAnne shot, too?"

"No. As far as Bryant could tell, she died from the injures she sustained when their wagon turned over. And she did survive long enough to tell Bryant that she did not know the men who attacked them." Richard paused to regain his composure. "We have not told either father or mother that Fountain was shot. We wanted to wait until after the funeral to tell them."

Mary nodded and sat back. She reached across the table for Richard's hand. They sat in silence for a long time.

"What is Bryant going to do with the children?" Mary asked.

Richard turned to face his wife and she knew the answer to the question before he opened his mouth.

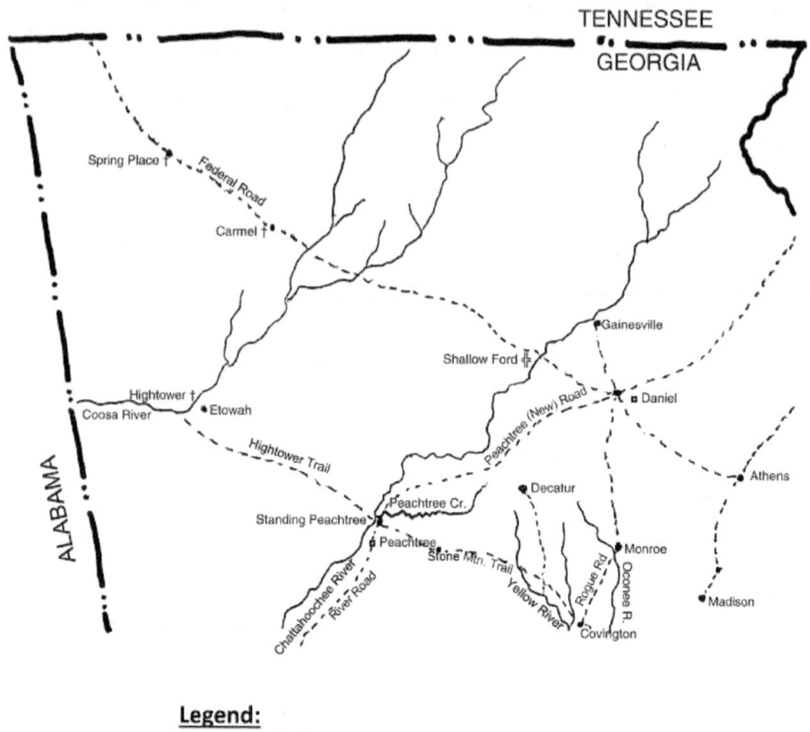

Map of North Georgia – 1828

The children had finished most of the morning chores when Mary and Richard gathered them together around the table.

Mary and Richard explained that Eugene and Betsy would be coming to live with them. Alice, too young to fully grasp the gravity of the circumstances, was generally happy that Betsy was coming to stay. The boys, well, they had questions – and there really was no time to answer them completely. And frankly, some of the questions went into details that Richard simply did not have the answers to.

They wanted to know how the wagon came to be turned over. Were the horses hurt? Had a doctor been summoned to care for their aunt? How were their grandparents? Were the other Aunts, Uncles, and cousins coming to the funeral? Why and why not?

Finally, after receiving blank stares from their parents and little in the way of information, James said to Paul with a grin on his face, "For having two intelligent, inquisitive parents, they sure don't know much…" which garnered a bright laugh from Mary, as she recognized her own words from the day before, and a slightly offended look from their father.

Mary winked at Richard and said… "I will explain it to you later" not knowing that the boys had already confessed to having met an Indian who would be calling on their father in the near future.

No one knew how much time they had. Richard thought that Bryant and his wife could easily pull into to Covington by noon, and possibly be at their home by mid-afternoon. So, in that time, furniture needed to be moved.

The family got to work.

First, the chest in Alice's room would need to be moved. For now, they would place a quilt on the floor, and the girls could alternate who slept on the bed.

Second, the loft had to be cleaned. There was plenty of space. Paul and James had to purge a few items and straighten up a bit. To make space for Eugene, Mary decided that he would be in the middle, and Paul and James would be on either side. While the boys objected slightly, Mary knew her sons and this would be best for Eugene. By putting him in the middle, there would be no whispering without him being literally in the middle. And her boys – they could scheme and plan, and when this took place, Mary did not want Eugene left out.

From this chaos, order quickly emerged.

Just as things were coming together a commotion was heard outside. It was Bryant and his wife, Sara, with Eugene and Betsy. They arrived earlier than expected, and there were two wagons. Both were loaded with household items. The second wagon was driven by a black man they did not know.

Richard was the first to step through the doorway and approach the wagon. Acknowledging his brother and sister-in-law with a simple smile, he approached the far side of the wagon and offered his hand to Sara.

"Thank you," Sara said standing. "It has been a long day and night."

Bryant hugged Mary and then turned to help Betsy and Eugene out of the back of the wagon. Both children seemed well, but rightly reserved and hesitant.

Alice ran to her aunt, who knelt and greeted her while the boys lingered on the porch.

Betsy and Alice quickly hugged and disappeared into the house.

Mary walked over to Sara, and after pleasantries were exchanged, the two walked a few steps away from the group, where a long and deep conversation took place. Richard had little doubt that Sara would relay to Mary far greater details about Fountain's death than Bryant had provided to him.

Richard turned to his brother and offered, "Bryant. This is a lot. I fear it is more than we anticipated."

"Well, there is even more to come in the weeks that follow, that is, if you want and need it," was Bryant's reply.

Fountain and Sara had been doing well on their farm. They had also been successful raising horses as well, and one was tethered to the back of the second wagon.

Walking to the second wagon, Richard asked Bryant, "Introduce me to your man."

"This is Boston. He is one of Fountain's slaves. He has a son, Simm, and a lady, Lucy, who can come to you as soon as you are ready."

Richard looked at Boston. His gaze was returned for a moment before Boston looked away. Richard also noticed that his brother was holding a whip and when he gestured toward Boston, he did so with the whip in his hand. This was new and unsettling to Richard, and it was no doubt a sign of his authority to the slave.

"Well, this is a lot to take on." He paused. "Mary and I, well, we are not sure we are ready for slaves. Frankly, I did not know Fountain owned slaves."

Bryant turned to Richard. "We both own slaves. We purchased the farmland between our two properties, and we are planting cotton. Oh, we will have enough corn to feed ourselves, the slaves, and our livestock, but we were thinking cotton will be the future for our families. So, over the winter, I purchased four, and Fountain purchased five. Boston, here, he is very skilled. He is good at carpentry, and with a wife and son, he has not been as ill-tempered as some of the others."

"I just don't know." Richard stared at Boston for a long moment.

Bryant turned to the mare. "Fountain had planned on bringing this mare to you. He knew you were looking for a brood, and he thought this filly would mix well with Banner."

"She is beautiful, and Fountain knew his horses. Thank you."

There was a pause.

Bryant turned to Boston. "Boston, hop down out of there and start unloading these items. That lady there," pointing to Mary, again, with the whip still in his hand, "She is the boss. Just do what she asks, and we will figure things out from there." Boston nodded.

Eugene brought the boys over to Boston. Neither Paul nor James had ever spent much time around slaves, and they were a bit nervous. It was obvious that Boston was strong, and he had the forearms of a man who spent his days challenging wood to yield to his will.

"And what do I call you?" were the first words Boston spoke as he looked at Paul and James.

Their mouths dropped and they continued to stare.

"This… This is James, and I am Paul. I am the oldest," Stammered Paul.

"Well, Eugene, it looks like you and I have two more ponies in our herd. Let's get to work."

The boys smiled at Eugene. Eugene shrugged his shoulders, "And you will like Simm too."

James asked, "Who's Simm?

Thinking Eugene would reply, they were shocked when Boston replied, "Simm is MY boy."

With that, Boston reached into the wagon and handed each of the boys of few items and they busied themselves unloading the wagons. Everyone quickly realized –whatever order had existed in the Lester home, was quickly undone. There were two dressers and two beds with feather mattresses.

It was immediately decided that Alice's smaller bed would be removed from the house, and possibly placed in the barn's loft or tack room for Boston. The two girls would share one of the larger feather beds that had just arrived from Fountain's home. Fortunately, this fit into the room, but there was little room for anything else. The dressers were placed in the corner of the hearth room.

A second feather mattress was placed in the loft between the two mattresses used by Paul and James. With great effort, a large trunk was placed beside Eugene's mattress that would hold his clothes.

With most of the major items unloaded, the adults turned around and the boys were nowhere to be found. The girls were playing quietly in their room. Bryant went out of the door and saw the boys in the barn – they were showing their hawk to Eugene and Boston.

⌬

While lunch was quickly cobbled together, the children were sent down to the stream to wash.

Bryant and Richard stood near the house and watched as the children waded and skipped rocks.

After a long pause, Bryant turned to Richard with a serious look and said, "You know, when we return to Covington, we will need to tell our father that Fountain's death was not an accident."

Richard, his eyes remaining fixed on the children replied, "I agree. And he will know best how to break that news to our mother." Again, there was a pause as both men watched the children at play in the stream. Finally, Richard said, "I just don't understand who would want to kill our brother. Are you aware of anyone holding animosity against Fountain, or JoAnne for that matter?"

Bryant thought for a moment. "No one really. But then, there is an awful lot of noise around the Creek and the Cherokee. You know, everyone acts like that mess with the Indians was all settled years ago at Talladega and ended at Horseshoe Bend… but it's not. The Indian Agent that the President appointed is stirring things up." Bryant paused. "There is going to be trouble. I don't know when, I don't know where, and I don't know who. But we are stuck right in the middle of it."

Richard stood in silence before finally speaking. "All right. But what does this have to do with our brother and sister-in-law?"

Bryant glanced down at Dried Indian Creek where the children were playing and replied, "It was certainly no accident. Fountain was shot. JoAnne, yes, she was injured when the wagon turned over, but she did not live long enough to shed more light on who killed them. Finding out who did this will be like navigating by the stars on a cloudy night. If you looked at Fountain's wounds, you would know, there is no doubt that he was shot. Unfortunately, we do not know whether the Indians shot him or if it was another settler. JoAnn was weak and there was so little time. The only things she told us was that she did not know the man who shot Fountain."

"Again, why would anyone want to shoot Fountain?" questioned Richard.

There was a brief silence before Bryant replied. "Fountain was trying to help the Creek Indians get the money they were promised five years ago after the Red Sticks were defeated." Bryant paused as he kicked a small pebble at his feet. "Our government promised to pay the Indians who were loyal during that whole mess. I am not sure of the amount, but I know this new agent has been no help to them."

"What's his name? I don't recall," asked Richard.

"David Mitchell. He used to be our governor, then he was the agent to the Indians, but he was dismissed by President Monroe."

"Why was he dismissed?" Richard asked.

"He was accused of smuggling slaves and using the Indian Mission at the Creek Nation to cover his illegal activities. Since the importation of slaves was outlawed 20 years ago, those who still import slaves are doing it through Florida and then up into the territory controlled by the Creeks. Because of the scandal, Mitchell was removed. I think he is a judge now." A distant look crossed Bryant's face that Richard had not seen before.

"So he was never punished, and some might say he was rewarded." Bryant nodded agreement. "Well, if anything, it is getting worse," Richard stated. "You have to wonder how much further the Creek and Cherokee will allow us to push before there is trouble."

Richard's statement hung in the air. There was no answer from Bryant, his mind was elsewhere.

Richard looked at his brother. "Bryant."

Bryant looked hesitantly at Richard.

"Is Boston legal? I mean, Fountain did not obtain him illegally, did he?"

"No. He is legal. Mine are too. I am pretty sure we can find the papers among Fountain's things. Heck, if you ask him, he will tell you. I think he grew up in Boston and came down to Charleston when he was a lad."

Bryant's eyes blinked as he wanted to change the topic of their conversation.

Finally, Bryant continued. "Well, you and I have a lot to deal with here. I am surprised Fountain put himself in the middle of all that. I did try to warn him against getting involved." There was a pause. "Do you think mom and dad will find out Fountain was shot before we return to Covington tomorrow?

Bryant thought further as Richard did not respond. "Well, we did what we could. We wrapped up his body and dressed the wounds. But, if they really look, there is no hiding it. He was shot in the chest, right in his heart. I am glad for mom that he was not shot in the head. You know how she is. She will unwrap his shroud and want to see his face."

The two men stood in silence for a long time. They could hear their wives talking as they prepared the food. At this late hour, it was understood that Bryant and his wife would be staying for dinner and spending the night.

Boston had unhitched the two teams of horses and was turning them into the pasture.

Richard turned and Bryant followed. Together, they pulled one of the wagons into its place – an open-air shelter adjacent to the barn. Satisfied that it would be out of the elements if it rained, both men returned to where they had been standing at the top of the hill and watched the children.

After a moment of silence, Richard looked at his brother and said, "Well, it is time to lay a little of our Father's Guilt on my boys."

A slow smile came over Bryant's face. "Well, dad was good at spreading guilt, so you had a good teacher."

Richard looked at him and said, "Yep. He taught us both well." He turned toward the creek and yelled. "Boys, Alice, Betsy, come on up here towards the barn." With that he turned and walked toward the barn with Bryant close behind. Boston came from the barn where he had been clearing out a spot for himself in the tack room. Richard walked to the Tool Room and pulled a bucket with nails and a hammer. He exited the barn and walked down the fence line to the place where the rail had fallen. He, his brother, and Boston inspected the rail.

Boston offered up, "Mr. Richard, I can fix that… that is not a difficult repair."

Richard turned to Boston. "You know, Boston, I am certain you could, and you would do it better than I will, but I have a problem. I asked my boys to repair this fence several times and several days ago… so, we are about to fix something more important than the fence."

With that, Richard began to nail the fence rail back to the post from which it had fallen. By this time, several horses, a mule, several goats, and five children watched as the men easily finished the quick repair. The cows did not care and ignored the proceedings.

Richard turned, looked at James and Paul and said, "Boys, I have asked you both to repair this three times. And you have totally ignored me." He paused for effect. "I will not explain to you how important it is to keep these animals in this pasture and not wandering about the countryside. But frankly, it is not just that. You had time to catch a hawk, but not do what I asked."

Both boys stared at him. This was not good. And it was in front of their uncle, Boston, Eugene, and Betsy, too. This was an unusual humiliation that seemed very public. Usually, this sort of correction took place in the cabin with only their mother and Alice as the audience.

It was at this point that Paul glanced over at his sister. Everyone, except her, had a look of concern on their faces. Alice was not happy, but she certainly was engaged with rapt anticipation over what would happen next, and there was a certain amount of joy in the fact that whatever was to happen next would not be directed towards her.

Richard continued, "Again, I do not like doing this and I do not do this lightly, but I need you to both go over to that thicket and pick out a switch. I need to make sure you two understand how important it is for you to do what I ask of you."

James protested slightly. But seeing his brother had already turned towards the thicket, he turned as well with Eugene close behind.

Bryant whispered in his brother's ear, "You are better at this better than our dad was."

Picking up the pail of nails and the hammer, Boston headed back towards the barn. This was not his place. Bryant held out his hands and took one of his niece's hands in each of his, and with his nieces looking up at him, followed his brother back towards the barn.

Searching for a switch is an art. You don't want one too thick because of the potential damage it could do. At the same time, if you pick one too small, you must endure the indignation and outright humiliation of being sent back to find a switch that your parent believes to be sufficient. So, the key is to find a stick that would be substantial enough to satisfy the parent, but at the same time acceptable to the child.

After a lengthy search and some conversation, both boys returned with sticks of relatively equal length and caliper.

Richard looked at both boys. Boston, having placed the pail and hammer in the tool room returned tentatively, but maintained a distance. Richard removed his coat. He placed his coat over the hitching post outside the barn and turned back to his boys. He reached out to both for their switches. After a brief inspection he handed them back.

The hawk, hearing the commotion from the hitching post in the breeze-way of the barn, flitted and fluttered. The hood had been removed from its head, so at various points in time, the bird would flap its wings wildly in an attempt to escape its leather bindings.

But at this point, the hawk seemed as interested in the proceedings as Alice.

With a stern look on his face, Richard said, "I obviously am not a good father, because you two are ignoring me when I ask you to do things. And again, it is not just the fence post. This is also about the safety of our animals." He paused. "I want both of you boys to strike me with your switch once for each year of your age. And, in that I am grown and your father, I expect you to each wield your switch like you're trying to move our mule. You under-stand me?"

Neither boy nodded that they understood, but it was obvious by the as-tonished looks on their faces that they clearly heard the directions.

At this, Alice's subtitle joy in what she hoped would transpire totally evaporated. She was horrified and began to cry uncontrollably. Betsy gasped, stepped back, turned, and ran towards the cabin, stopping on the front porch without going inside. The boys, with terror in their eyes, and tears welling, pleaded for their dad to not make them do it.

None of the Lester children could fathom striking a parent. Much less at their behest.

The pleas, of course, went unheeded.

Richard removed his coat and folded it lightly over the hitching post. Placing both hands on either side of his coat he said "Paul, you're first. Bryant, you count."

With his brother counting the lashes, Paul whipped his father 11 times, dropped his switch at his father's heels and backed away, tearful, but without sound.

Mortified, James stepped forward and again pleaded with his father to not make him do it. Richard turned, knelt, hugged his son, and whispered, "Do what I ask. We will both be better men for this."

With that, Richard turned, and again placed his hands on the hitching post. James lashed his father with tears so heavy, he could not see where he hit Richard Lester, and having lost all sense of how many times he had struck his father, he was only stopped by his uncle's hand.

"Here, son," said Bryant, "give me that switch."

The boys stood silently staring at their father, wiping the tears from their faces.

The sobs slowly subsided, and their father said, "Let's not do that again any time soon. All right? I will try to be a better father and you boys can do better doing what is asked of you. Now, go back down to the stream and wash your faces." The tears had streaked their dusty faces.

The boys nodded. Their father knelt, giving both boys a vigorous hug. He rose, picked up the switches, and looked at his boys. They turned and left quickly with Eugene and headed slowly back down the hill towards the stream.

Boston stood in silence trying to measure the man to whom he would now be yoked. This was a master of a different sort. He wondered silently what measure of correction would be dealt to a slave by such a man?

Richard turned, picked up his dusty, black coat and put it back on. He looked at his daughter, any amusement that might have been on her face had long disappeared. Now, tears silently trailed down her cheeks. He touched her forehead and said, "Take Betsy inside and help your mother and aunt prepare the meal."

The girl turned and walked towards Betsy, who was still standing on the humble porch of the cabin.

After a short moment, Bryant turned to Richard and said, "Well, if our memories are any indication of theirs, none of those children will forget that. It borders on cruelty."

"Cruelty to them or me?" asked Richard half joking. "I hate spanking them. They really are good boys. But, with everything going on around here, and with two new members to our family, I thought setting an example now might let Betsy and Eugene see how things should go, or better yet – not go."

Bryant held out his hand taking one of the switches from his brother. He swatted his own leg and flinched slightly.

Richard smiled and said, "In all seriousness, that really hurt."

Bryant said nothing, but silently agreed.

"You're a good father Richard, and you and Mary are generous to take in Eugene and Betsy."

"Well, just remember, if something happens to me, you get the whole lot of them," he smiled. He looked at Boston. "Bryant, let me have a word with Boston, will you?"

"Certainly." Bryant followed his niece's footsteps towards the house.

Richard closed the distance between where he was and where Boston was standing. The two men stood in silence for a long moment.

Surprisingly it was Boston who broke the silence. "Sir, I am not sure what to make of a father who allows his sons to lash him."

"Well, Boston, we are both in a quandary. Because I am not sure what to do with a slave." Again, a long silence followed. "Tell me, how did you come to be owned by my brother?"

"I was owned by a boat builder in Charleston where I repaired boats and mended sails. While there, I learned something about carpentry and wood-working. After two seasons, I was sold to an Indian as a young boy. I lived on his farm down near Macon and we repaired boats, houses, built some furniture. After the unrest several years ago, my master thought he and his family would be traveling south to be with the Seminole, so he sold me to your brother."

Richard thought for a moment. "So, you never lived in Boston?"

"No. Never been there," was the slave's simple reply.

"During the unrest, did you take up arms?"

"I did what I was told. I mainly dug ditches and cut wood, but yes. I fought."

Richard reflected for a moment. "Can you hunt?"

"Yes," Boston replied, "but frankly, I am a better trapper."

Richard thought about that for a moment before continuing, "And Boston. Why do they call you 'Boston'?" Asked Richard.

"I think that is where my first master was from," was the reply.

"I see. Did he treat you well?" As soon as he asked the question, Richard regretted it.

"Sir, I am not sure what to say," Boston said with reservation focusing on the earth between Richard's feet. "Under his foreman I learned carpentry, and boat repair, and there was plenty of that kind of work to do in Charleston. But he was a hard man. He was quick to anger. Many of the men around me were lent out to "Slave Menders" and when they came back, they were not of much use." He paused. "And if you were a slave with what the Masters call 'rabbit' in your blood, the Paddy Rollers around Savannah were worse than the Menders."

Richard had little knowledge of Paddy Rollers or Menders. But he decided to ask someone else.

"Can you read and write?"

Boston looking to the woods as if searching for an answer replied, "No. But I do know my maths."

"Lastly, tell me about Lucy and Simm. Bryant tells me you have a woman and a son."

At this, Boston straightened. "Yes, Lucy is my wife. We are bound together, and Simm is our son."

"You said 'bound.' So, you were married."

"Yes. We were married several years ago."

Richard paused and it was his turn to look to the forest for words. He could hear the wind approach. The wood creaked as the trees swayed and both men drew comfort from both the sound and the temperate afternoon breeze.

"Boston, my wife and I are not even sure we want slaves." He let the statement linger and then drift away with the wind. "You, Lucy, and Simm will stay here. And if my wife and I decide we do not want slaves, I will not sell you separately. I will see that wherever you go – you go together."

The men looked at each other. It wasn't a question, so Boston did not need to respond, and his agreement, well, that was not required.

"So, until my wife, family, and I decide what we are doing, let's leave it at this: There is so much that needs to be done. I need help. If you see something that needs to be done, do it. Beyond that, you will sleep in the barn and take your meals there as well. If you have questions, ask."

The two men stood in silence, and Richard continued. "Boston. Please do not call me 'Master.' Let's reserve that for Christ and maybe my wife." A brief smile crossed Boston's face revealing strong, shockingly white teeth. "You can call me "Mr. Lester or Mr. Richard. And, if you call me something else, don't do it around my children."

"Yes, sir, Mr. Richard," was the reply.

Richard turned to leave and then stopped. "… And Boston, don't run off. We will bring Lucy and Simm here. From my standpoint, you don't belong to me, yet. We are still working all of this out. Stay put, and my family and I will figure this out."

Boston nodded and returned to the tack room.

Dinner was finished and the dishes were being put away when there was a knock on the door.

Richard opened the door.

Standing before the door a few steps off the porch in the hard, packed earth stood the Indian that Richard half expected.

"Mr. Lester, I am Joseph McIntosh. I believe I met your sons yesterday."

By then a small crowd had gathered at the door behind Richard, including the boys. Seeing Paul and James, Joseph nodded to the boys and continued "How is your Hawk?"

"He is well," asserted Paul. "We fed him this morning just as you told us to, and he ate well." Pausing for a moment he added, "Thank you for the hood and leather straps – that was you, wasn't it, Mr. McIntosh?"

"Yes. Yes, it was. I thought those might help get you started. You know, we could try to fly him in a couple of days if you wish. Would that be fine with you, Mr. Lester?"

"Well, yes, I think we all would all appreciate that, particularly the hawk," replied Richard.

"Very well then." The Indian shifted his gaze, "I will come back in a few days, and we will see if your hawk is ready. Between now and then, though, you two should name it."

"Name? Heck, we do not know if it is a girl or a boy. Why do we have to name it?" asked James.

"Every good hunting companion, even a hunting rifle, should have a name worthy of the task," replied Joseph. Turning to Richard, Joseph asked, "Could I have a word with you before the sun sets? Alone."

"Well, certainly, but can my brother join us?" Richard responded, putting his hand on Bryant's shoulder.

"Yes. Absolutely yes. That would be good."

Richard turned to Mary and his sister in-law and said, "We will be just out front, if you need something from us, just let us know." Mary and Sara returned to the table where the children were gathering.

Mary sat down, removing her apron "Children, let's read something to your Aunt Sara. And afterwards, maybe walk down to the stream to cool off before getting ready for bed."

Richard and Bryant stepped forward into the dust, joining Joseph in front of the porch.

While Richard and Bryant were both tall, Joseph was taller. His hair was bound by a red and tan cloth wrapped tightly about his head. Dark piercing eyes seemed to soak in more than just what could be seen. His horse, which was close by, bore no saddle but there was a thick blanket and a satchel with two pouches, one pouch hanging over each side of the black horse.

Joseph smiled lightly and began, "Yesterday, in catching that hawk, your boys showed a great deal of…" and he paused searching for the right word.

Richard interjected, "What they lack in intelligence, they make up for with stupidity."

The three men laughed. "No, not at all what I saw," said Joseph. "I was going to say bravery, or at the very least your boys are more curious than mine."

"You have children?" asked Bryant.

"Yes, four. Two from my first wife who died several years ago, and two from my second wife, but they are not of our blood. Their parents are both dead and their mother was her sister. So, the responsibility fell to her."

Both Richard and Bryant looked at each other.

"One last question. By any chance, are you related to William McIntosh?" asked Richard.

The question stung, but it was not the first time it had been asked. "Why, no. Not that I am aware of." was the reply.

"Several days ago, I spoke with your brother Fountain, and he suggested that I speak with you. You're a lawyer, right?"

Richard looked at Joseph and then Bryant without answering the question.

"You know my brother?" replied Richard.

"Yes, we have hunted together, and last year I sold him three slaves," came the reply.

"I was frankly not aware he had purchased slaves until earlier today."

Bryant replied, "I believe he was planning on planting cotton this spring."

At that moment, Boston emerged from the barn. Seeing the movement, Richard, and Bryant both looked towards Boston, as did Joseph.

There was a brief hesitation.

Joseph turned to Richard, "That is Boston. One of the slaves I sold to your brother."

"Boston, come here!" Richard called across the yard.

Seeing Joseph, Boston approached Joseph swiftly. "I think you two know each other," Bryant said.

There was an obvious familiarity between the two men.

"Boston, you are looking well. How are you?" Joseph asked.

"Just settling in. Arrived here today," Boston replied.

Joseph turned facing Richard, not sure what to make of the changes.

Turning to Boston, Joseph asked "Was Fountain displeased with you?"

"No. Not at all," Boston replied.

Richard interjected, "My family, I mean my brother and I, we are dealing with a lot of changes right now." At that statement, Bryant looked at his brother and Joseph wondering why Richard did not tell him of Fountain's death. Richard continued, "How did you come to meet my brother?"

The Indian shifted his weight a little, "Fountain was hunting near my land, and we shared a fire. Since that time, we have hunted together several times. I enjoyed his company a great deal over the past few years. And, both Fountain and Bryant here have used our wood mill when that was needed."

"So, are you the man who showed Fountain how to trap the beavers on our properties?" asked Bryant.

"Yes, that would be me. It would be more accurate to say that it was Boston and me. Although I understand the beaver came back. The truth is, Boston is the trapper. I learned a great deal from him."

Boston shifted his weight. He disliked the attention, even when it was positive.

Bryant smiled and replied, "Yes, those beavers are the most persistent critters I have ever known. We have trapped and killed at least three families of beavers in less than two years, all in the same area. As quickly as we trap and kill them, and drain their pond, they return."

"Well, that is not all bad," replied Joseph. "A steady stream of beaver pelts has value to most men."

Richard returned the conversation to Fountain, "So, you spoke with Fountain, and for some reason, you then came to speak with me. Why did he send you to me?

At this, both Richard and Bryant would later recall, Joseph McIntosh's demeanor changed. "You may know, for over a decade we have been trying to get $300,000 your government owes my nation. And since that time, we have seen Indian Agents come and go, but no one can assist us. Every time we cede more land, more of my Indian brothers leave for Florida or lands in the West. We are now hearing rumblings that some of our land was given to the Cherokee, or at least they are claiming ownership. We are also hearing they may cede that land to your government. They do not have the right to cede land that they do not own in the first place."

"Listen." Richard thought for a moment. "I really do not know anything about this – and I believe this is something that you need to take down to Milledgeville, Savannah, or even back to the Indian Agent."

"I disagree," replied Joseph. "Your father is a Methodist minister. Certainly, he knows the Methodists living among the Cherokee and running the mission in Etowah. We think you, with a letter from your father, can help us resolve this quickly and quietly. You see, the mission in Etowah has grown, and many of the prominent Cherokees send their children there to learn. The men who run the mission are well respected and liked."

There was a pause before Joseph continued. "And I must say, while I do not know you, Fountain spoke highly of you. And I have never seen a man discipline his sons as you did today."

At that, Richard bristled slightly, he should have thought "others" would be watching, but he did not. Bryant laughed lightly at the thought of the Indian watching the proceedings from the cover of the woods that surrounded the farm.

"Well, as they say – the sins of the father are borne by his sons," Bryant said quietly. "Our father did something similar to us when we were little and not doing as he asked."

"I see," replied McIntosh. "That is a good lesson. I may instill that sometime soon in my children."

"Speaking of sins of the father being borne by his sons." Richard halted the conversation. "Did you know Fountain died two days ago? We are burying him tomorrow. That is why Bryant, and his wife are both here now. That is also how Boston came to be my slave."

McIntosh reeled. A long silence filled the air. He looked at Boston. Boston simply stood as motionless as stone. No one spoke as both Lesters saw the obvious confusion on Joseph's face as he absorbed the revelation of Fountain's death.

Shifting his gaze to the dirt between them, McIntosh asked "How did he die?"

Richard was quick to reply, seeing that Bryant was about to answer, "Frankly, we don't know much, but both he and his wife are dead. Their wagon overturned."

"And you say this happened two days ago?"

"Yes. That is right."

Joseph stood in silence searching for words.

After a long moment, Richard continued, "Joseph, please do not repeat this, but our brother was shot." He paused. Joseph did not seem surprised. "While it is true that his wagon overturned, Bryant here, saw the wounds. He was shot."

Joseph looked at Bryant and then at Richard. "This is unsettling. I can only imagine how this has impacted the two of you."

The three men stood in silence. Bryant knelt and picked up a small stone and tossed it, for no apparent reason, into the woods to the right and beyond the house.

The three men watched as the stone disappeared into the woods.

"Mr. Lester, we have a lot to discuss. You have a brother to bury. I need to return to my home as I have been away for too long. But you need to know, I am very sorry. With Fountain and JoAnne dead, frankly, my family may be in danger, too. Fountain was a calming voice and there are settlers who want my land, our land. There are also Creek Indians who are also calling for us to take up arms. I need to return home."

He turned to leave but stopped. Turning to face Richard and Bryant, he said, "I have no right to ask this, but I do need your help. We need your help. There are members of my clan that want to attack the Cherokee over what they are doing. So, the conflict here is not just between the new settlers and my Nation. There is also hostility brewing between us and the Cherokee. We need to stop this before it is too late."

"I will return," he continued. "Let me check on my family and let you and your family bury your brother and his wife. Again, I am so very sorry."

With that, Joseph McIntosh mounted his blanketed horse, nodded to Boston, and rode quickly up the dirt approach on which everyone traveled.

The men stood for a moment.

"Richard, I told Fountain to stay out of this mess months ago. I am frustrated that he did not listen."

"Well, there is a lot going on here. Let's go inside and get the children settled for the night. And we need to get up early and ride into Covington tomorrow, so we have a lot to do and think about."

They turned, the men to the cabin and Boston to the barn.

"Boston, we will need two wagons to travel to Covington in the morning, but I am going to leave you here to look after the farm. There is still corn to be planted in the upper field. I will be up early to show you where to plow and acquaint you with the mule and Danny."

Boston nodded and turned continuing towards the barn.

Mary busied herself about the kitchen. Once JoAnne gathered her bearings and understood what needed to be done, she began to help.

The two girls had helped briefly by setting the table, which with Eugene, Betsy, JoAnne, Bryant, Boston and now Joseph McIntosh, would be crowded.

"It has been a long time since I have prepared a meal for ten people," Mary said as they moved about busily. She had decided the meal would consist of stew, brown bread with nuts, and apples. She had wanted to prepare a roast, but the afternoon had been absorbed with other matters.

JoAnne replied, "Yes, ten people is a lot." She paused, turned, and began counting the places. "Wait. Mary, you are not planning on feeding Boston in here. Are you?" The question hung in the air. She continued "And sister," she and Mary often referred to each other as "sister" which both women liked, "you cannot feed a slave the same food that you give your family. That will not do."

Mary paused, "JoAnne, I honestly have not had time to think about this. I frankly do not know what is expected of me. I have never owned a slave, much less fed one."

"Frankly, Mary, that is the point. If you feed him too well, it will become expected. You cannot do that. If you do, your slaves will drain your stores and it will bring their ass to anchor." Mary was taken aback by the use of the phrase. "They will be of no use. You should give him a simple porridge or gruel. Grains and beans in hot water with bread. If you add a small slice of smoked ham when he has worked a substantial day, but even that should not be expected. Which, by the way, today he has not earned."

Mary turned, wiped her hands on her apron and then wiped her brow. "JoAnne, you are probably right. But with all the goings on around here, I do not have time to mix up porridge or gruel. So, he gets a portion of stew."

JoAnne pursed her lips and nodded. "I understand. It is a special day, and the slave probably would welcome a full belly. But be careful, you are going to ruin him for work."

"I know. You are probably right. My father says that a "bacon-fed" slave gets fat and useless." Mary returned to her work resolved to discuss the matter further with Richard.

The truth was neither Mary nor Richard knew how to treat Boston. And, if his woman and son were to follow, the problem would only grow.

Later that night when the cabin became quiet, the Lester couple resolved that the family would gather as many of Fountain's chickens as possible. The family would give some of the additional eggs produced by the chickens to the slaves.

Beyond that, Richard had thought the slaves would be given Saturday afternoon and Sunday to hunt and trap meat for the week. This would serve several purposes. First, the family had long had a rabbit, squirrel, and chipmunk problem that, at times, could ravage the family garden. By setting Boston to task in trapping these animals, the family's vegetable yield should improve. Second, by limiting the slaves' intake of pork, chicken, goat and the occasional deer and beef, the family's own stores of food would be preserved.

Richard would discuss the matter further with Bryant and others as to how they fed and treated their own slaves.

The lesson bestowed on his boys earlier that day and the fact that he did use a switch from time to time to discipline his children left Richard with the thought that, if needed, he could strike another grown man and discipline a slave when needed. "Discipline." This was the logic that the new slave owner employed to rationalize any future use of force. Force was the means by which "social order" was maintained on his farm. How else could he keep the man hin "his place." At the same time, he had not been in a fight since his early teens, and that had been a simple game that had become heated. It had involved more wrestling and pushing than punching. No blood had been drawn. It was the way they had been raised. You just did not strike another person.

Richard was not entirely comfortable with the notion.

He had not struck anyone out of anger in a long time. He thought about this and frankly could not remember the last time – it might have even been his sister when they were very young which had appalled his father. "We do not hit women. That is something a Lester does not do." His father had paused. He had never seen him this angry and the man who had a story for everything, seemed at a loss for words. "I know you are close in age, and being slightly older, she can get the better of you in an argument. But, if you ever strike her again, the consequences you will face will be grave." Richard had never struck anyone after that lecture, male or female.

It seemed, as he thought further, this was about to change.

When he was required to correct his children, he always sent them to get a switch. The reason for this was it allowed him time to clear his head and arrest his anger.

He was resolved to do something similar with his slaves. 'Yes, he thought, he did not want to strike any of them out of anger either.' Such was his justification for striking a slave. Feeble as that rationale might have been.

The thought that the slave would fight back was not a thought that crossed his mind. And frankly, as the number of slaves in the area grew, this fear would consume the slave owners of Georgia. It was one thing for a slave to be obstinate. What would happen if they all decided "enough" at the same time. In the not too distant future, this would become a debilitating fear among the slave owners.

As for his children, he only spanked them when they lied, talked back to their mother, hit a family member, or disrespected someone in authority. Such actions were never tolerated. At an early age the children had come to understand "the four things" they could never do. And if they did, a trip to the woods for a switch quickly followed.

Richard resolved that he would have similar rules for the slaves. No fighting. No disrespecting authority, and no stealing. If a slave refused to work, he would simply sell them to someone else. And he would never use a whip. He had been taken aback just by the sight of his brother constantly holding a whip in his hand while instructing Boston. While at his farm, he had not even slightly hinted that the whip would be used, but the gesture was undeniable to Richard. And Richard was certain that Boston had taken notice too.

Could Richard be different? Probably not, but time would tell.

Richard thought further about his brothers. Fountain and Bryant had both bought slaves. He had not known. No doubt, they had kept this from the family because they knew it would have brought disapproval from their father.

Each year, more members of German's fellowship had decided to own slaves. Recently, the fellowship had discussed whether to allow the slaves to worship with them. It was decided that separate services would be held and in another location. And while his father never spoke out against slavery, Richard knew that his father disapproved.

So often, for his father, it was not what he did, but what he did not do that left an impression.

German did not swear. He did not drink. He did not talk about women with other men. And while others spoke in support of slavery, even using scripture to do so, German never did.

Richard, while good at resolving disputes for others, had no desire to initiate a dispute with his father.

The night was sleepless for Richard as he thought through that future conversation with his father. There was no doubt in his mind that the conversation would not go well for him. He was certain that even the logic he used to justify correcting his children and applying that to a slave would be challenged.

Boston had only a few possessions. He had brought two blankets from Fountain's homestead with him on the journey to this new place. His clothing consisted of two short sleeved shirts, two pairs of well-worn pants, a pair of old shoes, and one longer sleeved shirt. Fountain had given him a woolen coat, but he had left this with Lucy.

Alice and Betsy had brought dinner to him and watched as he ate. It was as if they had never seen a man eat. The truth was, Alice had never seen a black man eat.

The meal consisted of the stew made of pork, potatoes and carrots, and a slice of brown bread with pecans. It was good, but Lucy could do better, he thought.

Once he had finished the meal, saying nothing, he handed the two girls the plate and spoon and they scurried back to the cabin.

Soon, darkness fell.

He laid on the floor of the tack room which smelled of leather, sweet feed, hay, and horses. He had seen at least one mouse already and was resolved that in the days to come, he would either get rid of the mouse, rig a hammock, and get off the floor, or both.

He left the door open to the tack room so that when the air stirred some of the cool night air would waft into his room… 'my room,' he thought.

Nothing was "his," and nothing ever would be. The first day had passed without a cross word from his new owners. He wondered how long it would last. Some owners whipped a new slave immediately – just to establish control. Others waited for a "reason" to do so. It was obvious to Boston that the Lesters were the latter. He wondered how long it would be before Richard Lester struck him. He wondered what his weapon of choice would be. Would it be a leather strap? Would it be a whip? Based upon the events of the day, he thought Richard might be a rod and cane sort. He was fine waiting to find out.

He thought of Lucy and Simm.

He thought of Freedom. While Boston was not educated, he knew what freedom was. He had fought alongside Joseph and the Americans in the War of 1812. In truth, he had primarily been tasked to carry supplies, care for horses, and when fortifications were built, he had dug trenches, ramparts and built palisades.

At the Battle of New Orleans, he had stayed back with the baggage and supplies. But as the wounded were carried into camp, he impulsively picked up a rifle and sword from a wounded man and entered the fray. He was not sure why, and when he thought about his actions that day, he only surmised that his life with Joseph and his family was comfortable. If the Americans lost or Joseph was killed, he had no doubt that all of that would change – and probably not for the better. It was a hunch. But that is what he had thought at the time. Joseph was truly the "master he knew." He had known others, and they had all been more cruel than Joseph. But even this had changed over time.

As Boston reflected on his life, he could sense that his own situation had deteriorated with the McIntosh's in the months before he was sold to Fountain. Much of this he attributed to the sheer number of slaves now working on the large McIntosh plantation. It seemed that every foreman or overseer with any authority was more harsh than the one before. And the number of slaves the McIntosh family had purchased exploded when the family purchased their own cotton gin. Boston had been relatively new to the plantation at the time, and he had seen how other farmers had reacted to the new device. It seemed to be changing everything.

He thought back.

There was his slave master in Charleston who was severe in the punishment he rendered. He had witnessed the harshness first-hand.

Slaves who had run were usually picked up quickly by the "Paddy Rollers" (slave patrols) and returned badly beaten. If you ran once, you were shackled. If a slave ran a second time, you were either sold, hobbled – intentionally maimed so that you could not run, or sent to a "Slave Mender" – where the treatment was harsh, and constant. The job of the Slave Mender was to extract any ill temper and free will from the slave. When they were returned, the slave was expected to be obedient and understand "their place."

This same owner had his foreman whip one of the female house slaves who was pregnant. The whipping was so brutal, the woman's water broke, and she went into labor. This seemed to only incite further rage in the overseer. Boston could still see the scene in his mind with hostile clarity. Neither the woman nor the baby had survived. While the scene was visually brutal, one of the most brutal things Boston had ever witnessed, it was the sound that haunted him. The screams of the woman being whipped combined with those of her young children as they looked on were seared into his very soul.

This harsh treatment seemed to only increase the desire for freedom among the slaves his Charleston master owned. For Boston, he had decided to bide his time. He would look for his moment and wait for the right opportunity.

Boston knew something of his value. Since 1808, the importation of slaves had been illegal. This meant that much of the slave trade involved buying and selling enslaved people already in the country. Because of the ban on slave importation, some slave owners began to purchase large numbers of female slaves and had become focused on "breeding" slaves – selling the children at increasingly young ages.

Joseph had seen to it that Boston had been trained in several ways and that he had skills beyond just being a laborer. This combined with the fact that there was no legal importation of slaves meant that his value had increased. Unfortunately, this was also true of Simm, and Boston was desperate to do everything he could to keep his family together.

And frankly, this was his greatest fear and when he thought about it, it was also his greatest source of anger. It was obvious to him that Richard Lester loved his family. Why was it that the Masters did not sense his love for *his* family?

He closed his eyes. They chose not to notice. They chose to think that their slaves could not share similar emotions. He had to contain his anger. There was nothing to be gained in thinking about it.

He thought back on the Battle of New Orleans. While it was true that he was late to the fray, when he joined the fight, it had been a strange and violent scene. At no point did he think he would die. He was certain that most of the men who died that day probably shared that same thought.

As he lay on his blankets in the darkness, he wondered to himself: 'what would I be willing to die for?' Lucy and Simm, that was a certainty. He had fought for freedom, and still was not free, so he was not sure of that. He knew stories of people who died for religion, and while he had some understanding of Christianity, that was a faith that was still not his own, so he was not sure he would die a martyr's death. No, sainthood was not for him.

He thought back to that morning in New Orleans. The fog, the mud, the blood, the smoke. He could still hear and smell the battle. It was horrible.

Had he followed Joseph? Was that it? Was he willing to die for a man who considered him property to be bought and sold? A man who could sell his son to some other plantation owner. He thought…

…He was wiser today. He would not be dashing into the fray today or at any point in the future.

But he had fought. No one had asked, he had just done it.

And, when it was over, he had returned to Joseph's home. He and Lucy had married and Simm had been born the next year.

His mind fixed again on freedom. Would that ever be given to him, or would he have to take it?

His mind returned to thoughts of home, Lucy, and Simm. He slept very little.

PART III

As one would expect, the funeral was a solemn occasion. German had steeled himself to lead the service, but intentionally keeping the service short to preserve his own dignity.

Catherine had wept openly, as had both Eugene and Betsy. Their sadness slowly ebbed as the day grew long.

Finally, the friends and fellow church members thinned so that German and Catherine were surrounded only by family.

Bryant and Sara were going to stay the night, but Richard and Mary were heading back with the children and would be leaving shortly.

Realizing the day was coming to a close, Catherine rose, "Well, we cannot eat all this food, and Mary, you certainly will not have time to cook. Let's send you home with some food." With that, she rose, went into the house, and emerged quickly with a large wicker basket and a ceramic pot. Sara and Mary rose to help her pack food for the trip and put the rest away for later use.

While they busied themselves, Richard rose and said, "Father, Bryant, and I need to harness the team and get the wagon ready."

He stood and the two men followed him to the small barn.

As the father walked with his two sons, it was Bryant who spoke first, "Dad, we have something to tell you."

German glanced back and forth at both of his sons, "What is it?"

They stopped.

"Fountain was murdered," Bryant said. "He was shot."

"And you know this how?" responded German ignoring the obvious response he was about to hear.

Richard nodded for Bryant to continue. "I saw the wound when we dressed him and bound him to bring him here."

German stilled for a moment. Neither son knew whether it was anger or sorrow that filled their father's face. It was neither. It was deeper. It was frustrated grief. The kind that wells up when something needless happens to end the life of someone you love.

German spoke next, "And dear JoAnne. Was she…?" his voice quivered.

"No sir. No, she was not shot. As best we could surmise, they were coming back from my farm to their home and there was an altercation that led to Fountain being shot, and his team of horses must have charged uncontrolled. She was truly injured when the wagon turned over."

"I… I…" German had no response.

Richard then spoke, "Father, I should make inquiries. At the very least, we should alert the State Sheriff. The state should know that one of its citizens was murdered."

The men turned to the horses and the harnesses. Working in silence for a few minutes, the three moved together in rhythm to complete a task that they had performed often and knew well.

Finally German spoke in a raspy, tired voice. "It does not make sense to simply leave this to the local Marshal. Our county is so new, we really have little hope of either satisfaction or justice in this matter. I agree. We need to journey to Milledgeville and meet with the Sheriff of the state. Bryant, can you travel with me there tomorrow? They will want to speak with you as you are the one who saw the wounds. You're the closest person to a witness we know of."

"Yes. Of course. I can drop Sara off at our homestead and we can continue to Milledgeville from there. Why don't you bring mother with you and stay a day?" Richard replied.

"We can ask her. Frankly, I am not sure how to tell her this," German said. "Maybe we can tell her tonight after Richard and the children have left."

Richard, Mary, and the five children climbed into their wagon.

Bryant shook Richard's hand and told him that he would be back soon to help expand the house. As soon as the planting season was over, he would come with men and material.

Richard tugged on the reins and the two horses lurched forward down the trail.

The children bounced in the back. Mary glanced over her shoulder every few moments to make sure no one had fallen off.

It was a long while before Mary spoke.

"So, are we keeping Boston?"

"I have been thinking about that," replied Richard. "I think we should."

He saw the look on Mary's face and realized that she had thought about it. The lady always had a plan.

"You said last night there is a woman, Lucy, and a boy, Simm."

Richard nodded.

"The truth is, with five children, I could use some help, and Lucy might be the answer. And my father would be pleased to know that we have at least made steps towards growing cotton – everyone else is."

Richard agreed. "It's not that we don't need help. If we do this, we will have three more people to be responsible for." The phrase lingered in the air.

"It's true. You're right. We will need to expand the garden and plant more potatoes and vegetables," Mary thought aloud.

Richard chimed in, "And, we can get another cow and some additional chickens from Fountain's farm."

"It would be nice to have the help. And Boston does seem able."

Again, the two settled into a silence.

It was a warm day, and the horses were beginning to labor as the trail climbed slowly up a hill. The sweat would turn to a light froth before the trip was over. When they spoke, the horses' ears would twitch, and their heads would turn slightly. Occasionally, a fly would land on an ear or rump of one of the horses and the horse's coat would lightly spasm to discourage the free riding fly.

The trip from Covington to the Lester farm was not difficult. The terrain largely followed what people in the area called a spine, a trail that seemingly followed the ridge of a small, but long mountain west then south towards Dry Indian Creek. Before they reached the turn to head down to their farm, they would pass several large, familiar farms. Both Mary and Richard could not help but note that increasingly, they saw black African slaves working in the fields. Farms that had largely been tended by families were now being expanded and worked by the new influx of forced, slave labor. They simply had not noticed the change, or, they had chosen to ignore it.

The dry rocky red-clay path wound from forest to field, and back to forest. This time of year, the air was heavy with pine pollen, which seemed to cover everything with a light yellowish-green hue. Then, there were the large pods that the poplar trees dropped that seemed to coat the trail, more densely in certain areas, that carried the wagon to the Lester's home.

In the back of the wagon, the children were quietly talking. While it was difficult to hear the entirety of their conversations over the sound of the horses and the wagon wheels as they turned roughly across rocks and pebbles, Mary picked out the occasional 'Simm does this; Lucy does that.' Undoubtedly, Eugene was giving her children an education on the newcomers. The hawk was mentioned several times as well, as the children's conversation turned towards finding a name for the bird.

After a moment Richard offered, "I need to see if I can help Joseph. There is something going on here with the Creek and the Cherokee, and if our family can help, we should. Not only that, but there is also more to my brother's death than just a wagon accident."

Mary, holding on to his arm and looking at his face, continued for him. "I know. Sara told me last night that Fountain was shot. She also said JoAnne was never conscious enough to tell them who was involved." She thought for a moment. "Richard, do you think you should really get involved with Joseph McIntosh? That isn't our problem. And it may well be the reason Fountain died. Sara told me that we should stay out of the whole 'Indian Affair' as she called it."

"You may be right. I share that thought. At the same time, Joseph is trying to do the same thing we are doing – he is raising four children, two of which are not his, but came to him because of a death in his family." Richard's voice tightened. "So many of us are just trying to provide a safe place for our families. Frankly, that is what Boston wants, too. He just has no choice."

He paused briefly before continuing. "You know Mary, I don't care who you are, white, black, red, Scottish, Spanish, Creek or Cherokee, all most of us want is to be safe and raise our families."

Mary squeezed Richard's arm before continuing, "You could set him free." Mary stated.

"Yes, we could. WE could. But where would a negro with no land or money go? And, the truth is, he is of value to us, and Fountain bought him free and clear from Joseph."

Mary sat up. "Did I hear you say Joseph sold Boston to your brother? How did Joseph know Fountain?"

"They hunted together. It was Fountain who suggested that Joseph come to see me. Fountain told him I might be able to help. You see, the last thing my brother said to anyone about me was 'go see my brother… he can help you.' How can I turn Joseph away?"

"But why does it have to be you?" asked Mary.

"Well, my father knows the men who run the Cherokee Missions. Most of them he has known for a while, and, in fact, his church has sent money and materials there to help build those missions."

"I see," said Mary. "So, the Creek think that, through your father and the missionaries to the Cherokee Nation, you can help bring about a resolution and avoid new hostilities."

Richard never answered. He was deep in thought as was Mary.

"These are dangerous times," he said. "We do not have to decide today."

It was late afternoon when the expanded Lester family reached the farm.

Boston stood in front of the Barn and moved toward the wagon to un-hitch the team as it came to a stop.

"Any problems, Boston?" asked Richard.

"None. I worked the mule in the field in the morning and Danny in the afternoon. I think we can finish the field in another two days. That field will be ready to plant before the week is out."

"The whole field?" asked Mary.

"Yes, ma'am. It will be completely ploughed. Corn-ready. If we had an-other day or two, your boys and I could walk the field and remove some of the larger stones and stumps, but frankly, the field looks pretty good."

"Boston, I think the boys can handle the rocks. If there is something too large for them to handle, they can put a stick in the ground, and you and I will spend a few hours or an afternoon and finish that task. Any rocks will be a good border for the field and, if we remove them now, it will improve the harvest and make next year's planting easier."

Boston nodded in agreement.

"Well, you all must be hungry. Give me some time and I will have one of the boys bring dinner out to you," Mary said as she stepped down from the bench of the wagon.

The boys headed into the breezeway to check on the hawk. Alice and Betsy followed Mary into the house.

The two men unbridled the horses and led them into stalls where they were fed and watered. The three boys then brushed both horses down.

With the new mare and the team of two horses that had drawn the wagon, all from Fountain's farm, Richard Lester now had five horses on his farm. He had growing concerns that his pasture would not support the number of livestock now on the farm. 'Expanding the pasture might be the next large project,' he thought to himself.

The men pushed the wagon back into its place, out of the way on the sunny side of the barn.

"Mr. Richard, I was thinking. I could build a room right here for me, Lucy, and Simm." He was pointing to the open air shed where they stored the wagon. "We would be close to the barn, and it would not take much time to build. There is already a roof and one wall."

"So, right here where we store the wagon. Where would we put the wagon?"

"When it rains, Simm and I would put it in the breezeway of the barn."

Richard looked at the location Boston had proposed before replying, "I think we can do better. Follow me."

They walked, crossing the hard packed earth in front of the cabin and approached the chicken coop. Beyond was a second, larger structure.

"This corn crib is bigger and does not smell like animals and hay. Would this work?"

"Yes, but where would you put the corn to dry?" asked Boston.

"Well, that is a problem. We have until harvest, July really, to build a new corn crib, one bigger to accommodate the larger harvest we will have because of the additional field we are planting."

Both men stood and stared at the crib. Boston paced the crib off trying to get its measurements.

"Well, what do you think?" asked Richard.

"I think we should build a replacement just there about twice this size," Boston stated.

Richard smiled. "No, about the crib. Will this work for you, Lucy and Simm?"

Boston fixed his eyes on the crib and replied, "Yes, this will work. Can I add a fireplace for warmth and cooking?"

"Why, yes. Certainly," replied Richard. He had not thought about that aspect. And in truth, Boston was right to inquire because many slave cabins did not have fireplaces.

"I will need to collect some stones to build a fireplace and then cut two windows for light and air but, yes. This will work."

Both men stood in silence as they surveyed the crib once more. The corn crib was actually quite sound structurally. It had to be in order to prevent smaller animals from ravaging the harvest.

Richard stepped forward placing a hand on the corn crib. Boston could not tell if he was blessing the structure or testing its integrity.

Finally, the farmer turned to Boston and said, "So, I guess you are staying."

There was a pause as the two men continued to measure each other.

"Boston, when it comes to owning slaves, you are going to discover quickly that we have not really thought about this." At this point, Richard could not look Boston in his eyes. Instead, he continued to survey the corn crib. "We are really pretty simple people and I think my instructions to you should be simple as well."

Boston did not agree or disagree. He simply stood and shifted his weight.

"Do what I ask. If you don't understand what I am asking of you, feel free to ask. Don't lie to us. And no fighting. If you get into an altercation with someone on the farm, I am not sure what I would do, but if the choice is between you and someone of my blood, you will be on the mule's end of that argument. Whatever you do, do not cross my wife. If you come between me and her, I will see to it that you are sold to someone else. Do you understand?"

At that, Richard lifted his eyes and they locked with Boston's. For the first time, Boston's eyes did not waver either. Boston nodded that he understood.

"Tomorrow, I will send you to the new mill with a letter. You will take Fountain's wagon and Paul to pick up the wood we need to build the new crib. I am in good standing with the mill owner, and he knows Paul. There are some logs that I cut down to a decent size. The logs are stacked up on the edge of the new field that you just plowed. You will take a load of those logs with you to the mill, and that will lower the cost of the hewn wood we purchase. I will help you load the wagon in the morning. The sooner we get this done, the sooner we can collect Lucy and Simm. You can also swing by Jordan's General Store in Covington and pick up some items my wife will need."

The two men stood in silence for a moment before Boston finally broke the silence. He turned. Looking over his shoulder at the pasture he paused, "Mr. Richard, your stallion and that mare, they are, well, your stallion is very interested."

"Is that a fact? Well. Then Boston, let's see if we can have a colt!"

As Richard turned to join his family in the cabin, he glanced at the horses in the pasture. By spring he could have six horses. Expanding the pasture would definitely be the family's next big task. Moreover, that wood could be used to expand the house.

The following morning, before breakfast, Richard and Boston hitched the new team of horses to the wagon that Boston had driven to the farm just a few days prior. The two men led the wagon into the field. There, they loaded an ample quantity of long, straight poplar logs into the wagon. The logs were between five and 10 feet long, which meant the longer logs extended out the back of the wagon about two feet.

Once the wagon was loaded, the two men led the horses back to the house where the children were busy with their morning chores. There, the horses were watered for the impending trip to the mill.

After a brief breakfast of biscuits and ham, Richard asked Paul to walk with him towards the wagon. There, he handed his son a note for the mill, and a short list of provisions needed from the mercantile store. Richard instructed his son to return with as much hewn wood as he could, without overtaxing the horses and the wagon. "If you come back with a lot more wood than you are taking to the mill, that is probably too much." Handing his son a small leather pouch, he continued. "The note should speak for me. Son, there are 20 Spanish milled coins in this pouch and a few coins of similar size and value with King George on them. They will be acceptable to the mill. When the miller deducts the value of the wood you are bringing to him from the cost of lumber, you should be able to get four boards for each log you are leaving at the mill, but you will have to pay for three of the boards. I am thinking you should spend about 12 coins on the lumber and bring home forty-eight boards in total."

Paul nodded.

"Put this in the pocket of your pants. You will need at least three of the smaller dime coins to purchase the items on your mother's list from the Mercantile in Covington. If your grandmother is home, go there and see if she can provide both you and Boston lunch. If she is not there, go to one of the taverns and purchase lunch for yourself and Boston. Boston should probably not eat in the tavern. I have never seen a black man in any of the taverns, whether he be freed or bonded, and I would not want that to be a problem for you, Boston, or the tavern owner."

"Yes, father. I understand," the boy replied with a seriousness that made Richard proud.

"Good. Off with you." Richard shook his son's hand and smiled.

Boston heard the conversation as well, but he was glad it was Paul who would be making the purchases. Until the proprietors of the local businesses knew who Boston was, he preferred not to deal directly with other whites. The truth was that whites preferred that as well. Many thought it beneath them to conduct commerce with a slave.

With a hug from his mother and a pat on the shoulder from his father, Boston and Paul climbed up into the wagon. Boston slid the family's old musket under the bench with the leather pouch and brass horn that held an ample measure of gunpowder.

Mary had been standing to the side, and before her son climbed into the wagon, she gave him a big hug and kiss. She walked around the front of the wagon, giving the horses and the rigging a light inspection as she did so. When she reached the other side of the wagon, she stepped back and crossed her arms, giving a stern look that Boston could not ignore.

Boston had done nothing to deserve a lack of trust. But for some reason, Mary was unsettled about sending her son on this errand with the new slave.

The night before, Richard had relayed his plan to send Boston and Paul to the mill, and Mary had protested vehemently. Her concerns were slightly arrested when Richard reminded Mary of Lucy and Simm, and because of this, the slave was "more bound to the Lester farm than anyone."

Boston did not know whether Mary Lester's demeanor was one of concern or anger. But he knew it was directed at him. Looking at the ground between Mary's feet Boston said, "Don't fret, Mrs. Mary. We will return with the wood and dried goods directly."

Mary's stance shifted slightly and her lips, which had been pursed loosened almost to a smile. She uncrossed her arms. No one called her Mrs. Mary. It was slightly disarming. 'This will do,' she thought to herself. She liked it.

Boston held the reins in his hands with Paul on his right.

The young lad was obviously excited by the responsibility of traveling to town with the family's new slave to make purchases. Paul quietly hoped that he would see someone he knew. A member of his grandfather's church. One of the neighboring farmers. Anyone.

The two traveled in silence up the dirt lane away from the farm as the horses and the wagon strained under the weight of the load. The sound of hoofs, wood and leather surrounded them. They passed the new field and the pile of timber from which the logs they now carried were pulled. After a short distance, the lane leveled out and joined a larger, well-worn trail that serviced all the neighboring farms nestled against Dry Indian Creek.

Once they were firmly on the road, Boston looked at Paul and asked, "How old are you?"

"I am 11," was the reply. "How old are you?"

"Oh, I reckon I am a few years older than your father. How old is he?" replied Boston.

"You know, I am not sure. I have never asked him." Paul was slightly embarrassed by this lack of knowledge.

"Well, I am not sure of my age either, but people tell me I was born in 1795, so, if my numbers are right, and they usually are, I am 33," Boston replied.

"So, you know numbers?" the boy asked.

"Yes. Enough to get by. Enough to help you at the mill if you need it… My previous owners taught me maths so I could do carpentry."

"It is strange that you do not know when you were born," the boy stated innocently.

"I guess it may seem that way, but it never seemed that important to anyone until today. And I am pretty sure they did not keep any record of it other than to note the number of slaves on the plantation where I lived had increased. Do you know numbers?" Boston asked.

"Yes. But I have never bought or exchanged wood we harvested from the farm for boards, and the only time I have been to the mill I was with my father." Paul's voice trailed off as he thought further about the transaction.

"Well, what did your father tell you?"

The boy reached into the pocket of his shirt and withdrew the piece of paper his father had handed to him. "He said the note would speak for me and him."

Boston, keeping his eyes on the road, glanced at the folded piece of paper Paul turned nervously in his fingers, and asked. "Do you know letters?"

"Yes, I can read."

Boston smiled at Paul and said, "Read the note so we both know what to expect."

Paul unfolded the note and began to read: "To Mr. Phillips or The Mill Foreman. I am in need of boards, 10 – 12 feet in length. My son Paul, and slave Boston, can speak in my stead if this note does not suffice. The last time we exchanged wood for lumber, you reduced the price of the planed boards by one-fourth to compensate me for the wood we harvested from our farm. If this is still acceptable to you, my son is authorized to make the exchange and has the coin necessary to complete the transaction."

Paul looked up at Boston. He then folded the paper and returned it to his pocket.

"So," Boston said, "if you and I can get the mill to reduce the price of the lumber a little further, your father would be pleased. We would have negotiated a better price than the one he did."

"Say that again?" Paul requested.

Boston thought for a moment before he began. "What your father is saying is for every three boards, we should get one free. The free board we get is for the wood that we are bringing to the mill. The wood in the back of our wagon." He paused. "Do you think we can do better?"

Boston could see the boy's mind working.

They rode in silence for quite some time, with Paul glancing over his shoulder at the logs in the bed of the wagon several times as he thought.

After some distance, they approached the Stone Mountain Road that led to Covington. Paul broke the silence, "Covington is to the right. The new mill is to he left and sits on the Yellow River. We should go to the mill first before heading into Covington."

With that, Boston encouraged the horses forward onto the well-worn road.

Crossing over Dried Indian Creek, the two traveled a short distance before turning south on the trail that deliberately followed the contours of the Yellow River and would take them to the mill.

Finally, Paul spoke again. "Boston, can you read?"

"No, I know a few letters. I can write my name. But I cannot read. I have never had much use for it, and certainly no time to learn it," was the answer.

In truth, this was not uncommon. Most whites believed knowledge would make a slave unfit to fulfill their purpose. Specifically, the slave owners believed teaching a slave could render the slave a threat to the owner and ruinous to the slaves around them while most likely bringing harm to the slave. Knowledge can be a powerful thing, and the masters did not want that knowledge shared with their slaves.

The mill sat astride the Yellow River and relied upon power from the water to turn its grist mill and saws that cut long logs into boards, beams, and usable lumber.

The new mill was a welcome enterprise to the area. Now, the Lesters could bring their corn here in large quantity and have it ground into meal. Visiting the mill had become relatively routine for the family in a short period of time.

As they approached the mill, both Boston and Paul noticed increased activity on the trail. As they drew closer, they could hear the sound of industry, water, and the indistinct voices of those who toiled at the mills.

They pulled up to the wood mill and waited in their wagon as two wagons were in front of them.

After a short while a man approached Boston and asked, "Are you here to sell wood?"

Boston, taking care not to look the man in the eyes, did not respond directly. Instead, he nodded at Paul sitting beside him, and quietly said "The young master here has been sent by his father. You best speak with him."

 "Wait, I know you. Where do I know you from?" the foreman looked closely at Boston, who sat silently looking at the reins in his hands.

"From the last time I was here, I guess," replied Boston.

"No, that's not it. I just got here. It is from somewhere else." Boston continued to sheepishly look away from the man and at the uninteresting ends of the horses hitched to the wagon.

Boston, trying to divert the conversation, looked at Paul and said, "Mr. Paul, this man is busy. Would you like to tell him why we are here?"

With that introduction, Paul leaned forward, looking past Boston at the foreman and said plainly, with only a slight hint of nervousness, "We would like to exchange the wood we have harvested for 10 foot, planed boards."

"What kind of wood are you looking for?" the man inquired, he was still trying to place Boston, but seemed to be losing interest in him.

"You know, my father did not say, but I think either poplar or pine would work for us. Would you agree Boston?" Paul waited for Boston's response.

"Yes, Mr. Paul, I think either of those would work for us." Boston continued, "Do you think we should get three poplar beams for the base and take the rest in pine board?"

Paul thought for a moment and looked at the mill's foreman. "That makes sense to me. Pine is less expensive than poplar, isn't it?"

The foreman shifted his stance slightly. "Yes, it is."

"The last time we were here, we exchanged harvested wood where for every three boards, we got one board at no cost in coin. In that we are getting three beams, and that requires less sawing, and we are bringing you poplar and taking mostly pine, do you think we might be able to do a little better?" The boy was pushing the negotiation.

At that, the man removed his hat and walked to the back of the wagon. Boston stayed on the bench, but he patted Paul's knee and with a tilt of his head, encouraged Paul to follow the foreman. Paul jumped onto the ground meeting the foreman as he surveyed the load of wood in the wagon.

"The timber is straight and true," Boston remarked, "and it is poplar."

The foreman looked up at Boston, who was still sitting in the wagon. He paced the length of the wagon several times. When he started moving the logs to get a better look, Boston turned in his seat and leaned over. With Boston's help, the foreman was able to move several of the long timbers so that he could inspect the wood more closely.

"Who are you?" the foreman asked without looking at Paul.

"I am Paul Lester. My father is Richard Lester and my grandfather, German, is the Methodist minister in Covington." Paul believed everyone in the area knew his grandfather, and for the most part, this was true; although Paul was not sure this man knew his grandfather. Something about the man led Paul to think that the man did not go to church on a regular basis.

The man looked at Paul, inspecting the boy further. Then at Boston. "Do you have coin or are you looking for credit?" asked the foreman.

"We have coin," replied Paul.

"I will give you five pine boards for each log you have in your wagon, and you will pay for the three boards with a silver sovereign."

Paul looked at Boston and back at the foreman. "Thank you. We will be paying for 36 boards then and two of the poplar timbers."

The foreman shook his head but did not smile as he knew the boy was pushing the negotiations further. "No, you will need to pay for the three beams."

Paul exhaled giving a sigh of relief, and at that the foreman laughed.

"You tell your father to come himself next time. He is probably not the trader that you are. Move along."

Paul turned to the man and said, "Thank you. I do have a question. You know this better than we do. Given the weight, do you think our team and this wagon can pull what we just ordered? Or should we make two trips?"

The man looked over the wagon and team of horses quickly then responded, "Your wagon and team are in much better shape than most. I think you will be fine. You can pull your wagon up in a moment and there is a trough across the yard where you can water your horses for your return." The man pointed across to the far side of the dirt yard. "We will load you up and have you on your way shortly. You will need to go inside to settle your account."

"Follow me and I will walk you inside." The foreman turned expecting Paul to follow.

Paul turned back to the wagon and whispered to Boston, "So, that should be 12 coins, right?"

"Sounds like thirteen to me because of the beams," Boston replied. "You worked a better deal than your father is expecting. If it is more than thirteen coins, ask them to write it down so that your father has a record of what we did. And Paul, you did not even need your father's letter."

Paul smiled and turned to follow the foreman. With his hand on his pocket that, as far as Paul knew, contained much of the family's monetary wealth, he followed the man toward the mill.

In short order, Paul returned with a smile on his face. And, as the foreman promised, the cut lumber was unloaded quickly: the three, rough-hewn poplar beams took their place first, with the sixty pine boards placed on top.

Boston climbed into the wagon expecting Paul to follow. The boy peered across the yard where the foreman was helping a man who sat in an empty wagon.

"Boston, please water the horses. I need to speak to the foreman once more." Paul turned and walked across the dirt yard and waited for the foreman to finish his latest transaction.

The foreman turned. Seeing Paul with his hand extended the large man shook the boy's hand. Paul noticed the man was missing two fingers.

"Thank you. We will be leaving. I know we will be back with more timber because we are clearing another field for cotton. I will see you then."

The man looked across the yard and saw Boston watering the horses.

"Glad you got what you needed, and I will be here when you return."

Paul walked across the yard and climbed up into the wagon. "My father will be pleased," he said, almost to himself.

"Yes, Paul. I think he will."

Paul looked at Boston and asked, "That man seemed to know you. Did you recognize him?"

Boston took a deep breath and replied, "Yes, I know him. He was the foreman at the McIntosh Mill. He was a hard man. He was only happy when his ox-hide whip was red."

There was silence as Paul thought about what Boston had said. As they traveled down the trail away from the mill, the young boy looked at Boston and asked, "Did that foeman whip you?"

"Oh, yes. He whipped me. He whipped Lucy and he whipped Simm."

Paul looked at the slave sitting next to him. Boston thought he knew what the next question would be before he asked it: "My dad whips me sometimes with a switch. But only when I deserve it. Did you deserve it?"

"Mr. Paul, if another man beat you or your mother with a leather whip, what would your father do?"

The question hung in the air while the boy pondered a response. None came, so Boston continued, "I know of no man who would let that happen, and I do not believe for one cluck that your father would stand by and allow it. So, when it did happen, I stepped in and stopped it. Slaves do not do that. When I did that, that foreman's anger would turn to me, and I was fine that. Well, as fine as a slave can be. So, I took the beatings that were intended for me – and when I could, I took the beatings that were intended for my wife and son as well."

Paul did not respond.

When Paul and Boston came to the Stone Mountain Road, they turned right, taking the road to Covington. Paul finally broke the silence asking, "Boston, how did you become a slave?"

"Mr. Paul, I was born into slavery. I have been bound my entire life. My mother was a slave, and it seems Simm will be a slave, too." This was the law. The status of the child was the same as their mother's; and everything the slave possessed: clothing, tools, furniture, were also the property of the master. Slaves had no rights to property.

It seemed to Boston that Paul had learned as much as he wanted to know about slavery for the day. The two traveled in silence, listening to the strain of the horses and the wagon as it lurched down the rough, well-traveled road.

The distance to Covington was covered quickly.

The mercantile store had all the items that Mary had requested: thread, needles, sugar, flour, and tea.

Leaving the wagon and horses at the mercantile store, Paul walked with Boston up the muddy road to his grandmother's house. The two dodged muddy patches, horses, horse-drawn wagons, and the manure left in the town's main street by the day's traffic.

The visit to his grandparent's was a welcome surprise to Paul's grandmother.

Catherine doted on her grandchildren. Paul, being Richard's oldest, was growing quickly. And, because the other grandchildren were further away, Paul was the grandchild she knew best.

"… and who is this you have with you?" Catherine asked.

"This is one of Fountain's men, Boston. He is our slave now." Paul replied.

Catherine looked at Boston and stepped forward taking Paul by his elbow. "I see. Well, what brings you two to Covington?"

"We had to go to the mill to pick up lumber for father, and then come into town to pick up a few things for mother."

"Well, you have had a busy day. I am so glad you came by. Have you had anything to eat?" she asked.

"Grandma, I am so glad you asked. I am gutfoundered, and I am sure Boston is too."

"I can feed you both." The old lady led them both into the large room on the left that served as both the dining room and kitchen. "Please, sit down. Your grandfather is going to be sad that he missed you. He had to visit a family of our congregation. They just had a baby a few days ago." Boston stood. He was not accustomed to sitting at the same table. Catherine, turned, seeing the hesitation, she pulled out a chair and said, "Please, sit here. Everyone is welcome at our table."

Paul and Boston watched as the Lester family's matron moved about the kitchen. Paul was always amazed at the woman's efficiency. There was an economy of movement about his grandmother that he did not see in his own mother. Maybe it would come with time. Or maybe it was just a talent that Catherine Lester had developed over years of opening her home on a regular basis and with no notice.

Hospitality – it was her gift. People would drop by with no notice or appointment, and food seemed to magically appear.

And today was no exception. The lady whirled around the kitchen while providing Boston and Paul with an update on all the news of Covington and Paul's extended family.

Boston and Paul had their fill of bread, butter, jam, apples, and smoked ham. For a lunch, it was a veritable feast.

Having their fill and with miles to travel in order to return home, Paul rose and crossed the floor. His grandmother heard the footsteps approaching and turned, pausing her work in the dry sink. He gave his grandmother a big hug.

Boston saw the old woman absorb the hug like dry earth. She closed her eyes and smiled. Boston guessed that the old woman would feed off her grandson's hug for several days.

"Grandma, thank you. That was the best lunch I have had in a long time."

"Oh, darling, thank you. It was a pleasure. And you are right, you better get on the road before your mother and father come looking for you both." She turned and looked at Boston. "And Boston, you are welcome here any time my son sends you to town." Catherine knew how negroes and slaves were treated in town, and it was unsettling to her. No doubt, if members of her congregation knew she had fed a slave at her own table, harsh words would be exchanged with her husband.

Paul smiled and Boston simply nodded. He could count on one hand the times a white person had extended kindness and warmth to him. Over the next few days, he would reflect on the simple act and realize the only other times such kindness had been offered it had been children, and often, when it happened, the children had been rebuked.

Paul led Boston from the house, and they walked back down the main street to where they had left their team of horses and the wagon.

The team was rested and the journey back to the Lester homestead went by without incident.

Upon their arrival, Paul handed his father the coin purse and a slip of paper from the mill.

Richard scanned the paper quickly. He shuffled the coin purse between his hands and smiled saying, "This is a bit heavier than I thought it would be. You did well."

"Thank you, father, but it was Boston's idea," replied Paul.

"Was it? That is good to know." Richard looked at Boston. Gradually, the two men were gaining the measure of each other.

In the days that followed, the farm was slowly and steadily transformed. To the outside observer, the change would have seemed slight. But to the Lesters, the changes were monumental. New routines were established.

The boys had taken longer than expected to remove the stones from the field, but that also meant that the job was well done. Around the edge of the new field, a low stone barrier had grown from their work. It was not high or structural in any way. There had not been enough rock in the field to yield a wall. However, in the future, when stone was needed for a project, this would be a good source of material for the family. For now, the low row of stones surrounded and defined the new field.

The children planted the corn as instructed. And with Boston, everything was easier. Boston and Richard had increased the size of the garden and started work on the new corn crib. The children had been told to each carry the largest rock they could carry up from the stream or the edge of the field, and they were to each do this three times each day. The stream rocks were smooth and of a better quality than those around the new cornfield. After two weeks of steady labor, the new crib had taken shape, and a large pile of stones had accumulated for a fireplace in the old corn crib.

One morning, Richard got up early and left for town in the family's wagon. He left the boys to assist Boston with watering the field, tending the livestock, and handing materials up to Boston as he completed the roof on the new corn crib. The girls gathered eggs, watered the garden, and helped Mary in the kitchen.

It was late in the afternoon when Joseph McIntosh arrived. As Mary expected her husband back soon, she asked Joseph to stay for dinner.

The boys took Joseph to the barn where Joseph inspected their hawk. He lifted the hawk off the hitching post and took him outside. After several minutes and a little discussion, it was decided that Joseph would see if he could attract the hawk to a squirrel skin lure.

This activity took most of the late afternoon.

As dinner was about to be served, the sound of horses could be heard on the lane leading to the farm, and Richard appeared cresting the hill. In the wagon were three people – Richard, Lucy, and Simm.

It would be difficult to describe the joy that Boston felt upon seeing Lucy and Simm. His departure from Fountain Lester's farm had been sudden. For this reason, he had been given little time to prepare, much less say goodbye. And, given his status, he had no say as to when he should depart, and whether or when he would return.

He had taken Richard Lester at his word – that he would be reunited with his wife and son, but as the two weeks had passed, he was beginning to wonder when it would happen and how long his separation would last.

Mary watched as Boston was reunited with his family, and the joy and warmth exchanged between the three was obvious. She was struck by how similar their emotion seemed to her own when she was reunited with her own family.

Boston, Lucy, and Simm were settling into the old corn crib. Richard had brought with him a few furnishings from his brother's home to help round out what he thought might be needed: A bed, a table, three chairs, and a chest. He had also brought some clothing that had belonged to Fountain and JoAnne as well as other household items that would be functional. Importantly, he had also loaded most of the tools his brother possessed, which would be needed to make Boston's work go more quickly. There were also several cages containing chickens and one milk cow tied to the end of the wagon.

Simm was older than Richard had expected. Richard guessed he was 13. Strong and intelligent, but shorter than his father

Lucy was small in stature, but very direct, particularly with Boston. Only slightly less so with Richard, which had taken him aback. In time, he would come to realize that the only person she cowed to was Mary. Around Mary, she was mostly quiet and slow to share any opinion. Lucy dressed plainly and the children would later agree that they never saw her without a bandana turban about her head. For years, the boys only assumed that she had hair, but none of the boys could verify either its existence or color.

After dinner, Joseph and Richard lingered at the table while the children went down to the stream with strict instructions to get clean, and a warning that Mary would follow shortly.

Joseph began, "I am glad Boston has found his way to you. Simm is a good lad and if you decide to, you could sell him for a profit in a year or two, if not now. And Lucy, she will make sure everyone, and everything is in its place – including you if you're not careful."

Mary smiled at that. These last few days had been increasingly hard. Even with the chores and the farm life that was never idle, the children just seemed to be everywhere and into everything.

"… and the hawk. The hawk is healthy. If they work with that lure each morning or night, they might be able to fly it soon."

Richard responded, "Well, we thank you for that. Frankly, I do not know anything about raising a hawk, much less hunting with one."

"By Fall, that hawk and the boys should be able to provide a steady supply of squirrel and rabbit if you let it," Joseph said with confidence.

Mary interjected, "Well, that is a good thing, cause with three additional mouths to feed, our larder will be empty before winter.

Joseph straightened. "Mary. Richard. Are you feeding Boston and his family the same food you eat?"

Richard looked at Mary. Mary nodded.

"That will not do. You cannot do that. They are slaves!" They should not eat as their masters do. You need to stop that and do so at once."

Richard looked at Mary, "We suspected as much. We will need to give them some measure of food each week. I know both Boston and Simm are trappers." There was a pause. "What they trap, they can certainly keep for themselves, but we are going through our stores rapidly."

"A hungry slave is a more loyal slave." The statement from Joseph hung in the air. Pausing, the three adults felt the tempo of the conversation was about to change. And it did. "Have you thought about helping us? Your crops are in the ground and if you can help, there is urgency. My people are upset on two fronts – the Cherokee Indians are about to transfer land that does not belong to them, and your government is not paying us what is owed from the assistance our nation provided in quelling the rebellion several years ago."

Joseph let it all sink in.

"Ride with me to Etowah," Joseph pleaded.

The statement hung in the air. "Ride to Etowah." Joseph made the request sound so simple. It was not. Etowah was north and west of Covington. It was a journey of at least a week there, and a week back. Three was more probable.

Richard looked at his wife, stood, and turned towards the embers in the larger walk-in fireplace. Kneeling, he thought of all the reasons he should not make the journey. Taking the small hay broom in his hand, he whisked a few of the ashes back into the depths of the fireplace. There was a large L-bar of iron on a hinge that Mary used for cooking. It was strong enough to hold their largest iron pot filled to its brim, and it allowed her to pivot the pot closer to the flame or away from the heat as needed. He placed his hand on the arm that cantilevered from the wall over the bed of the fireplace and the ebbing flames below. Even though the bar was still hot from the fire, he moved it back and forth thinking.

Joseph could not tell if he was inspecting the mechanism or not.

Richard rose, brushing the ash from his hands as he looked at his wife. She had not spoken, and the couple had not had time to fully discuss the journey and its dangers. The silence in the room was tense.

Mary approached her husband and quietly said, "Richard, surely you are not thinking of doing this." Although she said it quietly, the statement was made with conviction. She continued, "Your brother and his wife have just died. Your first obligation is to this family and these children. And the truth is, for all we know, Fountain and JoAnne were killed over this."

Richard nodded, stepped forward, and placed both hands on his wife's shoulders. He then turned to Joseph. He could tell the Indian was about to speak but he raised his hands.

"Can you give us another day to think about this. The truth is we have had very little discussion about this. Let us sleep on this one more night," Richard said. "I think Mary is right and that I may need to ask that you take this task from me. Whatever assistance I can offer would be subtle." He paused. "Frankly, I do not believe I will be any help in getting the government to pay your nation anything. I would not know where to start." There was a far off look on his face. "Is there any way you can return in the morning, and we can give you our final answer then?"

Joseph nodded. He knew he was asking a lot of Richard and Mary, particularly given all that his family had endured.

"I am camped not far from here. I will return in the morning." With that, the man turned and to leave.

"You are welcome to stay here in our loft," Richard offered.

Joseph paused for a moment and thought, "No, I think my campsite is nice and quiet. I will sleep there and return in the morning."

As they heard the sound of Joseph's horse recede in the distance, Mary turned and sat on the stool nearest the cooking stones and stared into the fireplace she knew so well.

After a short while, she stood, "I need to check on the children."

It was much later that night. The house was quiet and dark. Richard woke to find himself alone in bed. He rose quickly putting on only the pair of paints that hung on a peg on the wall by its suspenders. He walked into the cooking area of the cabin. It was empty.

He opened the door to the cabin and walked out onto the porch and turned left. Even in the shadows of the dark night, he knew the trail by heart. He walked the short distance down to the stream and found his wife.

She was sitting on a stone by the stream. The stone was odd for its size. Most of the stones along the creek were small. Even the largest stones could be moved by one man. This piece of granodiorite was quite large and because of its size it seemed out of place. It was like a giant had simply decided it had carried the stone far enough and dropped it there on the Lester farm where it would remain for eternity.

The stream found the stone immovable as well as it took a sharp turn at this point and diverted around the large obstacle.

Mary was seated quietly on the cool stone, her arms about her shins and her knees pulled tightly to her chest with her bare feet on the rock. Her chin rested on her knees as she stared into the water.

She did not turn as Richard approached. She had heard him well before he arrived at the stream's edge.

Richard sat gently next to his wife as the quiet water of Dried Indian Creek flowed steadily by.

It was a long time before either spoke and it was Mary who spoke first.

"You need to go. You need to do this."

Richard did not reply.

"We could send for your mother and father. They could come here for a few days each week to help me while you go with Joseph. Frankly, you should take Paul with you. I think it is time he followed his father and watched him work."

Richard had hoped she would come to this decision, but he was taken aback by the notion of taking his son on the journey.

"No. Absolutely not. This is no trip for a boy of eleven."

Mary turned and looked at her husband intently. "Richard, if you were a blacksmith or a cobbler, he would be working right beside you by now. It is time," his wife insisted.

She continued, "We can all return to your parents' house on Saturday so he can preach on Sunday."

"Work?" Richard creased his brows, totally ignoring the issue of his father having to preach on Sunday. "This is beyond me, Mother." He rarely called Mary "mother."

"No. It's not. Get the letter you need from your father to the mission in Etowah. The men who run those missions are good men, too. They know and respect your father, and no one wants a war between the Creek and the Cherokee. Father. Go."

Richard, stood, brushing imaginary dust from the rock off his pants, he glanced around the forest and back at the stream. This is what Fountain seemed to want him to do. After all, he was the reason Joseph had come to his farm in the first place. Now, this is what his wife wanted him to do. His father, when he knew the full scope of things, ever the peacemaker, would want him to go as well. And again, quietly, in his heart, it was what Richard had thought all along. Until now.

Now it was Richard who had reservations.

"Mary, a few days ago, you asked if I thought Fountain's murder could be related to this? Have you thought about that connection?"

"Yes. I have. Fountain obviously thought finding a resolution between the Creek and Cherokee a task worthy of pursuit and one, because of your distinctive talents, you are called to resolve."

Richard did not reply. He frankly had no response. He simply stood in silence looking for answers in the stream.

He sighed, placed a hand on his wife's shoulder and stood. He started up the trail towards the cabin.

"Husband. Is that it? You are simply going to leave." She stood, removed her nightgown, and slid into the crisp night water. She moved with beauty and grace. Richard did not. But what he lacked in grace he made up for with speed and utility. While Mary's body had produced a beautiful white silhouette against the dark forest that folded around the stream, Richard's body was a blur. This man did not need a second invitation from the woman he loved.

Mary laughed quietly as her husband stumbled and splashed into the water and into her embrace.

As expected, Joseph returned the next morning. The Lester children were up and busy about their chores. He approached the boys who were in the barn milking the cows and feeding the other animals. "Where can I find your father?"

James replied, "I think he is still in the house with our mother."

Joseph walked his horse over to the post in front of the house and tied the reins of his horse to the steady wooden hitch.

He knocked on the door and stood for a moment before Mary opened the door. She smiled and said, "Joseph. Come in." Stepping aside she continued, "You know, I must apologize, we should have insisted that you spend the night here last night. Please do not feel slighted by my lack of hospitality. In the future, you must plan to stay with us. It may not be a feather bed, but we can certainly do better than pine needles atop Georgia red clay."

"No. No, please do not worry. I did not feel slighted. My request of your husband is something that I know you two needed to talk about."

Looking past Mary, Joseph saw Richard standing next to the family's table.

Pointing to an open chair, Richard said, "Well, let's not make the same mistake again. Please, come in, sit, there are a few biscuits left from the morning that I rescued from the boys. They are for you."

"Thank you," Joseph replied as he sat in the chair.

Richard did not wait for Joseph to speak.

"Joseph, I will go. But we are not going to Etowah. We are going to Standing Peachtree. That is mid-way for all of us, and that is the customary meeting place for your two nations. Come back in two weeks. We will leave on a Monday. By then, I will have spoken with my father and mother, and I will have things settled here with Boston and his family as well. That will also give some time for my father's letter to get to the Cherokee Mission. Tell me, do you trust Boston?"

"Yes, with my life. We fought together in the conflict against the British. Boston will keep your family safe."

"And Simm. Do you trust Simm? He is basically a man."

Joseph thought for a moment. "Like most of us when we were his age, he is still figuring out where he fits in. He will find his way, but at this point, it is Lucy who holds Simm's heart at bay."

Richard thought for a moment. "Does the gathering at Standing Peachtree make sense to you?"

Joseph did not hesitate, "Yes, it certainly does."

Richard turned to his wife. "Mary, I am unsettled about leaving you with Boston, Simm, and Lucy – all three are barely settled."

Mary took a few steps to close the space between her and her husband. "I am not entirely comfortable with it either. But in truth, I feel better with them here than I have in the past when it was just me and our three children." She paused, realizing, by the look on her husband's face that Richard had never stopped to fully understand her fear when he was away. "If you are going to be gone two or three weeks, that is a long time no matter what comes our way. But, if your mother and father will come here for a few visits, that would give me a measure of peace."

"I am certain my mother and father will come. We will only be gone three weeks if we must journey all the way to New Echota. And I think it would be good for my parents as well as Eugene and Betsy." Richard said.

Mary smiled.

Joseph had not eaten a biscuit. He rose from the table and shook Richard's hand thanking him for his help in the future endeavor. Before leaving he turned and crossed the floor to Mary who, while listening to the exchange, had never really paused in the various tasks she was completing.

"Mrs. Lester. I think owe you thanks as well. I will be taking your husband from you for a time, and I am sure this will create added burdens for you."

At that, Mary paused, wiped her hands on her ash-stained apron and crossed the floor. Taking a piece of cloth, the wrapped the biscuits up and handed them to Joseph. She looked deeply into Joseph's eyes – and the Indian was slightly startled.

"What Richard did not tell you is, I am sending my oldest son along too. My husband can take care of himself. You just make sure my boy comes back home and you and I will be square."

PART IV

Joseph had left the Lesters in the afternoon. He would camp each night along the Ocmulgee River and be home before the sun reached its height on the second day.

He was troubled.

While his grief was certainly not as deep as that of the Lester family, he knew Fountain's death had impacted Richard and his family. He had liked Richard even before he had met him. He was just as Fountain had said he would be. Fountain had said that he often went to Richard for guidance and always found his advice sound; and, when he followed it, the fruits yielded were evidence of its worth.

On most fronts, Joseph had found dealing with the white settlers very frustrating. His father, being Scottish, did not have the same distrust. Even now, his father seemed to side with the whites.

Joseph's mother, on the other hand, was Creek. The Creek, being matrilineal, considered Joseph one of their own. The whites did not. And so, his dealings with the settlers were different than that of his father, even when working with people that his father had known for years.

There was a general lack of trust. At the same time, the Indians had come to realize that the settlers brought with them goods and ways of doing things that were to be admired, and in many Indian communities, Indians were developing trades that mirrored those of the white settlers. The McIntosh farm that he now ran for his father boasted a large blacksmith shop and a wood mill of its own.

However, when something at the mill broke, they still preferred to engage the services of a white tinkerer.

It was true, the tinkerers in Covington, Macon, and Milledgeville could fix anything. It was also true that even whites called the tinkerer's shops "clip joints." Most tinkers preferred to be paid in coin. Good coins went into the tinker shop, but only clipped coins came out. It was well known that many of the artisans would clip the edges of their coins, melting down the small amounts into small silver, copper, and in some cases, gold bars. Although these bars were small, they were valuable. And on the frontier, where coin was scarce, the bars acted as a secondary currency.

And recently, some of the tinkers had refused his request to journey to his farm to make repairs. The development seemed curious and slightly unnerving.

Who to trust?

Over the years, he had come to trust Fountain. Now, with his death, one of his primary links to understanding the white settlers and how they thought was gone.

As he rode towards home, he wondered if Richard could possibly be his new touchstone in this regard. For some reason, one that he could never himself understand, he simply did not totally trust Bryant.

The new Indian agent was worse than the man appointed by James Monroe before. What was his name? In the moment, the name escaped him… "David Mitchell…" that was the man, he thought to himself.

Mitchell had come to the Creek Indians in 1816. Before him, the agent was Hawkins. He had brought to the Creek Indians notions of "civilizing" the various tribes and clans. Five had followed this advice, including the clan to which Joseph's mother was a member, but following the War of 1812 and the Red Stick uprising, the Chiefs had been pressured to surrender much of their land. And, given the defeats at both Talladega and Horseshoe Bend, the militant factions within the Creek Nation had been silenced if not killed.

Because of those lands previously confiscated, the Creek were desperate to retain the rights to their remaining lands.

For this reason, this issue arising with the Cherokee was particularly troubling even though neither tribe would consider the amount of land in question substantial.

Joseph had no doubt that eventually, the white settlers would end up with most, if not all, of the Creek land in Georgia. However, if Creek land was ceded, the Creek would be the ones to do so.

Joseph settled into the rhythm of his horse. He longed to be home.

His farm was near a "Talwa," or a town called Ocmulgee, which stretched along the river of the same name. Many of the homes in his town were constructed of wattle and daub – a combination of mud and sticks. The Indians would lattice or weave the sticks together. This along with a mixture of mud and grass created a sturdy, insulated home. The structures were easily maintained and surprisingly cool in the summer and warm in the winter. Most of these homes were circular with a hole in the roof's center that allowed smoke to escape.

Like the majority of Creek villages, in the center of Ocmulgee was a large open space where the community would gather for important events.

Joseph was not a chief. He was certain that this slight was because of his last name. While he was not related to William McIntosh, many Creeks, regardless of their clan, still seethed over the treachery of William's agreement to cede land. And when it was learned that he had received money for his signature, the elders had sent Law Menders, led by Menawa, to execute William McIntosh for his treason. While no elder had said such directly, having the same last name was undermining Joseph even though his mother was a member of an entirely different clan and his father, as far as anyone knew, was not related to the traitor.

Having said this, his father, being a Scottish trapper and settler, had initially bestowed upon his son advantages that Joseph could not deny. Like his father, Joseph could communicate well in four languages: English, Spanish, Creek, and Cherokee. He had traveled widely with his father, who, while in his late fifties, maintained trading relationships in both Savannah and Charleston, and had recently moved to the new town, Milledgeville, that had sprung up to be the new capital of the state.

For almost 100 years, the Creek had traded willingly with the whites that clung to the coast like a spider to its web. The whites brought goods that the Creek did not make, including knives, iron pots, and muskets.

Initially, trade had been focused on deer, beaver pelts, and native grown crops like tobacco, corn, and squash.

Joseph's mother was a member of what later would be called the Lower Creek Indians, or Muscogee, and a member of the Raccoon Clan.

Initially, the Council of the Ocmulgee had sent Joseph north to measure if Fountain Lester or his father, German, would be willing to act as emissary to the Cherokee on behalf of the Creek. Most acknowledged that this should be the task of the Indian Agent, but there was such distrust of the agents appointed by the US Government, the Creek needed another ambassador. When Joseph had returned and suggested that the younger brother, Richard, act in this capacity, his recommendation was accepted.

What Joseph had not known was that as soon as he left for Covington, the Ocmulgee's Chief and two elders had departed for Cawita, the Creek's Capital, to seek approval of their efforts to reconcile with the Cherokee.

Word of the negotiations between the Creek and Cherokee was certain to get back to others who would seek to undermine the effort.

The following day, Richard's conversation with his mother and father had gone as expected. There were a lot of questions about Fountain's death. It was frustrating to both parents that between them and their sons, no one had answers.

Bryant, however, with some certainty, believed Fountain's death was entirely due to his efforts in assisting the Creek Indians in obtaining the monetary settlement they had been promised. He had strongly urged his father to stay clear of anything related to the Indians.

Now, Richard stood before him asking for his direct involvement. As he related to his parents, almost pleading, one of Fountain's last efforts was to convince them to help in keeping peace between the two tribes.

Initially, his mother's reaction had been one of shock and his father's bordered on anger. Slowly, his father regained his composure, and just as Richard had predicted, his father would not turn his back if there was a roll he could play in keeping peace between the settlers, the Creeks and the Cherokees.

He rose from his chair. He went to his desk, withdrawing paper, a quill, and an ink well. He sat for a moment before he began to write.

Who should he reach out to at the mission? He thought it best to compose a letter to James Jenkins Trott, he was the man he knew the best at the Etowah Mission:

New Echota, GA
Hightower Methodist Mission

Dear Reverend Trott,

It is my sincere hope that this letter finds you well and in the good grace of His Holy Spirit. It has been many years since we last met, breaking bread with Ignatius Few and his wife, Salina. I reflect fondly back on those times as I hope you do as well.

My work here in Newton County goes well. The school prospers with my wife, Catherine, as its primary teacher. We now have over two dozen students regularly, although, because of the planting season, these numbers fell dramatically over these past few weeks. Only now are these students stepping back into our school, returning their education to its previous station of importance.

The work with our congregation continues and we do hope our humble support of your mission is received in the Spirit in which it is given. It is upon this relationship that I write to you today.

Last month, my son, Fountain, was murdered. We have come to believe with some certainty that his death was conceived by parties desiring to sow discord between your beloved Cherokee Nation, and our Creek Indian neighbors.

My son, Richard, will be traveling with members of the Creek Nation, including Joseph McIntosh, in your direction. They are willing to come to Etowah, but I propose instead to meet at the old Peachtree Creek Fort near Standing Peachtree. It has been conveyed to me that this location is the customary Liminary Meeting Place for these two Indian nations.

My son and his companions intend to arrive there in two weeks.

We are hopeful that they will find their Cherokee counterparts there and of like-mind, seeking avoidance of any future conflict between the two nations.

We will continue to pray for your efforts in Etowah and ever endeavor to further His kingdom.

We do hope to see you soon and offer encouragement to your efforts as a devoted witness to The Good News.

Yours in Christ,
German Lester

Once the letter was completed, Richard took the letter himself to the Brick Store in Winton and placed it on a stagecoach that would make the journey as quickly as possible to Etowah on the road that linked Savannah to Northwest Georgia and the new frontier state that was Tennessee.

If all went as planned, the letter would be received in New Echota in less than one week's time, and the Cherokee contingent would have ample time to travel down to Standing Peachtree. That is, if they were of a peaceful mind.

Joseph had passed the emerging village of Macon early in the morning and arrived at his family's home as the heat of the day began to settle on his family's farm.

His home, much of it built by his father and passed on to him, was hewn out of logs harvested years earlier. The farm sat on a bend in the Ocmulgee River. By most standards it was a large house as befitted a man of his standing.

The farm was large. It sprawled – following the contours of the Ocmulgee River. His father had hired a foreman to run the farm, which allowed Joseph to focus on the other businesses.

The blacksmith shop was a going concern. Originally, it had been built to service the needs of the farm. As those needs had been satisfied, the family had allowed the shop to take work offered to them from other nearby farms. Some of these farms were owned by fellow Creek Indians, others were owned by white settlers. Recently, for some reason, the white settlers had stopped bringing their horses, wagons, and other items to the family's blacksmith.

The wood mill was the newest business for the family. It was located near the river, as the water powered the wheels that turned the saws. The mill operation had steadily grown and, again, until recently, was providing a satisfying profit to the family.

Joseph's father had moved to Milledgeville, which, as a city, was growing rapidly. From Milledgeville, his father could broker wood for the mill as well as trade pelts which would be sent to Savannah and from there to Europe. This fur trade had been the mainstay of his business from the very beginning. While he and Joseph were both excellent hunters, the two men had realized that they could make more money buying pelts from their Creek friends and neighbors and carting them to the coast, than they could possibly earn hunting and trading just what they were able to harvest from the woods of Georgia.

The wealth that this trading had produced allowed his father to purchase the large estate Joseph now called home. It also allowed the family to be an early adopter, converting much of their farmland to cotton and purchasing slaves.

Joseph's father did not share his son's concerns over the white settlers. This was natural, as he was white. Having said this, since the War of 1812 and the Red Stick Rebellion, both men had come to realize that the family may need to exit Georgia entirely. For this reason, they had begun to slowly sell both acreage and slaves, and his father was actively exploring land in Florida on which the family could settle. Both he and his father had friends within the Seminole Nation.

In Joseph's mind, if the Creek could not negotiate a satisfactory settlement to the land dispute with the Cherokee, the momentum to sell the rest of their farm would accelerate. Joseph believed his father was of the mind that the mill was a business he would keep, and they could manage it from Milledgeville or Florida if need be.

As he arrived, Joseph's wife, Talease, was tanning a deer hide, drawn taut on a frame of four saplings.

She smiled and rose to greet him.

They embraced for a long moment.

"I am so glad to be home… to you," Joseph said, taking a long look at his wife.

"Oh! You are? Then why are you gone so often?" was her wry reply. "You must be hungry, as am I. Come, I have some salted fish in the house. You can prepare a plate for me and tell me about your journeys."

Joseph smiled, understanding that his wife must have been exhausted by the children in his absence. He would be serving dinner for a few days. "Better yet. Where are the children?" Joseph asked, expecting at least one or two to be nearby.

"They have gone for a swim down at the river. I was just about to check on them. Why don't we join them?" Talease suggested. At that moment, the two adults heard the faint splashing and laughter of their children.

"I can think of no better way to wash the dust off." He took her hand in his and they headed towards the sounds of his children and the clay-stained water of the Ocmulgee.

Reverend Trott had just returned from riding his missionary circuit of fellowships in the mountains of north Georgia. An energetic man, he was rarely in one place long.

Arriving at the one-room mission near New Echota, Hightower, he was immediately handed a letter. He took the letter and placed it in his coat which was laid on his saddle and continued the work of watering and feeding his horse.

"Aren't you going to read that," inquired the young Indian student who had handed him the correspondence.

"No. I thought I would just ask you what it said." With that, Trott turned and smiled at the young man.

Looking at his feet, the young man replied, "I was just practicing my letters. I did not intend any offense."

"It's fine, your no bottle-headed fool, and I am a simple man with little or nothing to hide. What did the letter say?"

Excitedly, the youth stepped forward, "A Methodist preacher down south has been asked by the Creek to arrange a meeting. They thought you could help." With that, Trott stopped the chore before him. It could wait.

He pulled the letter from his coat and read the note from German Lester. It was as the youth had conveyed. He turned to the youth. "Have you seen any of the elders in New Echota in recent days?"

"Why yes, there is a Council meeting this week and the Supreme Court will convene next week."

"I must ride as if fetching a mid-wife. I need a fresh horse." Trott turned to find a horse.

The ride was not far, but it was entirely unexpected. Arriving in the emerging town late in the afternoon, Trott acknowledged to himself that he most likely would be spending the night.

Trott was not unknown in New Echota. However, he was not Cherokee, and he knew his place. He waited outside the Council House for a long time.

As he leaned against the hitching post, he was amazed at how quickly the town had emerged. The town boasted a print shop, and Council House, and based upon the progress, the humble building for the Supreme Court would be completed soon.

Suddenly, he could hear the shifting of bodies and the door opened. Men blinked as they entered the sunlight and their eyes adjusted.

One of the first to emerge was William Hicks.

Hicks tolerated Trott. And since his brother's death, his attitude toward Trott had worsened. His brother had been chief, and William fully expected to succeed his brother in that same role – which he did for several months. However, once the Cherokee Nation ratified their constitution, an election was held, and he was replaced by John Ross.

William Hicks seemed the only one to be surprised by the election of Ross. In his heart of hearts, he knew both his brother and Pathkiller had held Ross in high regard, and many believed the two previous chiefs had been training Ross for the post. But the rejection by his own tribe stung.

Seeing Trott, Hicks lowered his eyes hoping to evade the preacher. He had no time to hear more about the suffering savior of the whites today.

"Mr. Hicks, are you and the other elders through with the meeting."

Hicks only heard the word "other" and he bristled. "Yes. We are done for the day."

"Can you lend me your ear for a moment?" Trott asked.

"I have been in that room all day. I really must be on my way." Hicks replied.

"I understand," replied Trott, "but I have received a letter of importance to the Cherokee, and I need advice."

The words still hung in the air as Chief Ross emerged flanked by several men.

"And I thought we had just discussed everything of importance." Ross said, standing in the doorway of the Council House before stepping down onto the hard earth. "What brings you to New Echota Parson Trott?"

"This letter," Trott said, handing the letter to Ross.

Reading the letter with interest, Ross paused, and handed the letter to Hicks. Hicks was immediately gratified by the gesture.

Ross turned stepping back into the Council House, "It seems we have one more item of interest to discuss." Looking over his shoulder at Reverend Trott, he said, "Mr. Trott, I think you should join us."

Since he had become Chief of the Cherokee Nation, he had become more aware of the opinions that polarized his people.

John Ross was the first chief to be democratically elected. While this consensus provided Ross with a level of confidence, he was also aware that there were Cherokee who were dissatisfied with not just his election, but with the leadership that had seen their nation's strength dwindle. Moreover, they saw the adoption of a constitution as something of an afront to the freedom they had always enjoyed. This faction seemed to be gravitating toward William Hicks.

Trott did not know all the elders or councilmen in the room. He scanned the room. The men he knew the best were all there – that included John Ross, William Hicks, and Major Ridge.

Major Ridge had gained his title by fighting alongside Andrew Jackson against the Red Sticks at Horseshoe Bend. Both he and William Hicks were successful farmers. William's farm was close by in the Oothkalooga valley.

Chief Ross summarized the letter and asked Trott to shed light on his relationship to German Lester. Trott relayed that his relationship was cordial and one of shared faith. He did not go much further as he knew many of the men in the room were not Christian and further explanation might simply steel any resolve against him and the request made by German Lester.

With little to add, Ross thanked Reverend Trott and asked him to step outside while the council deliberated further.

Standing outside, Trott could hear only mumbles. From time to time, however, he could discern voices in Cherokee that seemed to swell with passion.

Again, there was a stirring of footsteps and then the door opened.

The men emerged. Few acknowledged Trott as they left.

Ross, Hicks, and Major Ridge approached.

It was Ross who spoke first. "I will go with you to Standing Peachtree and several others will join us as well."

"Again, I want my voice heard, we should not do this," Hicks protested.

"Your voice was heard. As was mine," Major Ridge stated, "but the council has spoken. We must abide by their decision."

"Mark my words," Hicks paused, "No matter how we dress, what language we speak," he then looked directly at Trott, "or what God we profess, nothing will bring peace. The white settlers will come. They want our valleys. They want our streams. They want our fields and what grows in them as well as what lies underneath. They are coming."

"Enough. That is enough. Your voice was heard. Your vote counted." Ross said sternly. "Say no more."

Hicks eyes dug into Ross's for a long moment. Then, he turned, leaving nothing but anger and dust in the air.

Ross turned to Trott, "Obviously, we are not united on meeting with the Creek. Many of us fought against the Creek and we wish to distance ourselves from them as much as we can. We think we know of the land in question. In our minds, it was given to us for our assistance in the War. But we have reason to want peace between our nations."

Ross continued. "Return here in four days. I am sure you have affairs to settle at home, as do I. We will journey with you to Standing Peachtree."

In the two weeks that followed, the new corn crib was completed, the expanded vegetable garden had sprung to life, as had the newly expanded field of corn. Fountain's mare had been named Abbey, and the hawk had flown untethered from post to lure daily. Boston, Simm, and Richard had completed the fireplace in his family's cabin, and all agreed that the fireplace would provide ample heat for Boston and his family on a cold night and would be sufficient for Lucy to use in cooking.

For the first time in their lives, Boston and Lucy had a bed. Up to this point, they had basically known only straw on the floor with only a blanket to sleep on. Lucy liked the bed. Boston was still unsure.

Simm was quiet, but diligent. Paul, James, and Eugene seemed to naturally look up to him, and their attention was entirely unwanted. Alice and Betsy were enamored with the older boy as well. Mostly, he worked alongside Boston, and if there was free time, he sought refuge in the woods, where, like his father, he would set traps for various animals. Frequently, he would return with something that could be made into a meal.

This sustenance was not needed for survival initially. However, as the days passed, the rations provided by the Lesters had dwindled. Success in trapping small game would be needed to sustain the family. It also seemed integral to both Simm's and Boston's nature. It was certainly proof that they could and would survive without the Lesters. Lucy, too, enjoyed the yield from Simm's hunts. While the Lesters provided food and Lucy certainly helped in its preparation, the quantity provided to Boston and his family varied greatly, and there was no "Allowance Day" on the Lester farm. So, without the allowance of food, Boston and Lucy really did not know what to expect from day-to-day.

On many plantations, each week, slaves were given an "allowance" of cornmeal, molasses, salt, and perhaps other staples as well. From this allowance, the slaves were expected to provide their own meals. Rarely was meat provided. In fact, meat was typically only rationed in the allowance on Christmas and Easter.

For this reason, Boston and Simm had both taken up trapping small game to supplement the meager rations that they were allotted.

The Lesters did not understand the concept or custom of "allowance" as it was applied to slaves. Initially, the couple had simply assumed that Boston and his family would eat what their family ate. Mary had increased the amount of food she cooked.

At the same time, Mary and Richard both realized that they were running through the family's store of food more rapidly. Richard had retrieved an additional cow, pigs, chickens and goats from Fountain's estate. The increased livestock would be needed to sustain the family and the addition of slaves.

Moreover, the Lesters had also decided that the slaves would be responsible for gathering their own meat, reasoning that Boston and Simm could hunt on Sunday. On most days, they were given eggs.

Mary and Lucy had settled into a routine where Lucy would take the girls in the morning after breakfast, spending most of the time watering the garden, weeding, and harvesting what could be pulled.

With one of the fields of corn well over a month old, the stalks were tall enough to provide cover for hide and seek… with the girls doing most of the hiding while Lucy pulled weeds and pretended to seek.

Boston was told to plan on expanding the barn as well as the pasture in the winter, as Richard wanted to be able to stable all the horses and cows. There were now five horses, and three cows, this could change as soon as Richard could bring more of Fountain's livestock to the farm following the harvest, including the family's dog, which excited both Eugene and Betsy.

It was late in the morning, and everyone was busy. Richard was in town drafting a will for family friends when the first real altercation took place.

It had rained, and there were several areas of mud about the homestead that invited attention. Seeing the clay adhere to his shoes, Eugene stated, "You know, I think I could roll in this mud and then in the hay and fly like that hawk of yours."

"You think?" said James.

"Absolutely" chimed Paul.

Simm, working in the barn, turned and walked out into the sun. He looked up at the door to the loft high above the barndoor and said, "Yep. If it were me, I might want some height. I am not sure jumping off a stool or a stump would do it. But if you jumped out of the loft, it just might work." With that, Simm turned, winked at Paul, and left the conversation to the younger boys.

Eugene did not need much persuasion. The fact that Simm, being older and assumedly wiser, had essentially endorsed the idea, was all the encouragement the young boy needed. Without further thought, Eugene was rolling in the mud. He was quickly covered from head to toe. James and Paul helped him climb to the loft where they covered him in hay before climbing down the ladder in order to return to the front of the barn and observe the flight.

"Don't jump till we get down there to see it," yelled Paul excitedly as they ran through the breezeway of the barn.

There, Simm, James, and Paul stood watching Eugene, wondering if the lad was brave enough to jump.

Now, to be clear, the height was about 10 feet, and the boys had jumped from that height before and lived to tell about it. This was different. This was frontier science.

At that moment Lucy came out of the Lester home and looked up. "Eugene. Boy! What kind of mess you up to? Come down."

"Watch Lucy. I am gonna fly!"

At that, Eugene jumped from the loft and began flapping his arms and legs in a frantic motion. For a brief moment, the boy hung there in the blue sky, suspended by invisible strings from heaven.

Mary entered the doorway just in time to see her stepson prove a basic tenet of frontier science. Frontier gravity.

He landed squarely in the mud that marked the well-trodden entrance to the barn.

Both Paul and James laughed. Simm shook his head and went back to work.

It was Lucy who got to Eugene first. Dazed, the wind knocked out of him and battered all over, but nothing broken. He was not badly hurt.

Then they caught the glare of their mother as she approached with a speed that was shocking. She grabbed both sons by their ears and demanded, "What did you boys put him up to?"

Paul replied trying to pull his ear away without losing it – "Nothing, mother. Nothing. He said he thought he could fly. It was his idea."

"Well! Someone here should have the sense to talk a man out of something so foolish."

Simm emerged from the barn. "Ma'am, is Eugene alright?"

Exasperated, she looked at Lucy and Lucy nodded. "I think so" Mary said with relief.

Simm looked up at the loft, back at Eugene, smiled and said, "You know, Eugene, there for one moment, I truly thought you were going to fly." He smiled. Everyone, except Eugene, laughed.

As penance for allowing their cousin to exercise his own, frontier stupidity, Paul and James had to do Eugene's chores for three days. They also had to clean off the mud from his clothing.

Eugene got an extra slice of pie.

As promised, Joseph had traveled with his two companions from Ocmulgee. Three other men had come from Cawita (Coweta). It was a modest group of six men, including Joseph.

Cawita was known to be the center of power for the Creek Nation, and it was a sign of the gravity of the times that three elders were joining in the trip. It was also important for Joseph because memories of treachery, not just that of William McIntosh, were present in everyone's minds.

None of the men would be acting on his own accord. No one wanted to be visited by the Law Menders of the Creek Nation. Having received both instructions and the blessing of the council, the Nation had confidence in the group they were sending to Standing Peachtree.

The group had camped close to the Lester homestead the night before, arriving before dawn at the farm.

Boston and Simm were up early. They had saddled Danny, which, being slower and less "frisky," would be Paul's horse, and Banner, which would be Richard's horse. One of Fountain's horses was also packed with provisions for the journey which included two pots, several blankets, a hatchet, rope, smoked ham, and corn biscuits. More than Paul and Richard would need, but it was the list that Mary had given to Boston and Lucy.

Paul had not been told of the journey with his father until the morning before. His excitement was barely contained.

Initially he had wanted to bring everything he owned, including the hawk. Richard quickly corrected the pile, reducing it to a spare shirt, a pair of pants, two blankets, and a hunting knife. The clothing was rolled tightly and stuffed into a leather saddle bag. An oversized leather jacket was tied to Paul's saddle. The small knife, he proudly wore in a sheaf on his belt.

The Lester men mounted their horses after saying their goodbyes, but it was the last item that Mary brought forward that surprised both Richard and his son. Walking to her son's horse, Mary pulled an old flint pistol that had been concealed under her apron. "It's loaded. I know you know how to fire it. If you keep the powder dry, and check it once each day, it will be right here in your saddle bag if you and you father need it." She patted her son's leg, turned, and walked back to Alice, Betsy, James, and Eugene.

Richard beckoned to Boston to approach his horse. He leaned over and whispered into his ears, "Boston, I don't know you well. Everything I love, I am leaving in your hands. If you need anything, you get my family to Covington. We have friends there who will take care of my family and yours. You know where my parents live?"

Boston nodded that he did.

"If you need to, go there."

Boston looked at Richard, and back at Mary. No response was needed or expected.

With that, Richard turned his horse up the slow slope and the lane leading away from the house, with the pack horse in tow and Joseph on his right. Paul fell in behind Joseph, with Danny locking into the pace set by Joseph's horse.

Each day, the men traveled twenty miles, and on the third day they reached a highpoint on the trail that descended towards the Chattahoochee River. Years later, someone would nail a buck's head to a large oak tree, and this would become the first stagecoach stop out of the newly emerging town of Atlanta. But for now, the area was largely unsettled and wooded. A short time later they arrived at Standing Peachtree and the site of the old, abandoned fort.

The original fort's importance had been eliminated years earlier when the newer palisade, Fort Peachtree, had been built just south of where they stood, on a bluff overlooking a bend in the Chattahoochee River.

Now, Standing Peachtree was just a trading station located at the junction of Peachtree Creek and the Chattahoochee River. It consisted of a dock to which several boats were tied, and for a few coins, a boatman could be found to row a man across the Chattahoochee River. The ferries, of which there were several, were further north on the waterway that sliced through the middle of Georgia.

Around the old fort, several small dwellings and trade huts had sprung from what had originally been a place for peaceful assembly and trading. And it was held as such by both the Creek and Cherokee nations. On irregular intervals, chiefs and elders of both nations had found reasons to convene at this location to settle disputes ranging from trading, hunting rights, and matrimonial settlements. But neither nation had built a permanent settlement on the site until the white settlers arrived.

The fact that white settlers found the site convenient was not a surprise. The fact that they decided to build a fort was.

Standing Peachtree Fort was ill-conceived at the outset, and both Indian Nations knew it, but never warned the aspiring white settlers. You see, the site was prone to flooding on a regular basis.

So, it was. After several floods, the new state Governor ordered a group of soldiers to build a second fort on higher ground, three miles south – this would be Fort Peachtree.

However, the two Indian Nations had never relinquished their rights to the site, and still believed the land at the convergence of Peachtree Creek and the Chattahoochee River a convenient place to meet and settle disputes.

When they arrived, there was no sign of a significant Cherokee contingent and no word that one was on its way. The Creek delegation quickly agreed to wait a few days to see if one would arrive.

Since the conclusion of the War of 1812 and the resolution of the Red Stick Rebellion, like its predecessor, Peachtree Fort was relegated in importance as well, and, for long periods, abandoned. The focus of both the state and federal government had shifted west. The fort was rarely garrisoned. Although, in late 1827, the previous governor, Governor Forsyth, had ordered minor repairs be made to the fort and appointed a Commander, Buford Rogers, to fully garrison the fort in both the spring and summer until further notice.

News that six Creek Nation elders were waiting to meet their Cherokee counterparts had reached Commander Rogers and the Sergeant on station at Fort Peachtree. On the morning of the third day, Commander Rogers ordered Sergeant James McConnell Montgomery to ride to Standing Peachtree on the pretense of securing a boat for a crossing later in the week. Upon his arrival, he was surprised to see Richard and the young Paul Lester among the group.

"I am curious, why are you and your son here?" inquired Sergeant Montgomery.

Standing, the two men shook hands, "I am just a scribe for this group. They have asked my help in settling and recording a small land dispute between the two nations."

"I see." Sgt. Montgomery pondered. "Well, I have to wonder how much land is involved and where it is located?"

"Frankly, I don't even know. For you and me, this is a good thing because the last thing we want are these two nations fighting over something that could have been resolved quietly and quickly." Richard paused. "We live near Covington. My father is pastor of a small Methodist fellowship there and he knows a few of the Cherokee Missionaries well. Our family is hoping we can help foster a resolution. My brother Fountain died trying to get this done."

"So, you say? How did he die?"

"He was shot," replied Richard plainly.

"Well, that sounds like a matter for the state to investigate. Has this been reported?"

"I know my father and older brother have made inquiries at the state capital. As will I when I return. But the only witness, my sister-in-law, JoAnne, died when their wagon turned over during the attack. And in that Fountain was a citizen in good standing and had a thriving farm, I agree, inquiries should be made, and I would appreciate any help you can offer."

"I see." The sergeant thought for a moment, removing a small leather-bound book and the stub of a charcoal pencil from the pocket of his vest, he made a few notes. "Well, I should report this to my superiors. It is not in our jurisdiction, but when a landowner is murdered, we must make sure a bed of snakes isn't waking."

"What do you mean?" responded Richard.

"If your brother's death is isolated, then we must wonder what would possess a man to murder another. Was he in dispute? Had he wronged a neighbor? If that is the case, the murder was isolated. If that is not the case, there is something larger at work, and frankly, with you here, with these Creeks waiting on the Cherokee, I have concerns that I must report to my superior."

Both men stood in silence for a moment.

"Well. I would not be here if it was not for Fountain," Richard finally responded. "He had suggested to his Creek Indian friends that because our father knew missionaries that the Cherokee trusted, and because I am a Reader of the Law, we might be able to find a resolution."

"I understand. Well, you deserve more than fiddler's pay for this, that's for sure."

By this time, Paul was standing at his father's side and the conversation turned to Paul's fascination with the sergeant's gleaming sword, which Montgomery graciously offered to Paul for a test.

After a few hearty youthful swings, the sword was returned. Hands shaken and with a cursory measurement of the situation taken, the sergeant mounted his gray horse and rode back up the trail from which he came, without negotiating any boat passage.

It was less than two hours later that nine men representing the Cherokee Nation arrived, one of whom was Reverend Trott.

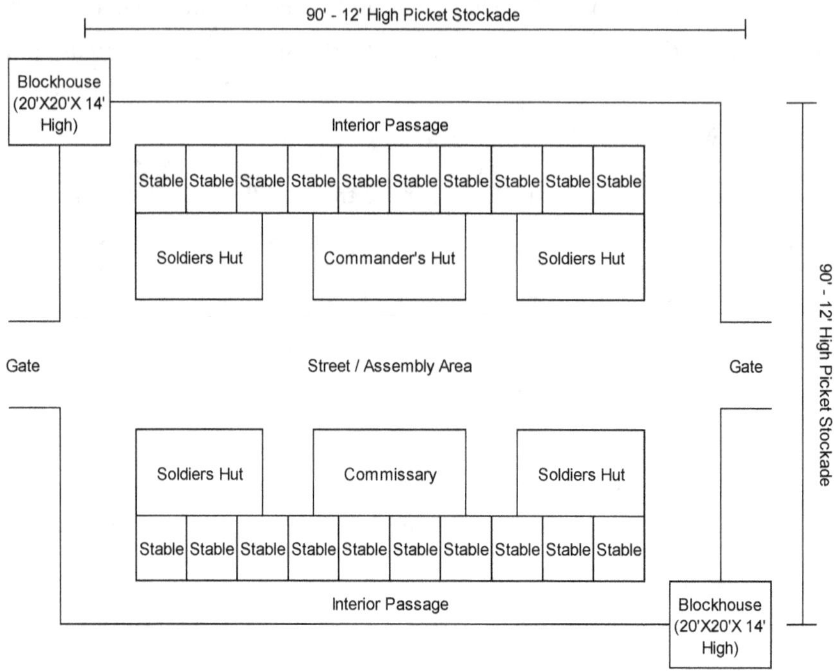

Typical Frontier Fort Layout

Upon his return to the fort, Sgt. Montgomery entered the palisade and tethered his horse in front of a small cabin that served as the command post. There were several other horses tethered to the hitching posts as well.

He scraped his boots of mud, stepped onto the large steppingstones that represented a porch, and knocked on the door.

He waited for what seemed an eternity before hearing the entreat "Come in."

He did not recall a time when he had seen the room this crowded. The room contained a small desk, three chairs, and a small cot that Commander Rogers rarely used, preferring to sleep in a cabin he maintained close by. Of the men in the room, he only recognized two. Commander Rogers was standing. Seated behind the desk was George Rockingham Gilmer, who had, for a brief time, been commander of the fort – before being elected to the State Legislature, and currently serving in the US Congress.

"What is it, Sergeant Montgomery?" Commander Rogers asked.

"I am here to report on a gathering of both Cherokee and Creeks down in Standing Peachtree." He paused.

It was George Rockingham Gilmer who replied. "We know. Sergeant. Have all the parties arrived?"

He looked at his commander and back to Gilmer. "The Creek Indians are waiting on the Cherokee. There is a lawyer there, Richard Lester. He is there to document a settlement."

"I see" replied Gilmer. "Please keep your commander informed. Let him know when the Cherokee have arrived."

Montgomery stood for a moment, looked at his commander – only to be dismissed with, "That will be all, Sergeant Montgomery."

With nothing else to say, he turned, closed the door, and returned to his horse.

What Gilmer may have lacked in stature, he made up for in intelligence. The man was intellectually imposing. Trained as an attorney, he had also served in the War of 1812 and served under Andrew Jackson in putting down the Creek rebellion that followed. With a retreating hairline that revealed a large forehead, the man was formidable.

As the sergeant left the cabin and fort, he realized the order he had been given was not from his commander, or even a man currently in the military. He paused for a moment wondering why the man he reported to was deferring his authority.

To say that the elders of the two Nations exchanged pleasantries would be incorrect. The two tribes had been on opposing sides too often for there to be much of anything pleasant to exchange.

Most recently, a faction within the Creek Nation had been supplied arms by British traders and the Spanish and risen up against the United States. The Cherokee, Choctaw, and many of the Lower Creek Indians had allied themselves with the young United States government. The animosity born out of this hostility ran deep.

Despite this deep-seated hatred, both Indian nations now found themselves in similar and tenuous situations. The two nations believed it prudent to avoid further confrontation. Increasingly, they were coming to the realization that their enemy was not native-born.

There were factions in both nations that were ready for war and actively sought to agitate their clan and entire nation to action. There were also men from both nations who had negotiated treaties, without the consent of their Nation's Councils, that had ceded land. Most of these so-called leaders had been killed or exiled.

Represented at this gathering were men who could speak for their nations. Five of the Creek clans were represented, and seven of the Cherokee clans were present.

It was late in the afternoon when Joseph McIntosh broached the topic at hand.

"There is land south of Fort Daniel that we all know to be Creek. We want it confirmed that the Cherokee will relinquish their claims to this land. The treaty you are about to sign would transfer ownership over to the United States and includes this land, and you have no right to it, and no right to transfer it."

At that, one of the Creek elders brought forward a piece of deerskin parchment that had several well-known landmarks on it. Everyone around the fire, regardless of their affiliation, could identify both where they sat, and where they had come from. But most importantly, there was a line that indicated what the Creak Nation believed to be the boundary between their Nations – that line followed the contours of the Chattahoochee River.

In the afternoon light there was no issue reading the map, which indicated a line extending from Fort Daniel, in the north, to Fort Peachtree and west toward Talladega.

There was a great deal of discreet mumbling in at least two native tongues, none of which was familiar to Richard. Trott was listening intently to the Cherokee as was Joseph McIntosh.

Finally, one of the Cherokee elders spoke. It was John Ross. "I am new as Chief of our Nation. In the years that followed the death of Chief Vann, we have come to realize that our two nations should be working more closely together." He looked at his fellow elders. "Let us speak amongst ourselves as we know this land well. We will return tomorrow morning and discuss this further."

Everyone understood. No one, on either side, was going to speak for their Nation without counsel from their peers.

Joseph McIntosh responded. "That is well with us. Just don't be too distracted by the bushel-breasted women that work the waterfront at night."

The men shared a laugh. "Truer words need not be spoken," replied Rev. Trott.

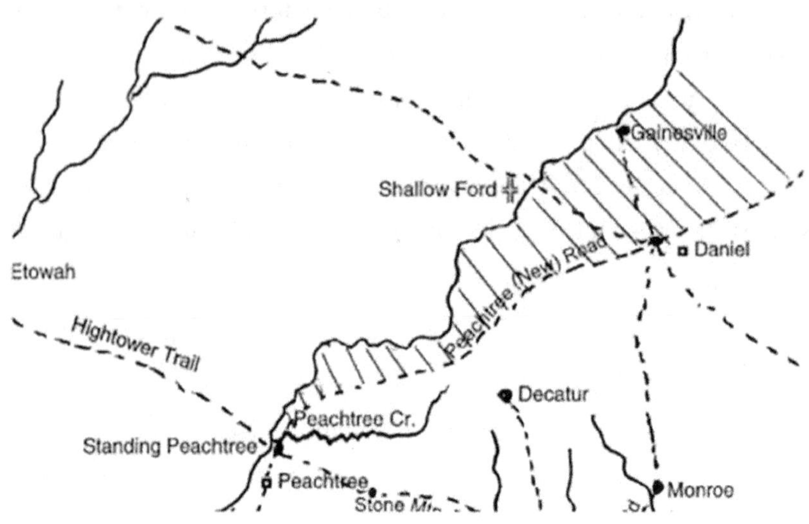

Map of Creek & Cherokee Land Dispute – 1828

The sergeant had barely closed the door to Commander Roger's cabin at Fort Peachtree when one of the men stepped forward out of the shadows that had shrouded him in the corner of the small room.

"My brother was NEVER supposed to die! That was never part of the plan."

"No, it wasn't," Gilmer said, turning to Bryant Lester. "But you… you were well paid, and you said you could keep your father and the rest of your family out of this mess. You have failed. And now we hear that another Lester has inserted himself in this. I can assume he is your brother too?"

Bryant nodded. "Yes. But your men did not just intimidate Fountain. They shot him. And, they should have at least waited and confronted him when his wife was not there." Everyone could see Bryant's frustration mounting.

"Yes. Brothers of the blade can often be quick to violence. But there is so much at stake here. The Government will not send troops in without cause. We must instigate a conflict between the Creek and the Cherokee." Looking at Bryant, Gilmer continued, "Look at us. We have had one white man's death and there are already complaints amongst us."

With that, Bryant leapt forward enraged. "He was my brother!" It was Commander Rogers and one of the other men in the room that stepped forward to restrain Bryant.

"Yes! And you have been paid. Your brother's death was unfortunate, but he will not be the last brother to die before this is all over. And let's not forget, your brother did profit from this too. He just did not know where the money had come from. Surely Fountain did not believe that the state militia was simply paying him for horses." There was a pause. "Bryant, I am surprised at you. Frankly, you are saddling the wrong horse here. If you are angry, you should be angry with yourself."

Bryant was still being restrained, but the two men were able to loosen their grip as Bryant glared at Gilmer.

"The blood that has been spilt has settled our accounts. I am done with this enterprise." Bryant jerked his arms free, glared at the men in the room. Turning to David Mitchell, Bryant looked tired and desperate. "I should have never met with you in the first place. Everyone knows you are still importing slaves through Florida and the trails that lead through the Creek Territory. I should have known better than to associate with you. For that matter, with any of you."

Mitchell bristled slightly. "Bryant. Watch your tongue. I have been accused of many things that have never been proven."

Bryant took a breath, looked at the floor and then again at Mitchell. "Yes. What is proven in a court and what is known by everyone to be true is not always the same."

Still, one man remained restraining Bryant's left arm. Bryant shook it loose and turned to leave.

"And Bryant…" Gilmer said quietly, "No word of this to anyone… or your father will find out how you and Fountain found the resources to buy your slaves. The whole community will know."

Bryant paused, then stepped away from the desk. The two men loosened their grip on Bryant's arms. Without looking back, he left the room. The door closed with a loud thud of wood meeting wood.

Mitchell looked at Gilmer and said, "I think the wrong Lester was killed. That man could be a problem. He could empty the bag on all of us." At this mention, several men in the room nodded agreement, with one stepping toward the door and cracking the cabin's door to peer outside making sure no one could hear the conversation. Satisfied, he closed the door and returned to the center of the small room.

Gilmer replied, "No, he cannot bring testimony against us without implicating himself. Bryant Lester is just a simple farmer. He will go back to his farm, and we will never hear from him or about him. Besides, I understand he has taken to slave ownership with zeal and has been quick to take up the whip on them at the slightest hint of insubordination. Of the Lesters, he is the most corruptible."

The man who had held Bryant to the last spoke for the first time. "Yes. His brother was breeding horses. Bryant has plans to breed slaves. All the women he has purchased are young and of childbearing age."

Gilmer smiled wryly adding, "Yes, in a few years, the slaves on his farm will start to look like him."

A few of the men in the room stirred.

"What? You don't? They all do. We all do eventually," Gilmer said.

The assumption that Gilmer was making condemned them all, but mostly himself. The fact that there was no objection confirmed the accusation that many assumed, but no one talked about – the slave owners were sleeping with their slaves. And this fact did not lessen the probability that some owners, eventually, would be selling their own offspring.

Breaking the awkward silence, one of the men returned the conversation to Bryant Lester, "Still, are you certain he will stay silent?"

"I think we should send a stern message to Bryant to make sure he understands the peril he is in. I think it is time to pay the warden at the stockade a visit."

There was broad agreement from the men in the room.

The room was silent until Commander Rogers asked, "Does Bryant know?"

Gilmer reached into the leather pouch that hung across his shoulder and falling at his waste that usually held ammunition. He withdrew something. Placing a large nugget of gold on the table he replied, "Bryant Lester has no idea."

Night was falling when Richard found his son a few hundred paces up Peachtree Creek, away from the site of the old fort.

They sat for a while watching the water flow past.

"Father. Why is the water here black?" Paul asked.

"Oh, son, that is the trees. See these tall trees? Most of them are oaks. Their leaves and branches fall into the water, and their roots are in the water too. See there?" Richard pointed to the opposite bank of the creek. There, on the water-worn bank, they both could see the roots of the large trees, some of which were completely submerged below the water. Paul nodded. Richard continued, "Where there are oaks and creeks or streams like this, the water is black."

Paul leaned forward looking at the water. "I can see myself more clearly than I can in the water at home." Both men were now looking at their reflections. "Can I drink this water?"

"I have, and it was fine."

Richard looked at his son and their reflections for a long time. Both sat back and settled against trees near the stream. For a long time, neither spoke. They just sat in the silence and enjoyed the sound of the forest and the black water.

After a long while, Richard stirred. The peaceful moment was gone. "Let's head back to camp. I need to speak with Reverend Trott before it gets too late."

∽

Reverend Trott was a man with a quick mind and wit. He had served the Methodist Missions to both Hightower and New Echota for several years and had earned the respect of many in the north Georgia frontier.

Unlike the Creek, the Cherokee had openly encouraged several denominations to open missions within their Nation and simultaneously encouraged prominent leaders to send their children to the schools run by the missions. The missions at both New Echota, the Capital of the Cherokee Nation, and nearby Etowah were well attended, boasting over 25 students each.

The leadership, from Chief Vann to the current chief, Ross, was of the mind that if the Cherokee adopted much of the same dress, some of the customs and language, that their nation could survive. It had been barely a year prior, in 1827, that the Cherokee Nation had adopted a new Constitution that intentionally mirrored that of the nation that now seemed to press in from all directions.

Chief Vann operated a ferry and a large plantation that took over 100 slaves to operate. In many ways, these enterprises mirrored the best and worst elements of the New World. Despite all of this, Chief Vann had been murdered several years earlier.

Now, led by John Ross, and armed with the legitimacy of a constitution, the Cherokee Nation was trying to rediscover its footing.

Like Joseph McIntosh, John Ross's father was Scottish as well. His mother was Cherokee. He had been appointed as the US Indian Agent in 1811 and served as such in the years leading to the unrest that was to follow. Like so many other leaders of the Cherokee, he had even served under Andrew Jackson as well, and for this, he was well-respected within the US Government.

Ross was one of the few Cherokee leaders who had made the trip to Washington, DC. He had traveled there as part of a Cherokee delegation to negotiate land ownership issues. For this reason, the Creek considered Ross a formidable adversary on the issue of territorial boundaries.

But Ross also knew he needed peace. He had seen Jackson's response during the War of 1812 and the Red Stick rebellion firsthand. Moreover, his service had not garnered either him or his nation any preferential treatment in the years that followed. The response had been brutal. The victory total, entire villages had been laid waste; and now, white settlers were making claims to fields that had been sown by the Creek and the Cherokee for centuries.

Like Chief Vann before him, Ross owned a tobacco plantation in Tennessee just north of Chattanooga Creek and operated a ferry that everyone knew as Ross's Landing. Chief Ross was a man among men, even though relatively young and in his thirties. At the same time, he had worked hard, and had no intention of his life ending as his predecessor's had. He needed a consensus. Without a consensus, he might not make it home. And, as a newly elected chief, he understood that he needed the support of his fellow Cherokee elders and leaders more than his Creek counterparts.

In any culture, Ross would have been considered a force to be reckoned with. He was bilingual, speaking both English and Cherokee fluently. He was wealthy. And in so far as an Indian chief could be politically connected, Ross was that man.

With piercing eyes and a strong set chin, Chief Ross presented a noble appearance. His demeanor was that of a man who had seen much, and once he had assessed a situation, he could divine an outcome acceptable to those around him.

His rise to chief had come when both Pathkiller and Charles Hicks had died in 1827, just a year earlier.

James Trott had lived among the Cherokee for five years. Over that time, he had developed a strong relationship with the nation and its leadership as a "circuit rider" who preached what he called "the primitive Gospel" with a dedication and zeal found only in one so young. He had recently married a Cherokee woman in Georgia, Allie Adair.

Rev. Trott was originally from North Carolina. His family had moved to Tennessee in 1815 when James was still a teen. There, he had been baptized and placed his faith in Christ and joined the Methodist Church.

Believing the missionary effort to the Cherokee worthy of support, German Lester and his congregation had sent a reasonable sum, substantial for a fellowship of its size and means, to the missionaries for several years.

Finally, in 1826, a call went out to the churches in Tennessee, Georgia, and North Carolina that sufficient inroads had been made, and that the Cherokee had agreed to allow the missionaries to build a mission. The mission would be a place where the missionaries could gather, but more importantly it would also be a place where they could offer schooling to the local children.

Responding to this call for support, German Lester's small fellowship had stepped forward, lending both men and materials to the building of the mission, which was completed in 1827 and boasted an initial class of 12 eager Cherokee students.

While James Trott looked familiar to Richard Lester, he could not recall that they had ever met. His father had only met him twice. Since that time, the two preachers had only corresponded by letter, but the exchanges were always cordial and well-received.

It was early in the evening when Richard and Paul found James Trott alone, sitting outside a cabin in the heart of what everyone called Standing Peachtree. He was wearing a white shirt and dark pants held above his waist by well-worn suspenders.

"Is this where you are staying?" asked Richard as he and his son approached.

Standing to greet the two Lester men, Trott replied, "Oh, no. I have set my canvass up over in that clearing," he said, pointing into the trees. Richard and Paul could only assume that there was a clearing buried somewhere in the woods.

The three shook hands.

Turning to Paul, Trott said, "What brought you on this trip with your father?"

Paul looked at the minster. Then at his father. "I think I am here to keep my father away from those women," he said nodding in the distance where several women were standing.

"Your mother was wise to send you, although I trust your father is a faithful man in that respect." Turning to Richard, he continued. "It is always nice to receive a letter from your father. However, that last letter did cause me pain. I was sorry to hear of Fountain's death. How are your parents?"

"Frankly, they have been so busy, I am not sure they have had time to shed tears over their loss. Having said that, I think they are staying at my house, and seeing Fountain's children without their parents – I think that may be when they start to grieve."

"So, you have taken in your brother's children?" asked Trott.

"Yes. My wife is a saint among saints."

Both men thought for a moment before James Trott continued, "Well, I am newly married. We are hoping to have children soon."

"It is a blessing," Richard said, looking at his son.

Paul shifted in his shoes at the reference, recalling that just two weeks before he had "blessed" his father with a switch, but he kept the thought to himself.

"Well, I thank you for receiving my father's letter in the spirit that it was sent. We have carved out a nice life among the Creek Indians and have found them to be good neighbors. Frankly, we were not sure your delegation would come. Much less, one that is so large," Richard said, looking at Paul and back to the Reverend Trott.

Looking over his shoulder where the activity seemed to be getting more jovial and boisterous, Trott said, "Let's walk towards my tent." Leading the way, Trott explained that as a circuit preacher, he had grown accustomed to sleeping on the ground and his linen duck tent was one of his prized possessions. Thick as sail fabric, linen duck was made of cotton and very heavy. Because of its double weave, the fabric was an excellent barrier to poor weather. As they bobbed and weaved between trees and evaded low-hanging limbs, the men came to a small clearing where there was a humble campfire and tent, guarded by Trott's horse.

It was here that Trott confided, "It is best that I sleep here. The Cherokee, they accept me. They are kind to me. But I must be clear, on the matter before us, they will not ask my advice and frankly, I should not give it."

Richard nodded, "I understand, and I am in the same position. Frankly, I think the only reason I am here is because I am my father's son, and I can write down whatever is decided."

All three had settled on the ground, close enough to the fire to benefit from the light, but far enough away to not suffer the heat, as the night was not cold, the fire was only needed for cooking, light, and the smoke – which would help keep some of the insects away. Trott nervously tended the fire, tossing a few small logs and twigs on the flames, which excited a response of both flame and sparks. Both of which settled quickly.

"Truthfully, I am not sure the issue is really the land," Richard said. "So much land has been surrendered already, I think both nations are trying to hang on to every piece of dirt that they can."

"I agree," James Trott replied… a thoughtful pause followed. "You must know, there are two or three men in the Cherokee contingent that believe the land in question was granted to them as a spoil of war – payment to the Cherokee earned out of their forbearance. Those men believe the land was earned out of their loyalty."

There was silence. "Richard, what do you think happens here? What I am trying to ask is, and I think what Ross and the Cherokee delegation want to know is, they don't want two enemies. They want to know that the Creek will not rise against them."

"I understand," Richard agreed. "Both nations have lost so much in the last twenty years, there really is not much left to lose."

Trott leaned forward, "There is more… There is something you must know."

Paul shifted, as did Richard. The look on Reverend Trott's face had turned grim.

"There are rumors that gold has been discovered in the hills north of here. And those hills are Cherokee hills. I have not seen the gold myself, but that is the rumor. At present, these are just whispers, but such a discovery would no doubt hasten confiscation of additional land."

"I see. And of course, you are right. Chief Ross must be under tremendous pressure." Richard reflected.

"That is a certainty. But again, I am not sure the rumor is even true and if Chief Ross has had any confirmation…" Trott thought for a moment before resuming. "The interesting thing is – they discovered gold in North Carolina. So, given the proximity, it is not a far-fetched notion. And, even if it is not true, the rumor itself will increase pressure on the Cherokee Nation to relinquish lands."

"And here I am with a delegation of Creek Indians asking them to do the same," Richard thought aloud. "Relinquish more land."

"Exactly." Trott said with finality.

The three sat in silence for a long time.

"Well, we best get back to our own place of rest. We will see you in the morning." With that, Richard stood, and Paul followed his father's motions to leave. Reverend Trott stirred to stand, and Richard placed his hand on the man's shoulder, "Keep your seat. Enjoy your rest." Bending slightly, he and Reverend Trott shook hands.

Once they were away from the glow of the fire and alone, Richard placed his hand on Paul's shoulder, "Son, you understand that you are not to repeat what you just heard to anyone, under any circumstances. What you just heard is a rumor at best and we don't repeat rumors." Pausing, he saw his statement had sunk into his son's ears. He continued, "Rumors like this, well, they can start a fight. Wars have been fought over less. People could get hurt, even killed."

There was a stillness in the woods about them with only the sounds of insects and trees bending in the slight breeze.

Richard could see that his son was forming a thought.

"Do you think this is why my uncle was killed?" asked Paul.

"It is more than possible," replied his father.

PART V

A low haze covered the entire Chattahoochee River basin the next morning. Being slightly elevated, the new fort was spared, while down closer to the river, Standing Peachtree was covered in a light, lazy fog. Despite this, anyone familiar with Georgia knew the day was going to be warmer once the cool dew from the evening melted away.

Over in Fort Peachtree, Gilmer had just arrived back at the commander's cabin. The commander had completed his rounds at the fort, and as Gilmer walked into the cabin, he could see David Mitchell arriving, framed by the gate as he entered its confines.

While he thought they had traveled separately, Commander Rogers wondered if the two had met secretly before coming to the fort. It was just a thought. "Why couldn't he trust them?" he thought to himself. It was too late to remove himself from this plot, and frankly, there was too much to be gained. If he could extricate himself from this intrigue, he was not sure he would want to.

Both men secured their horses to the hitching post and entered in close succession.

"Any word from our Sergeant on the proceedings down in Standing Peachtree?" prompted Gilmer as he seated himself behind the desk.

The fact that Gilmer assumed he could sit in his old chair in the presence of the fort's current commander was more than an annoyance to Commander Rogers. On several occasions he had come close to reminding Gilmer that he was just a US Representative, and in this fort, he was no longer in command, but he had held his tongue. He knew George Rockingham Gilmer was a powerful man. While the commander could quickly muster 35 armed men, Gilmer could, within several days, muster the entire Georgia Militia.

"The parties have all arrived. They met briefly last night and are meeting again today." Commander Rogers continued, "There does not appear to be much urgency or animosity."

"Well, that is unfortunate and will not do." Gilmer replied. Turning to David Mitchell he asked, "Did you find the men we discussed."

Mitchell, who had been standing, turned to pull a chair closer to the desk, sat down and settled in. "Yes, I have the men we need. We have four men who were Red Sticks, and the warden is certain they can be convinced to do our bidding. In return, we are going to give them pardons and they are to disappear to Florida and will promise never to return."

Gilmer looked satisfied. But for clarity he asked, "They understand that no guns are to be used."

Mitchell cocked his head. "We have not fully explained the details. But the warden is certain that all of the men are proficient with bows and arrows. And they will be told that if they ever return to the State of Georgia they will be hung for insurrection and murder."

Michell nodded again and added, "Frankly, we are the least of their troubles. If they return and the Creek get to them before we do, their demise will be more horrific."

"When will the deed be done?" asked the commander.

"As soon as the meeting at Standing Peachtree is concluded," was the reply.

Commander Rogers was well known at the stockade because the garrison that manned the prison was also called upon to help guard the newly reopened Fort Peachtree. This was particularly true during planting and harvesting seasons when manpower was hard to find. Mitchell was only known by a few of the people at the prison.

The stockade had two buildings: a kitchen, and a larger building that housed the prisoners. Outside the pilasters that contained the prisoners were a barracks, a cabin for the warden, a stable for horses, and a commissary for the guards.

From Mitchell's point of view, there was very little difference between the guards and the prisoners. Everyone was ill-tempered, dirty, and smelled of human filth. When you entered the prison stockade, you were immediately struck by the fact that everything was a shade of brown. Mitchell curiously thought that he did not realize there were so many shades to the color of mud.

Sanitation conditions were non-existent for the prisoners, and this meant that even after one left the stockade, whether you were a guard, a visitor or a short-term prisoner, the smell did not leave you – it traveled with you for days.

As the Commander and Mitchell arrived, the prison warden was about to flog a prisoner. The warden considered it his duty, some would say his privilege to deliver this type of punishment.

The prisoner was secured between two large posts with his arms outstretched. His bare back exposed to the morning sun, the warden, and the approaching men.

"What have we here?" asked Mitchell.

The warden turned not knowing who was approaching.

"Isn't it obvious!" the warden replied with a tint of annoyance in his tone. Seeing Mitchell, his demeanor immediately changed. The guards of the prison could tell the warden was intimidated.

"It has been a while since I have flogged anyone. May I?" Mitchell asked knowing his request would be granted.

"Certainly, the honor is yours." The warden handed his whip to Mitchell.

Mitchell reached out taking the whip from the warden with his aging hand. He tossed it lazily at the ground. The whip had five strands of leather. In the end of the leather strands were tied various pieces of metal. Two looked like musket balls, the other three simply looked like flat, thin spurs.

"What is this man guilty of and how many lashes is this man entitled to receive?" asked Mitchell. He had stressed the word – entitled.

The warden looked disdainfully at the prisoner. "He brutally beat his wife. His wife's family and the community have asked us to make sure he gets a message that this will not be tolerated."

"And how many lashes were included in his sentence?" asked the commander.

"Ten, but from the looks of his wife, she received more than that?" replied the warden.

Mitchell walked towards the prisoner who had been glancing over his shoulder.

Mitchell looked at the man who stood defiantly straight and glared at the man who would issue his punishment. Mitchell thought he even detected a slight smile.

In truth, the prisoner was somewhat relieved when he saw Mitchell. At this point, David Mitchell looked his age, and the prisoner thought lashes from the older man might be a relief.

The prisoner was mistaken.

"Oh, you have the look of a man who does not understand the wrong he has committed." Mitchell whispered as he neared the wife-beater, "but you will. Trust me, you will." Mitchell walked behind him and around the other side so the prisoner lost sight of him for a moment. Now standing on his right, Mitchell leaned close. "I am an excellent horseman. I can flick a fly of my horse's ear and he will never break stride." He smiled, "Unfortunately for you, subtle skill like that will not be needed today. But before the day is over, trust me, flies with gather about you like bees to a flower, and you will wish I was here to flick them away with my whip."

Mitchell walked back, handed his hat to Commander Rogers, and removed his coat handing it to the warden.

Taking a wide stance, he flicked the whip a few times to better gauge its weight and length.

He took a deep breath and then the punishment began.

At first, the prisoner simply exhaled and grunted in defiance when he was struck. Gradually, his clenched teeth and his defiant stance was replaced as the number of lashes mounted and the prisoner's back became cracked and lacerated.

The warden was known to enjoy seeing others suffer, but even he was taken aback by the violence directed toward the prisoner.

Finally, there was a pause. Mitchell wiped his brow. "I simply need to catch my breath. I know we are not counting, but I think that was 5." The warden thought to himself – 'it was closer to 25.'

The prisoner was now hanging. Arms totally outstretched and unable to stand on his own. The only things keeping him from being prone on the ground were the ropes that bound him to the posts. He gasped.

Mitchell whipped him five more times before stopping. He exchanged the whip for his coat and looked back at his handiwork.

"That should stop him from beating his wife. At least until his wounds heal."

No one said it, but everyone, the commander and warden included knew that these wounds would never fully heal.

Mitchell turned, leaving the prisoner to the guards and whatever meager aid would be offered to the prisoner before he was released the following day.

As instructed the day prior, the warden had selected four prisoners. All four were Creek Indians. All four were self-confessed hunters. None of the men had been convicted of killing a white settler. This was important to both Mitchell and Gilmer as both men believed there would be fewer questions asked if the men released were not murderers.

The men were still wearing heavy, iron leg cuffs when they approached the Warden, Commander Rogers, and Mitchell.

The commander looked at the warden and said, "Give me the keys to the shackles?" Handing the keys to Commander Rogers, Mitchell said, "That will be all, Warden."

The warden raised his brows, handed the keys to Rogers, and turned towards the kitchen.

Once he had left the six men standing together, Mitchell was the first to speak, "Do you speak English?" Two men nodded, the other men, stood motionless with blank stares which Mitchell took for "no," which essentially meant that Mitchell would need to speak to the men in Creek, which he could do.

"You each have over two years remaining to serve out your prison sentence. Is that correct?"

The men nodded, shifting, and looking at each other as they did so.

Mitchell was still perspiring from the flogging he had administered. For a fleeting moment, he wondered if the four men had seen his work on the prisoner. He continued, "The State of Georgia will give you your freedom. But you must agree to do something in return."

The men looked at one another again. It was the shortest of the four that spoke.

"What do we have to do?"

"You must kill a man. And then, you must leave the State of Georgia. You can never return."

A second, taller man asked, "Who do we have to kill?"

"I will tell you that in a moment," replied Mitchell, "but first I want to know if you will do it."

The shorter Indian replied, "Why do you want this man killed?"

"He is an enemy of the state. He and his family are creating problems," Mitchell responded. "That is all you need to know."

"Then you should have some of the guards of the stockade kill him. Why don't you get them to do it for The State?" The Indian spat the last two words with disdain and hate.

"We can't. We need you to do it. Or someone like you."

Commander Rogers now spoke for the first time, "Listen, if you will not do this, we can find others who will. We will leave you here to serve out your sentence."

The men looked at each other.

"Will the man we are to kill be armed? Is he a soldier?"

"No," replied Mitchell. "He is a lawyer. The son of a minister. And, yes, he will be armed – just like anyone else who would be traveling on the Stone Mountain Road."

"Will he be traveling alone?"

Mitchell and the commander looked at each other. Mitchell Responded, "He will be traveling with his son, at the very least. There may be others with him. We don't really know."

The commander jumped in, "You can pick the time and the place. It simply needs to be done in the next three to four days. He lives in Covington. Do you know of Covington?"

Several of the men nodded.

"Kill him before he gets home if you can. Frankly, we do not care when or where, but it does need to be done quickly."

The largest of the four now spoke, "You have taken everything we had. We will need arms and horses."

"You will be given both," The commander replied.

There was a lull and Mitchell could not tell which way this conversation was going. It was obvious to him that the two men who spoke knew each other, or at least, were familiar to one another. The other two men seemed to be listening as they whispered amongst themselves for a few minutes.

Shaking the keys he said, "time to decide. Do you want freedom? Or do you want someone else to be free."

The small huddle broke slightly, with all four Creek Indians again facing Rogers and Mitchell. The smallest man spoke first, "I will die in here if I stay. There is no food or air worthy of my spirit. I will do it." With that, the other three agreed as well.

Mitchell handed the keys to Commander Rogers, "Unshackle the men." He ordered.

The commander knelt, and with some difficulty, the shackles were un-locked. He collected the shackles and carried the leg-irons and keys over to the kitchen where the warden was standing, having watched the entire conversation from a distance.

"We have what we need. Thank you. Complete the notations needed on the prison's roster, will you?"

The warden replied, "And commander… when the sergeant leaves, I will get his post at Fort Peachtree."

The commander sighed. "Yes. When he leaves. Please have your man bring the four horses from the stables to the hitching posts out front."

The warden stood and followed the commander towards the gate.

The gate to the stockade was opened and the seven men stepped through. The change in the air and the scenery was stark. The men were immediately glad they had made the decision. It was true, very few people survived more than a year or two in a frontier stockade. And while there was a rumor they were going to be moved to the new prison in Milledgeville, there was no confidence that conditions there would be an improvement.

The warden continued past the corner of the stockade. The Indians did not know what he was doing.

The prison guards closed the gate that was almost twice as tall as the men.

Mitchell waited for the men to settle and made sure the warden was too far to hear anything that was said. He finally spoke. "You are to kill Richard Henry Lester. The commander will travel with you as far as Standing Peachtree and point him out to you. You can kill him with knives if you wish. Whatever you do, you must put at least one arrow in him."

"An arrow?" The largest of the four Indians looked puzzled.

"Don't you see. They want it to look like Indians did it." The smallest Indian was the smartest of the group, and he was quickly piecing things together. "This is going to bring trouble to my family and my nation."

Both Mitchell and the commander could see the resolve of their new recruits weakening.

A third Indian spoke up for the first time. "Well. We are Indians. And frankly, our tribe did not come forward to defend me when I was arrested. Did they defend you?" The Indian looked at the other three. There was no reply.

As Mitchell continued to describe the mission he had for these Creeks, he was increasingly annoyed that the smallest man in the group, known as Harjo, was continually whispering to his taller companion, Talof.

Finally exasperated, Mitchell barked "Is there a problem? You two hearing me, or will I have to repeat myself?"

The short Indian glared at Mitchell. It was unsettling to the man who thought himself self-assured. "No. My hearing is fine. I just do not care for the sound of your voice."

As the two men stared at each other, the warden rounded the corner of the stockade followed by a guard. Each was leading two horses. None were saddled, but each horse had a rope bridle, blankets and heavy clothe saddle bags.

Handing the reins to the Commander and Mitchell, he said, "As you requested. Each saddle bag has rations for four days, fresh clothing, a knife, and here are the quivers and bows you asked for."

The warden stepped back, eyed the four former prisoners one last time, and retraced his steps to the prison gate.

Knocking on the gate, one of the doors opened slowly and both men disappeared inside.

The men were now looking through the bags and inspecting the horses.

"We need rifles." One of the Indians stated.

"No. You don't." replied Mitchell firmly. "We said we would arm you. This is it. You each get a bow, arrows, and a knife. When you kill Richard Lester, you can take whatever he has on him – although I would be careful what you take. If the items can be identified as his and you are caught with it, you will hang." There was a pause. "We are giving you a task. How and when you complete this task is up to you, but, let me be clear. Leave no witnesses. If there is anyone around, you must kill them as well."

With that, Mitchell turned, untied the leather bridle for his horse, and begin to mount the animal. Mounted, the man now towered over the odd, small gathering. "Men. Do not return to Georgia. If you do, I will personally hang you for murder. And commander, get them cleaned up. They have the look of men who have escaped the gallows." He kicked his horse and rode away from the stockade.

The commander was now left alone with the four Creeks. He was nervous and wanted to put distance between himself and the Indians as quickly as possible.

He mounted his horse and led the men away.

He rode in silence. It was obvious to him, too, that the smaller Indian and the larger Indian were close.

"Hey, we would like to wash. Can we do that?" Again, it was the smallest of the men making the request.

"That will be done. There is a bend in the trail further up where the trail is close to the river. You can wash there."

When Bryant had left the fort, he had stayed close by. Watching the comings and goings.

He had followed Mitchell when the meeting at Fort Peachtree had concluded. He was more than troubled.

Fountain was dead and his own actions, putting it bluntly, had led to the death of not only his brother but his best friend. Initially he had been despondent.

Immediately, he had jumped on his horse and was heading back towards Covington and home. He was only a short distance from the fort when he stopped his steed. He was filled with so many emotions: anger, grief, frustration. What could he do? He had to do something.

He thought, 'why do those men want a conflict between the Creek and Cherokee? What could possibly be the motive?' He knew land was at the heart of the issue. But there must be more to this.

He turned his horse and headed back down the River Road in the direction of Fort Peachtree.

From the cover of the trees and removed from any trail or path leading to the fort, he waited and watched.

It did not take long. Gilmer was the first to leave.

Bryant waited. Gilmer was a US Representative. If there was dirty work to be done, it would not be him, it would be either the commander or the Indian Agent, David Mitchell. He would follow the next of those two men to leave.

He only had to wait a short while. In his fallen state, he was not sure he deserved it, but both the commander and David Mitchell emerged from the fort together and headed on a trail that headed south on the eastern bank of the Chattahoochee.

They were in no hurry. Bryant waited a few minutes. Then, with little urgency himself, he mounted his horse and followed.

The trip was not long. They traveled along the rough wagon path for a few minutes and arrived at the stockade. While the stockade was not large, it housed many of the state's most undesirable inhabitants – most were Indian. White settlers where now mostly taken directly to the newly constructed state prison. The small frontier prison was substantially smaller than Fort Peachtree, enclosed by a stockade that was about sixty paces in either direction.

While Bryant had not seen either man enter the stockade, he thought he recognized their horses tied to the hitching post outside the gate.

Again, Bryant waited from across a grass and mud clearing. After a short time, the commander emerged with Mitchell and five men. While Bryant did not recognize the five other men, he thought four of them could be Indian. The fifth man disappeared around the corner of the stockade.

The four prisoners, the Commander and Mitchell stood outside the fort where a heated conversation ensued. While Bryant was too far away to hear the words, there were moments where he could tell that the men were at odds and not in agreement. As the conversation seemed to subside, the man who had left returned with another man from the side of the stockade with four horses.

The commander had knelt down and removed shackles from the prisoners' legs.

The reins to the horses were handed over to four of the men. They were also handed what appeared to be bows and arrows, but at that distance, he could not be sure.

After a brief conversation, Mitchell mounted his horse and continued up the path towards Fort Peachtree. Commander Rogers lingered briefly with the four men, but soon, they were mounted and riding in that direction as well.

Again, Bryant mounted his horse. And, as before, there was no reason to hurry as there was nothing of note between the fort and the stockade aside from a few small farms and one large plantation that fronted the river.

As he assessed what he witnessed, he could not fathom what was going to take place. All he knew was that two men of power had released four men from the prison and then equipped them with both horses and what he believed to be weapons.

Now, they were heading back in the direction of Standing Peachtree.

Bryant was resolved to get his brother to leave Standing Peachtree with his son as quickly as possible. At the same time, he could not be seen in Standing Peachtree.

The truth was: Bryant did not want anyone to see him.

Upriver at Standing Peachtree, the fog had been slower to lift and was being replaced by a sticky heat. There was little doubt that the day was going to be hot, and with the river close by, humid as well.

Chief Ross and his contingent along with Reverend Trott had arrived early. To the embarrassment of Richard, the Creek were slow to arrive. And when they did, they did so without apology.

Once greetings were exchanged, it was Chief Ross who spoke first.

"I want to say that we have spoken at length about the land under dispute. For clarity, we want you to agree that the land north of the Chattahoochee River from where we are seated out to Fort Daniel near Hog Mountain is Cherokee land. The land you are concerned about is the land north of the New Road and South of the Chattahoochee River."

The "New Road" linked two fortifications and would be known initially as "Pitch Tree Road" – because the pine trees felled in constructing the road were an excellent source of pitch. And, being so close to the river, the pitch was needed to seal and waterproof the various vessels that plied the Chattahoochee River. At some point after its construction, the road's name changed to "Peachtree".

It was a question that needed a response. Direct and Simple.

Joseph leaned towards the men seated to his left and after a long moment, he turned and in Cherokee, so that there would be no doubt, replied, "Gohiyhdaneha," and for Richard's sake he repeated "It is agreed."

All the Creek men nodded.

Ross, in return, shifted in his seat so that he could see the faces of the men seated nearest him. Most nodded their consent. The man closest to Chief Ross leaned towards him and said something that was inaudible to the rest of the group. Chief Ross listened. After a brief pause, Ross continued. "It needs to be said aloud. We bear no animosity at this time with the Creek Nation. Today, and going forward in our histories, we need to work together when possible. As both of our nations have given up much and now that there is less and less for us both to govern and call "*our own*," each parcel of land that we have is even more dear than ever."

There was wide agreement.

Ross continued, "We will not argue about the land in question here today. I was say aloud, the land we are talking about was granted to us by the Whites for our loyalty during their war with the Nation across the sea. And, in truth, both of our nations have hunted on these lands." He paused. The faces and the tenor of the meeting had become tense. "It is also true, that we never believed the Whites had the right to grant us that land." This statement brought a relief that could be seen on the faces of the small Creek delegation. "But in return for relinquishing our hunting rights south of the Chattahoochee River to Pitch Tree Road, we want your assurance that no Creek Indian will lift arms against the Cherokee. In return, we will pledge the same." Again, he paused, reading the faces of the men in the small circle. "Going forward, the Creek are not the enemy of the Cherokee, and the Cherokee are not the enemy of the Creek. This piece of land is important. But more than that, we desire peace with your nation." He paused. "Both of our nations have hunted this ground for generations. We will relinquish our rights, but we must have peace between us."

An ease fell over the circle. There was no dissent.

"It is done," Joseph spoke. "Our man will write this on parchment. Once you and your men have approved the terms, our elders have authorized us to sign on behalf of our nation."

"That is well with me. I am sure Mr. Lester and Mr. Trott can capture our words correctly. Once it is completed, I will sign the document on behalf of the Cherokee Nation," Chief Ross said with a sense of finality. Turning to Richard, he said, "Do you need anything more from either of us to prepare the document we need?"

Richard looked at Trott, and back at Ross, "No. I think I have everything we need. It should be an easy document to craft and a relatively simple document for you to review."

With that the men rose and left the small ring of stones where they had been seated, leaving Reverend Trott, Richard, and Paul.

Richard turned and lifted his satchel removing a quill, ink, and a piece of parchment. Paul had been sent to the nearest cabin, and, with the help of one of its inhabitants, had returned carrying a small square table.

Before any sentence was added to the parchment, Richard conferred with Trott concerning the language of the phrase he was about to transcribe. Trott added only a few comments, but mostly agreed with the wording that Richard proposed. Quickly the one-page agreement took shape with the major statements being that the land south of the Chattahoochee and north of the

New Road belonged to the Creek; and no land north of the Chattahoochee River belonged to the Creek. In return, the Cherokee agreed to never raise arms against the Creek, and the Creek agreed to never raise arms against the Cherokee.

As Trott read the brief agreement a final time, a man approached the three and asked, "Are you Richard Lester?"

"Yes, I am," was the reply as Richard stood.

"A gentleman asked that I get this note to you quickly." He handed Richard the note and left as suddenly as he had come. Richard placed the note in his pocket.

Trott watched the man leave, "How odd. Don't you want to read your note?"

Richard raised his brows and opened the note. Without reading a word he recognized the handwriting immediately. It was from Bryant. The note contained one sentence: "Please return home in all haste."

He closed the note and looked at Paul. "Son, we are about done here, and we need to hurry home. You go gather our things and pack the horses. I will be along behind you in a few minutes."

"Yes father." Paul rose and headed to gather the few items they had brought with them and saddle their horses.

He handed the note to Trott so that he could read it. "We need a second document so each tribe has one to carry home with them to their nations."

Trott read the short note quickly. "My, that is curious… and it is not even signed."

Richard nodded. "It is from my brother. I recognize his script."

Taking a second piece of parchment out, he began preparing a second copy of the agreement in silence, pondering what the note meant. Once the second copy was completed, he stood. "I need to find Joseph and make sure this agreement is as he expected." He paused. "Reverend Trott, it has been a pleasure meeting you here today, and frankly, I thought there was going to be more involved in creating this document." Trott shook his hand and smiled as Richard continued, "And, with what you related last night, I am certain there are some things that have gone on here both said and unsaid that were helpful to both the Creek and the Cherokee."

"Richard. This is no small agreement. What you have just written down is a peace agreement between the Creek and the Cherokee. What started out as a simple land dispute is now a peace treaty between the two largest Indian Nations in Georgia." Trott said. "Blessed are the Peacemakers!"

Richard looked at the document and sighed, "When it comes to the Indians, I fear there will be no victories only delayed defeats."

Trott stood in silence as the statement lingered. After a short moment he turned and said, "I will go find Chief Ross and will meet you back here as soon as I can return."

Both men turned to search for the men that they needed.

Richard easily found Joseph McIntosh and the other Creek elders. He showed the parchment to Joseph and related that the document had been reviewed by Trott as well – who was collecting Chief Ross as they spoke.

Joseph read the document, turned to the other Creek elders, and related that the document was ready to be signed.

After a brief discussion, each man stepped forward and signed the document. Three of the men could read, and they paused, reading the document, and nodding as they did so.

As they concluded, Chief Ross approached with Reverend Trott. "I am told the document is in good order." He paused as the other men stepped back. Joseph, keeping a hand on the document so that it remained flat, watched as the chief read the agreement.

As he finished reading the document most of the Cherokee contingent arrived. Several read the document as well. With no objection, Chief Ross signed the document and stepped back. Looking at Joseph he said, "It would be good to have a second identical copy of the document so that both Nations can possess one."

Richard stepped forward, "Reverend Trott and I had the same thought." He handed a second identical agreement to Joseph. Joseph smiled, and each man stepped forward to again sign the twin agreement.

As the signing concluded, there was a great deal of satisfaction from both parties. Joseph McIntosh stepped around the table and offered his hand to Chief Ross. "Thank you for making the journey from New Echota."

Chief Ross took his hand gladly. "We are all busy. And when Reverend Trott related to me that your nation was concerned about its northern boundary, we did not want the issue to fester."

"It now seems like such a small matter." Joseph replied.

"No. When it comes to our ancestral lands, there are no small matters," Chief Ross said as he rolled the parchment and pushed it into a leather cannister for the trip home.

Richard approached both men, "I trust our business here is concluded." Both men agreed. "I need to return home as I received an urgent message from my brother just this morning."

Joseph looked beyond Richard and now noticed that Paul was approaching with two horses saddled and the third horse packed for the return journey. Nodding in Paul's direction he said "You are in a hurry! I will pack quickly and catch up. I don't want you making the journey alone with your son."

"I thank you, but there is really no need." Richard responded.

"It is the least I can do. Besides, we must pay you for your services. You two get started and I will catch up."

With that, Joseph turned, handing the parchment to one of the Creek elders and walked down the muddied road to gather his horse and belongings.

Bryant was heading towards Covington. He had sent the note to his brother; and, from the cover of the woods near Standing Peachtree, he had seen Paul saddling and packing their horses. He decided he would move down the Stone Mountain Road towards Covington. He had not decided if he would wait for them or quickly ride to Covington in front of them. He would set a leisurely pace, and if they caught him, they would travel together – at no point did he encourage his horse to move faster.

If his brother and nephew caught up to him, what was he going to say to Richard? How could he explain his presence?

Bryant thought for several minutes and after a few short bends in the trail he decided that he would tell Richard the partial truth.

He would tell Richard that he had delivered four horses to the fort that Fountain had sold to the army. This was true. He had delivered four horses. While there, he had overheard men talking about unrest being stirred up between the two Indian Nations, and he had sent the note. This half-truth would give him time to decide what else he would tell Richard about his involvement with Gilmer and Mitchell.

The original plan had been simple. And to keep it simple, Bryant had not told Fountain about his conversations with the scheming duo. The fewer people that knew, the better it would be.

Mitchell, had approached him, and he was certain others had been approached as well.

The task was not complicated. For $4,000 in silver coins, a huge sum to him, he was to stop trading with the Indians and encourage others to do the same. An equal sum, slightly reduced for his trouble, he had given to his brother. Additionally, they were to not use any Indian owned businesses until told otherwise. It was a broad, targeted boycott. If an Indian owed money – which was not the case with Bryant, those notes were to be recalled as well.

The whole plan, at least as far as Bryant knew, was to put financial pressure on both the Creek and the Cherokee to leave Georgia entirely.

Because of Fountain's close friendship with Joseph McIntosh, it had been difficult for him to justify not using Joseph's blacksmith or mill. The rationale was that: there was a mill that was closer – which was marginally true. In truth, they were about the same distance apart. Topographically, it was slightly easier to get to the white-owned mill. But it was also true that the McIntosh Mill had been the primary source of lumber for both Bryant's and Fountain's farms for quite some time.

As the boycott gained strength, financial pressure on the Creek had mounted and this, in turn, compelled the Creek to increase their efforts to obtain the money promised by The United States following the Red Stick Rebellion.

For Fountain, Bryant had negotiated the sale of four horses each year to the State of Georgia for the next four years at a slightly inflated price, which had pleased Fountain. He had been breeding horses for several years, and a contract of that size would be easily fulfilled. And Bryant had relayed that part of negotiating the sale of the horses was for them to not use the McIntosh Mill.

When Bryant had agreed, he had asked Mitchell why this was being done, and the reply had been – "It's time for the Indians to move west. There is ample land beyond the Mississippi."

So, Fountain did not fully understand why he was not buying lumber from McIntosh, and Bryant did not fully understand why the Indians needed to move west.

Bryant was now on the Stone Mountain Road. This would be the road that Richard and Paul would travel on their return to Covington. He was certain of it. There really was no other reasonable route for them to take.

The departure from Standing Peachtree had taken longer than Richard had wanted. Reverend Trott had left his humble camp to return to New Echota quickly. Richard did not want to leave the trading post without purchasing some additional salted fish and deer jerky for the ride home. He thought if they pushed the pace, they could certainly be home in three days, but he hoped to be home late on the second.

The heat… the heat would slow them down as they would need to stop at any crossing and water their three horses.

The Stone Mountain Road was normally busy. In some places it was wide enough for two wagons to pass each other. At its most narrow points, it was certainly wide enough for a wagon and a rider heading in the opposite direction.

For much of the ride up to the Piedmont Ridge from the Chattahoochee basin, Richard and Paul said little. They were both surprised by how steep the trail was as it climbed away from the river. As is often the case, neither of them had noted the change in elevation just days before as they had traveled this same path.

As they passed others heading the opposite direction, Richard would guide Banner and the pack horse to the side of the trail. Paul would follow on Danny, and they would wait for the pilgrims to pass. Given the traffic on the trail, the initial pace was slow.

Gradually, the noise, smoke, and smells that one associated with civilization were replaced by the noises of the forest. While hot, there was a light breeze as the cool air was replaced by the heat from the higher elevation of the ridge, as it had been in the sun since its rise that morning. The trees swayed slightly, yielding a woody creaking noise that was pleasant. The smells of humanity were replaced by that of pine and honeysuckle.

That same morning, Mary had risen and set about her early morning chores. Before the children had woken to the smell of bacon and biscuits, she and Lucy had cleaned the cooking hearth, and collected eggs.

"Lucy, my husband, and son should be back in two days or so. And I am not sure who will be with him. I would like to prepare a nice meal for him. "

Lucy thought for a moment. "On the edge of the horse pasture I noticed a patch of blackberries. Do you think they are ripe enough to make a pie?"

"It seems a bit early. After breakfast, take the girls and see if they are ready."

That would be a nice departure of the routine of the day for both Lucy and the girls.

Mary and Lucy would prepare breakfast together. A portion of which Lucy hoped to carry to Boston and Simm, and they would eat their meal either outside on benches that Boston had made, or inside the slave quarters. Mary had found that whatever was cooked was consumed by the slaves. She was shocked at how much more food was required to feed both her expanded family and their three new slaves.

The children would wake up, gather around the table for breakfast, and then head outside to do their chores.

The garden next to the house, being larger, took longer to tend than before, and Lucy and the girls would generally do this in the morning. If it had not rained for two days, they would also water the garden. After the garden was tended, the two girls would set out to collect eggs. Despite the simplicity of the task, this seemed to take a little longer each day as the girls would get distracted.

The boys were to milk the cows and turn them out in the small pasture nearest the barn. They would then feed the horses and turn them out as well. The pigs were always the last to be fed and tended.

Once this was completed, they would work with their hawk. The hawk had yet to fly free. It had only flown to a lure, tethered to a hitching post. The tether, however, had been lengthened so that even Boston and Simm were impressed by the distance the hawk would fly on command.

The boys had named the hawk "Hatchet" because of the way it cut through the air.

Simm and Boston were tasked with watering the larger fields in the morning.

These tasks took most of the morning.

They would break for a brief lunch during the heat of the day and then in the afternoon, Simm and Boston had been ordered to begin clearing the forest adjacent to the pasture so it could be expanded.

Clearing a field was hard work, but each day trees were felled, and the trees that were large and straight were pulled to the side of the lane that led to the farm where they were stacked to dry. Boston was sure Richard would want to use the logs to expand the home at some point. Or, if other slaves from Fountain's farm followed, another slave cabin would need to be built.

James and Eugene were supposed to take the smaller branches to a separate pile. They would be used for firewood. But the truth was, neither boy was big and strong enough to really carry anything of size, even working together. Boston and Simm found their "help" superficial at best.

However, when German and Catherine Lester arrived late in the afternoon, that changed. For four days they had stayed, and the work went quickly. German said little to Boston or Simm. With German's help, the boys were able to harvest a larger number of the branches. On the last day, German had hitched the mule to the wagon, and several large loads of wood were moved and stacked neatly close to the house and next to the slave cabin as well. The stacks would provide the needed fuel for cooking and winter warmth. It was late in the afternoon when Boston stopped and removed his shirt, and Simm did the same that German, James, and Eugene first saw the backs of their slaves. The lash marks on their backs were unmistakable, and they caused all three of the Lester boys to pause and stare. James and Eugene would later recall the first time they saw the damage that had been afflicted by prior masters. There was never a discussion about the lashes that might be needed from them as present masters. But they all knew that if the family-owned slaves, that day would certainly come.

During that same time, German's wife, Catherine had taken it upon herself to take some of the clothes that had belonged to Fountain and his wife, and tailor them for use by Richard, and Mary. Catherine quietly hoped that a few of the dresses would be set aside for the girls to use when they got older. Without Richard there, some clothing was set aside to be altered later. But by the time Friday morning arrived, Mary had a new dress and Lucy was given on old dress that seemed beyond repair.

As German and Catherine were planning to leave the next morning, it was not until Thursday night that Mary found both the courage and opportunity to ask her in-laws what had happened when they had journeyed to Milledgeville with Bryant.

German spoke softly, trying to speak in tones that the children would not hear. "We spoke with the Marshal there. He promised to make inquiries. But, frankly, with no witnesses and no known antagonists having ill-will toward Fountain, I am not sure what he will find."

Mary looked at her mother-in-law and saw tears dripping off her cheeks on the clothing she was mending. She rose to cross the room and knelt. The two women embraced for a long moment.

German stood from his chair and walked to the front door. Pausing to look behind him, he stepped outside, closing the door behind him.

German and Catherine spent Friday morning at the homestead before loading their own wagon and heading back to Covington.

The Grandparents hugged their grandchildren, promising to return before the sun set on Sunday afternoon once the Sunday gathering concluded at church.

Mary promised that as soon as Richard and Paul returned from their journey – they would again be joining them on Sunday mornings in church as a family.

With a snap of encouragement on the reins, the old team of horses lurched forward and began the slow ascent up the trail away from the Lester homestead.

The further away from Standing Peachtree, the fewer the people on the trail. They had crested the rise and begun the long slow passage on the crest of the Piedmont. The good thing about this was the travel was easy. The problem: water was scarce. And, on such a hot day, they would need to water the horses.

They had been on the trail for about three hours, when Richard shared with his son that it was time to find water, rest the horses for a few minutes, and eat something themselves. Paul was glad to hear it. Even though he was just sitting, he was tired, hot, and thirsty. Danny was too.

They turned off the main trail and made a slow, short descent to the north of the trail. Richard was certain, given the steep topography, they would find water as the trail dropped.

And, just as they hoped, after several hundred paces, the terrain leveled out in front of a wide, gentle stream.

Paul jumped off his horse and tied him quickly to a low branch.

Richard quickly corrected him, "Son, water Danny first. There will be plenty of water for you. We will want the water to settle in their stomachs before we mount up for the afternoon."

Both men led their horses to the bank of the slow-moving stream. Richard took a cloth from one of the saddle bags on the pack horse and soaked it in the water. With water dripping heavily, he put the cloth on Banner's neck and let the water cool the horse. He did this several times and soon the sweaty, milky froth was replaced with a wet, brown sheen.

Handing the cloth to Paul, Paul did the same while Richard led the pack horse to the stream.

It did not take long for all three horses to have their fill of water. Paul sat on the ground with his back to a tree. His father reclined, resting the small of his back against the trunk of a tree.

"What do you think your mom, brother, and sister are up to?" Richard asked.

Paul shrugged, "I just hope they are taking care of Hatchet."

"Hatchet? What is 'Hatchet?'" his father asked.

"Oh, that is what we named the hawk. It was the only name we could all agree on. And, since we did not know if it was a boy or a girl, that seemed to work either way."

"Who came up with that?" his father asked taking a bite of smoked jerky and turning a slightly bruised apple in his other hand.

"You know, I think it was Eugene. Yeah, I am pretty sure it was his idea," Paul said with some uncertainty.

"Well," replied his father, "that is a good thing. I am glad you and your brother are letting him into your world like that. Eugene must be missing his mother and father, and he is going to look to you and James as to how he should behave and where he fits in with our family." He paused. "Paul." He paused again, this time waiting for his son's eyes to lock on his, "You are a good son. So is your brother. Treat Eugene like you do James. No better, no worse. Just like family… just, do what you are asked, because I really don't want all three of you hitting me with switches any time soon."

With that, both laughed.

There was a long silence.

Danny was the first to stir. He had been standing on three legs, with his fourth leg slightly bent and his lower lip drooping as though a long sleep was about to descend upon him. He shifted his weight standing firmly on all four legs, and his head was now erect and his ears alert, cocked forward as he looked back up the hill and into the forest.

Richard shifted too, as all three horses were now standing alert. "They hear something. Time for us to move. Saddle your horse." He rose, and in two swift moves he had placed the blanket and the saddle on Danny, leaving Paul to tie off the saddle.

Richard followed the same motions, putting the blanket and saddle on Banner. Simply because of repetition and adult dexterity, his horse was saddled first. He turned to help Paul.

As he turned an arrow flew past his shoulder, barely missing. Instead, it was lodged in a nearby tree.

Pulling Paul to the ground, Richard said, "Son, listen to me. I am going to put you on Banner. Ride him into the stream and go downstream, with the current, and across to the other side as quickly as you can. I will follow. Head back to Standing Peachtree. If you keep the stream on your left, you will eventually come to it." With that, he stood, slid the rifle out of its leather sheath, hoisted his son on to Banner, and handed him the reins.

Suddenly, a second arrow barely missed his son.

"Keep your head down and ride!" With that, Richard slapped Banner's rump and the horse leapt frantically into the black-water stream with a loud splash.

Paul held the reins in one hand, but he had both arms around Banner's neck as the horse splashed in the mud and crossed the stream. Fortunately, the stream was not deep, the depth was concealed by the black water.

Paul was now ten horse lengths down the stream. He sat up, glanced over his shoulder, and saw his father. His rifle was in one hand and reins in the other. Both Danny and the pack horse splashed wildly as they entered the stream following behind him.

By now, Paul and Richard could hear several voices as they yelled at each other. Richard could not make out what they were saying, but he thought he recognized the language. Unfortunately, it was not Latin.

Banner struggled up the bank on the other side through the laurel and ferns that hugged the stream. Paul looked past his father, and he thought he counted three, possibly four men. All of them were armed with bows and moving quickly through the woods.

One of the men drew his bow and Paul saw that its aim was true. The arrow struck his father in his left shoulder.

Paul yelled, "Father!" It was not a word. It was the only utterance he could find, and it leapt from his throat.

Richard again yelled, "Ride, Paul! Ride!" He lifted the reins to his teeth, turned and raised his rifle, aiming it at one of the men standing on the bank just yards away. Richard pulled the trigger.

Banner leapt, startled from the shot, but grabbing a fist full of the horse's black mane, Paul stayed in his saddle.

Richard saw the man fall. He could not know if he was dead. He only knew that he could now see two men bobbing and weaving along the opposite side of the bank.

A fourth, large man jumped into the stream in front of Richard and was rushing toward his son and Banner as they struggled through the trees and dense underbrush of the forest.

While Paul's horse was getting further and further away from the stream, for the first time since the attack began, doubt entered Richard's mind as he desperately wanted his son to get away.

Through the branches and low brush, Paul saw Danny and his father struggle up the bank just behind. It was then that a second arrow hit his father. Paul saw the look on his father's face. And he saw him mouth the words "Ride." There was no sound. The arrow had pierced his throat. His father leaned forward on Danny as the horse continued to struggle up the bank, and back into the stream. Paul saw his father drop his rifle and lean forward against Danny's neck. He saw one man in the stream climbing up the bank ahead of him.

At that moment one of the men running in the water neared Richard's horse. Leaping from the water, he grabbed the arrow lodged in his father's shoulder and pulled.

The pain shuttered through Richard Lester's body as he put the flint pistol his wife had placed in the saddle bag to the Indian's chest and pulled the trigger.

The man, with an astonished look on his face, fell back into the dark water.

Richard pulled on Danny's reins, turning him back into the stream. Both horses now splashed their way down the stream, as a man continued to follow on the far bank.

Richard looked to his right – he could no longer see Paul, and with all the splashing that his horses made in the stream, there was no chance hearing him.

The stream bottomed out, reducing the depth of the stream, and the height of the bank as well, Richard turned his horse toward the bank and felt a third arrow pierce his back, the tip exiting just left of where his shirt was buttoned.

Paul stayed low to the neck of his horse as the horse weaved through the forest. Looking to his left, he saw a large man approaching quickly as the man darted, dipped, and weaved, running through the trees, reaching out for Paul and his leg. Paul felt his foot leave the side of his horse – his foot had not been in the stirrup, as there had been no time to adjust them for his shorter height.

The sudden approach of the large man had startled both Paul and Banner.

He heard the tall man say something but did not understand the word or words.

Banner continued to move through the trees as Paul hung on to the horse's mane.

Paul saw the man's face clearly. For a moment, their eyes locked one to the other. He was surprisingly tall.

At that moment Banner lowered his head and neck and kicked at the man, but his grip held onto Paul's pants. If anything, it tightened as Paul, the tall Indian, and Banner moved through the woods.

Paul reached with his right hand and pulled the knife from its sheath. Letting go for a moment of Banner's mane, he quickly moved the knife from his right hand to his left and swung the knife wildly in the direction of the man's forearm.

He had cut the man, but in doing so, he dropped his knife. His fleeting thought was one of frustration as he lost his knife, and the cut was not deep. It merely irritated the large man.

Paul returned both hands to Banner's mane with even greater purpose.

The horse, now unguided, went between two trees. Paul felt his on grip on the horse loosen, but his right leg was firmly in the right stirrup. He was now precariously not seated in the saddle. Using the stirrupped footing as leverage, he pushed up, regaining his hold. At the same time, he felt a tree on the left wedge firmly against his left leg and Banner's ribs… a godsent tree. There was no room for the man. He lost his grip and fell to the ground.

Paul looked back as the tall Indian quickly stood.

To Paul's shock, the man did not move. He simply watched as Banner forced a path deeper into the woods.

The last thoughts of a man are fleeting. Richard thought of his wife. His children. He could see all three plainly. His brothers and sisters, his mother and father. Ironically, his last thoughts were associated with water: of Fountain and the cool, black water that would be his final baptism.

Bryant thought he heard a gunshot. Maybe two. He had stopped during the heat of the day to rest his horse as well.

He waited.

Whatever sound he heard had come from further down the trail, back in the direction he had just traveled. Back towards Standing Peachtree.

A few minutes passed and there was no further disturbance. He stood to saddle his horse. Both he and his horse had needed the rest. With the horse re-saddled, he placed his foot in the stirrup to renew his journey.

Just as Bryant was about to turn his horse onto the trail, he recognized the sound of riders approaching. Whoever it was, they were riding hard and fast. He guided his horse further to the side of the trail.

Then he saw them. Two men. Four horses. Both men, armed with quivers of arrows and bows. He was not sure, but he thought these were two of the men from the stockade; but where were the other two men? As the men passed, he got a closer look at the four horses. He was certain he recognized the horses – they were the horses he had delivered to Fort Peachtree.

With that, he turned his horse back towards Standing Peachtree, but now, he was riding with speed and purpose.

In his haste, he rode past the lightly traveled trail that could have taken him down to his brother. He rode on, staying on the road that connected Savannah to Covington, then Standing Peachtree and on to the new state of Tennessee. He passed a couple in a wagon. He passed two men on horseback, and slowed to see if, by chance, he could recognize them. He did not. He sped on, descending off the Piedmont towards Standing Peachtree.

He rode into Standing Peachtree as Joseph McIntosh was about to mount his horse and ride out in hopes of catching up to Richard Lester and his son.

"Bryant! What a pleasant surprise. Are you looking for your brother and nephew?" asked McIntosh.

"I am. I was hoping to ride back to Covington with them. I just dropped four horses off at the fort that Fountain had promised to deliver," was Bryant's reply.

"Well, I am about to head out. I am hoping to catch up to them by nightfall. They left in the morning. So, we have some distance to cover if we are going to catch them." Joseph said, turning to see the commotion behind him, as he had lost Bryant's attention.

It was Paul Lester. Both he and his horse looked as though they had ridden through a thicket of thorns. The boy's shirt and trousers were torn. The horse was bleeding from several scratches on its legs, chest, and thick neck.

Paul's eyes were wide, and he was obviously upset.

Bryant jumped off his own horse and ran towards Paul and Banner. Placing his hands on the reins, the horse continued to stomp and raised up, lifting its front hooves off the ground, tumbling Paul to the ground below.

Releasing the reins of his own horse, he lifted his nephew to his feet. "Paul, are you injured? Where is your father? What has happened?" his uncle asked.

Paul looked at his uncle and then at Joseph.

The boy could not speak. He began to shake. His uncle knelt and put his arms around the boy as Paul began to sob. Bryant closed his eyes and held the boy.

Banner continued to stomp his hooves and shake his head violently.

Joseph walked slowly to the horse, speaking quietly in his native tongue. Gradually, the horse became less agitated.

The boy had returned without his father. Bryant knew just by his nephew's appearance and the poor state of his horse, the boy had ridden through purgatory in his retreat to Standing Peachtree.

The tall Creek Indian, Talof, made his way back to the stream.

The shorter Indian, Harjo, was already making his way back to their horses.

He passed Richard Lester and the body of one of his fellow conspirators. By the contortion of their bodies, and the fact that the latter's face was face-down, firmly submerged in the water of the stream, he could tell both men were dead.

On the bank opposite them, one of their number struggled to prop himself against a tree. He had a belly wound which ran with black blood. The wounded man knew, no one had to tell him, his liver had been pierced. The wound was fatal. The tall Indian paused as the man struggled to sit up. The men's eyes met in silence. There was nothing to say. They both understood – no assistance was needed. None would be offered or given. The tall Indian went back into the stream and waded against the current, to the horses.

When he got to the shorter Indian, the one to whom they had all deferred, Harjo was already mounted on his horse and had tied off a second horse to his left wrist.

"The boy saw me." Talof stated.

"What?"

"The boy, he saw me," he said as he mounted his horse and tied off the reins of the last remaining horse to his wrist.

"Talof." it was the first time he had used his friend's name. "You should have left him alone. Why did you go after him? We had no quarrel with the boy – only his father."

Talof thought for a moment, "The truth is, we had no quarrel with the father either, I just did not want the boy to get away and bring help. And you heard the man at the fort, we were told to not leave any witnesses who could identify us or bring people back here."

Harjo looked down the stream at the bodies of the two men in the water. He looked up the stream as if searching for something and back at Talof. He thought for a moment. "Well, we need to get away from here as fast as we can.

I want to put as much distance between me, this," he nodded downstream, "and those two men we met at the prison. There is no helping either of them." He paused, "And if that boy saw you as well as you think he did, I may need to put distance between you and me."

He turned his horse and, with a second horse following, he guided both swiftly away from the stream. Talof followed.

He and Harjo were from the same clan, and they had become friends during the Red Stick Rebellion.

While of different temperament, both men had grown close. It was a friendship whose strength had been tested time and time again. Forged out of conflict. Cured when the two men had lost their families.

Both men had grieved their losses together, although, as Talof reflected on it in this moment, they had never really talked about their losses.

The losses were more than just family, as Red Sticks, many of the Creek Indians in Georgia resented the hostility that the conflict had brought on the entire Nation. For this reason, the two men had felt ostracized, exiled by their own people. Reviled by their tribe, both men had lived on the fringe of their own society, finding camaraderie in the few other survivors of the brief movement for Creek sovereignty.

Talof respected Harjo because of his intelligence.

Similarly, Harjo knew no one of Talof's size and physical ability. The man had the strength of three men.

As iron sharpens iron, the two men had become stronger in combining their diverse talents.

The further they got away from the stream, the flatter the trail became. Glancing over his shoulder, Harjo saw Talof was having no trouble keeping up. With that as assurance, Harjo kicked his horse, and both horses labored into a trot as the trail peaked.

Harjo thought they needed to maintain a quicker pace for a period of time to put distance between themselves and anyone who might follow in pursuit.

～

Sgt. Montgomery had left his home early that morning. In that his home was located close to the main postal route that ran from Augusta to Standing Peachtree, and there was no official post office in the area, the post riders and stagecoaches often left mail for the area with the sergeant.

As Montgomery traveled his way to the fort, he made several deliveries, dropping off various letters at the homes of neighbors along his way. He spent a few short minutes at the fort and left there in the still heat of the mid-day. Over the past two days, he had provided daily reports to his commander, Buford Rogers. All of which had been received with feigned indifference.

The first report relayed the fact that all the parties had arrived. The second was that an agreement or land treaty between the Creek and Cherokee might be drafted by Lester and Trott. Today, he hoped to learn if the agreement had been written and signed.

However, the indifference reflected by Rogers was poorly hidden, because after each report was made, he had mounted his horse and quickly left the fort.

The sergeant was a seasoned veteran of many years. His father, Captain James Montgomery, had allowed him to follow during the Revolutionary War as a young lad of eight years old. While he had grown up in South Carolina, the battle he witnessed was fought on Georgia soil in Burke County.

As an adult, Sergeant Montgomery had served under Gilmer during the War of 1812. While serving in that war, Montgomery had overseen the construction of a small fleet of boats at Fort Mitchell in the southern end of the state. Following the war, he had stayed on at Fort Peachtree.

This experience in building boats served both him and his family well. After the War of 1812, his father had moved his wife and family of 14 to Standing Peachtree as well, which, at that point in time was considered deep in the frontier of Georgia. With his father, Sergeant Montgomery had purchased 1,000 acres of land near Standing Peachtree that included land on both sides of the Chattahoochee River. They paid $3,600 for the land, and, together, they had started a ferry service. For many miles in either direction, this was the only ferry crossing into the Cherokee land north of the Chattahoochee.

While Montgomery was loyal to Gilmer, he was not blind to Gilmer's actions. And, at various times during his career, he had tried to distance himself from his commander's decisions.

Buford Rogers was a different matter. He neither liked nor trusted the man. When the orders came to reopen the fort, the command had been offered to Montgomery. He had turned it down. His family's businesses required more and more of his attention.

Since the War of 1812 had ended, Montgomery and his brother had been employed by the federal government to prevent white settlers from encroaching on Cherokee land.

Wearing as many hats as he did made Montgomery sensitive to both the white settlers, who were trying to find suitable land to farm, and the Cherokee Nation, which was under tremendous pressure to simply exist.

Like many others, his family's businesses were expanding rapidly and included a grist mill.

For Gilmer's part, he was aware of Montgomery's growing influence in the area and considered him an important ally. And, because of these other ventures and his advancing age, Gilmer thought that it was only a matter of time until Montgomery resigned as sergeant.

Montgomery visited the fort briefly and left, riding into Standing Peachtree by early afternoon. As he arrived, a large contingent of men was gathering in haste.

Montgomery, staying on his mount, inquired what the commotion was about.

The man did not respond. Rather he pointed in the direction of John Ross, a man Montgomery had met, but did not know well.

He slowly dismounted and led his horse over to Chief Ross. He waited, as the three men were in a deep conversation.

Once the conversation ended, he stepped forward.

"Chief Ross, my name is Montgomery, we met once before up in New Echota."

"Yes. Yes. I recall," replied the chief.

"It seems there is a bit of a stir here this morning. Is there any assistance I can offer?"

"There may be. It appears a man, Richard Lester, was attacked earlier today. We are going to travel upstream with the man's son and try to find him." Chief Ross paused. "His son returned and is in quite a state." At that he pointed to a young boy seated on the ground and a man sitting near him. The two men walked over to Paul and Bryant Lester.

"I am Sergeant Montgomery. Chief Ross tells me there has been an attack."

Bryant stood. "Yes. Some men attacked my brother and his son. My nephew and his father left here earlier this morning and were traveling back to Covington when it seems four, maybe more men, attacked them."

Ross turned to the sergeant. "We believe two of the attackers were injured. Is that right, Paul?" The boy nodded. "Bryant believes he saw two Creek Indians heading south on the road who may have been involved."

"What makes you think they were involved?" asked the sergeant.

Bryant stood. "They were riding horses I delivered to Fort Peachtree yesterday. And I saw four men mount those horses at the stockade. Let me state this more plainly. Men were released from the stockade, given arms and horses; and those same men then killed my brother. Who holds that kind of authority? Why is this happening?"

"Before we start rumors, there needs to be some confirmation. I urge you to let me go back to the fort. I will gather men and horses and we will pursue the men with you."

Bryant looked at Ross and back to the sergeant. "What you don't know is, my brother Fountain Lester was murdered several weeks ago. These two incidents do not seem to be isolated. We need help. You can ride to the fort and gather more men, but I cannot wait. My brother is out there, and I need to go find him. Once I have my brother, I will help you find the attackers."

Sgt. Montgomery replied, "Wait. Richard Lester was attacked… and you are Richard Lester's brother?" A shocked look came across Bryant's face as the man continued. "I spoke with your brother briefly just two days ago and he told me of Fountain's death. I wrote a letter and sent it to Milledgeville just yesterday."

"Letter! That letter is going nowhere. My father and I have already been to Milledgeville as well, and forgive me for saying this, my family and I do not expect any justice to come out of Milledgeville." The condemnation hung in the air before Bryant continued. "Do what you must. We cannot wait."

Bryant turned to Paul. He lifted his nephew up and placed him on a fresh horse.

Bryant, Paul, and five other men mounted their horses and darted up the road out of Standing Peachtree.

Ross turned to Sgt. Montgomery. "You must know, we are going after those men Bryant saw riding hard to the south."

"Who is we?" asked Montgomery. Montgomery looked beyond the chief where seven men were already mounting horses. One of them was McIntosh, who was holding the reins of a saddled, riderless horse.

Without answering Montgomery's question, the chief turned, taking the reins for his horse from McIntosh, he mounted the animal.

"Sergeant. We intend to catch the men who did this. According to Paul Lester, the boy who just left here, they were attacked by Indians. According to Bryant, those Indians were armed and supplied with horses by white men. Men you probably know well. You and I both know, if Indians did this, there will be a response against our nations. Probably against both the Creek and the Cherokee. Richard Lester was a friend to us. We must help the Lester family find justice. We cannot wait. If we were to wait, I am afraid of the violence your government might bring against both of our nations."

The chief turned his horse, and with a light kick, headed up the trail in pursuit of two men none of them knew.

As the sergeant watched the group ride away, he could not be sure, but he thought the men captained by the chief consisted of both Creek and Cherokee Indians.

Hours later, with help from the people of Standing Peachtree, the sergeant would collect the bodies of the two Indians from further upstream, returning the bodies to the stockade.

When he arrived at the stockade, the warden was nowhere to be found.

The guards at the gate knew the sergeant. Dismounting his horse, he walked to the horse that was carrying both bodies and lifted their heads. "Do you know these men?"

One of the men stepped forward. Taking a closer look, the guard was able to identify the men as prisoners who had both been paroled just one day prior. "I believe they called this one Yaholo and the other Kikkikwawason."

A cursory examination of the prisoner log revealed that four men had indeed been released. The names of all four were listed. The only good outcome of the visit to the frontier stockade was the fact that the Sergeant now had four names: Harjo, which means "Brave." Talof or "Bear."

If the guard was correct, then the sergeant knew who he was tracking: Talof and Harjo.

As the sergeant left, the warden was returning.

"I have brought the bodies of two men back to you. It seems that they were released yesterday." The warden did not like the accusatory tone.

"We did release four men yesterday." The warden replied.

"Who ordered their release?" the sergeant continued.

"I don't recall, it should be on the log."

The sergeant glared, "It is not, and you say you don't recall."

"That is exactly what I said." The warden turned and walked away, offering no further explanation.

The two fugitives had left the river quickly.

Their tacit "agreement" did not include killing the son, and there was no use in retrieving the two men who had been shot. If they were going to survive the day, the wounded would only slow them down.

The horses had value. And they needed to ride fast. Each man having a spare horse would be a true asset.

During their imprisonment, the two friends had made plans. Once released, they had planned to head to Florida where they hoped they could be free. They both were like-minded and did not trust the current leaders of the Creek Nation. To them, it was obvious to anyone and everyone: the Creek were going to be pushed west and possibly eliminated entirely.

When the white men had come forward and offered freedom if they left the state, the choice was easy. The men were basically telling them to do what they already intended to do.

They both mounted the horses they were initially given, grabbed the reins of the horses for the two fallen men, and darted up the faint trail away from the stream.

Neither man had spoken to the other until they arrived where the trail crested the hill. They had a choice, they could return in the direction of the Chattahoochee River and Standing Peachtree to the River Road that would take them directly home to Coweta, or they could head east and then head south on the Rogue Road.

Neither option was good.

If they headed back towards Standing Peachtree, they would certainly be back in Creek territory more quickly. That was the most direct route home. However, in order to get home by that route, they would be required to pass both Fort Peachtree and the stockade from which they had been released. Neither man wanted to go near the stockade. It would just be too easy for them to end up jailed again.

They turned east and south toward Savannah on the Stone Mountain Road.

The two men had ridden hard throughout the day. When they came across water, they would let the four horses drink and then change horses. But even doing this, their horses would need to rest soon. *They* would need to rest soon.

Both were resolved to ride hard until they absolutely had to rest. There was a thin, less traveled hunting trail that they could take south. Since both men were on horseback, they did not need a wide road made for wagons. A trail, even a hunting trail, would do.

After a short distance, they came to the trailhead that could take them south along the Flint River and to what the settlers called The Alabama Road. This road would take them directly south and then southwest toward Coweta and on to Florida. Both men were known in Coweta, which was largely inhabited by Lower Creek Indians. Being recognized would not be helpful because, eventually, men would surely follow searching for them.

Those who knew them would also know that they had been imprisoned for illegal trading of both pelts and rifles. The trade of deer and beaver pelts was taxed by the state, and only men with permits were allowed to conduct trade. Neither Indian had obtained a permit. And, when they were found with a large quantity of pelts and guns near Augusta, justice had been swift. Both men had been sentenced to three years in prison.

Obtaining a permit to do something that they had always done and continued to do on their own land was an injustice. Many Indians refused to bend to a law imposed on them by a government that was not their own.

The two men stared at the trail. It seemed so lightly traveled that their speed would be reduced.

For the most part, the two men wanted to avoid people until they got into Florida and were among the Seminole.

Finally, the Bear said, "Where did they say Richard Lester lived?

"Covington," Harjo replied. "That is at least another hard day's ride east."

The taller Indian thought for a moment. "I think I have to kill the boy." He made the statement without emotion.

The silence that followed was only broken by the sound of the woods at night and the horses as they stomped their hooves and as their tails slapped at flies.

It was then that Harjo noticed the slight wound on Talof's arm. "How did you get such a gash?"

Talof shrugged. "The boy, he had a knife."

Harjo shook his head, "He was close enough to knife your arm? That is a problem. I see why you think you need to journey on to Covington."

There was a still in the forest. Only the sound of finches and a low hum from insects.

"That is not my journey," the shorter Indian replied. "I will leave this road to you, and I will head south on this trail. It will take me longer, but I think splitting up will help us both leave this mess behind. Surely, anyone following us will be looking for two men." He looked down the trail as his words hung in the forest air.

Harjo continued, "I will travel to the town the whites call 'Fayetteville,' and circle back towards Milledgeville. If I can, I will sell or trade one of the horses for a gun, money, and clothes. I will then head north and look for you on the Rogue Road between Covington and Milledgeville." He looked at his friend. He pointed towards Talof's arm, "When you have a chance, you should bind that wound. It is not good for a man to be covered with his own blood."

Talof nodded. "Your right. I will do that. The blood will simply call attention to me. I will bind it."

Both men now looked down the road from where they had come.

"We part here, then," Talof said, consigned to travel to Covington alone.

The two men parted. Harjo taking the hunting trail along the Flint River towards Fayetteville. Talof taking the Stone Mountain Road to Covington.

"I will see you soon. If I don't find you on the road between Covington and Milledgeville, I will look for you in Florida. Safe journey." The two men went their separate ways.

John Ross and the contingent he led had overtaken Bryant, his nephew and the five men who rode with them.

Because the son's description related that Indians had ambushed his friend, McIntosh was pushing the pace. This attack was very personal to him. He had considered Fountain one of his closest friends. In a short time, he had come to care for Richard Lester and his family. Joseph and Richard had come to realize that they had a lot in common. Beyond this, he had promised to return Richard's son to his wife unharmed, and while it was requested in passing, he had taken the promise seriously. Moreover, because he was the person who personally asked Richard for help, Joseph felt responsible for the events that were unfolding. He could not fathom why men from his own nation would attack the Lesters. When the group of men came upon other people traveling the opposite direction, they would slow their pace and inquire: "Have you seen two men, each riding a horse and each with a second horse in draw?"

They were relatively certain they were on the right trail because people continued to point them in the direction they were headed.

Invariably, as they pulled away, either Ross or McIntosh would ask, "How long ago did you pass them?" Early afternoon was the consistent reply.

Neither Ross nor McIntosh believed they were gaining on the two men they were pursuing.

Paul had found the faint trail that just a few hours earlier, he and his father had traveled.

"Are you sure this is it?" Bryant had asked.

"I am certain." Paul said. With confidence the boy kicked his horse and sped away. Down the hill towards the unseen stream that the boy knew was there. The other men did the same, following the boy deeper into the woods.

When they arrived at the base of the hill, Paul was nowhere to be found, his horse was lightly tethered to a branch and drinking from the stream.

Bryant heard splashing in the stream. He saw Paul in water up to his young waist, struggling slightly in the streambed. "I see Danny! I see our pack horse!"

Bryant stayed on his horse, encouraging him into the stream, as did four of the other five men. The fifth had jumped off his horse and had pulled an arrow from the trunk of a tree. He continued to search the woods, finding a second arrow.

Paul stopped. He was going no further.

Three of the men had drawn rifles. Bryant had not. He left his horse and jumped into the black water of the creek holding onto the reins. All of them were now more alert than they had been.

Bryant saw his brother. Next to him was the body of a man he did not know. Both men were in the water entangled in the same fallen tree. He could see three arrows in his brother. He tapped Paul on his shoulder and handed him the reins to his horse.

Stepping past Paul, he knelt beside Richard, pushing the dead assailant into the stream, and the Indian slowly drifted away. A short time later that afternoon, the sergeant from Fort Peachtree and his search party would find him.

Placing both of his hands under the arms of his brother and with great effort, he lifted Richard's pale, cold body out of the water and partially onto the bank. He then pulled himself out of the water, bent over, and dragged his brother further away from the stream.

Paul had yet to look away from his father. Looking at his nephew, Bryant stepped toward the bank and offered a hand to the boy, pulling him up the slick bank and out of the water.

"There is a man here!" came a shout from one of the horse-mounted men in the stream.

The man following on the bank approached the wounded man. "I think he is alive," he said as he knelt. "He will not be for long."

Bryant looked at Paul and said, "You stay here." Paul did not respond. He was not leaving his father.

The other men and Richard now surrounded the dying Indian. "Why did you do this?"

There was no answer. Only a grimace.

One of the Indians stepped forward and knelt. "Where is your honor. You attacked a man and his son. Why?"

Another man spoke, "Did you not know that Richard Lester is a friend to our Nation?"

At that, the man blinked, tilted his head back against the tree, and closed his eyes. He swallowed deeply. But still there was no answer.

Bryant stepped forward. He stepped on the wound in the man's stomach. This evoked a response. "You will answer our questions."

At that the Indian kneeling withdrew a knife and showed it to the wounded man.

"I will skin you. You know I will. You do not have long to live, but it will be painful if you do not answer our questions. We have little time. You have less. We can give you a quick death, but you need to answer our questions."

After a brief moment, the Indian looked at the man he had knelt beside.

"I am thirsty." There was a pause. No one moved to get the man a drink. "We wanted to be free. They promised us we could be free," was the reply.

"Who promised? Who said you could be free?"

"I don't know his name…. I… I think he was the governor or the general."

Bryant stood. Only one man remained by the dying man's side. He was whispering to the man in Creek. And the man nodded. Bryant thought to himself. All of this had been orchestrated by Gilmer and Mitchell. Unknowingly, he had been complicit.

"Is there anything else you need from this man?" asked one of the Indians.

"No. It does not make sense. The Governor. The General… There is no General," thought Bryant out loud.

The man stepped forward, removed a pistol from his belt, and shot the dying man between the eyes. Looking at Bryant he said, "No reason for him to suffer. No reason for him to live any longer and poison our air."

The other Indians looked sternly at the man who now replaced his gun in his belt. "Don't look at me like that. I left him his eyes. He will not stumble about in death. He will be able to find his way."

At that, one of the men brought forward the arrows he had found. "I found these back up the trail by the stream. They could be Creek, but they are poorly made."

"And him," Bryant said pointing, "was he Creek or Cherokee?"

"I know him." One man offered. "He is Creek. He was a Red Stick who survived the war. I frankly thought he was dead or in prison."

"He was in prison. Until yesterday. I saw him leave the stockade myself." Bryant replied. He rose and crossed the stream.

His nephew had not moved. He simply stared at his father.

Bryant bent down beside his brother. He brushed some of the wet leaves from his face, hair, and clothes. He gently closed his brother's eyes. Then he took a bandana from around his neck and tied it beneath Richard's jaw and head so that his brother's mouth would remain closed.

"Paul, let's head back to Standing Peachtree."

Paul blinked. Looked at his father and walked past him into the woods. He was getting further and further away from his uncle. About the moment Bryant was going to yell for the boy to return, he saw Paul kneel to the ground and pick up his knife. Returning to his uncle, he also retrieved the rifle his father had dropped.

With help from the other men, they placed Richard's body on Danny and led the horses back across the stream. After a short distance, they found where they had entered the stream and retrieved Paul's horse to begin the journey back to Standing Peachtree.

As they turned to travel up the trail, one of the men rode forward to Bryant, "Do you want one of these arrows. I pulled them from the forest."

Bryant looked at him and thought for a moment. "No. If we need one, we can pull it from my brother."

In the light of day, the pace was relentless. As night fell, the pace had slowed, but was still steady. While they had stopped several times to water the horses, and there had been a lengthy stop as the sun fell, all the men agreed to ride for a few hours in the dark, so long as they could make out the road and their horses held up.

By riding for two or three additional hours in the dark, Ross and McIntosh were confident that they could close the gap between the group they led and the two Indians they were chasing.

During a stop at a small stream as night fell, McIntosh had approached Chief Ross. "I just don't understand why Creek Indians, men of my own Nation, would do this?"

Ross had simply turned and walked away from the small fire and McIntosh had followed.

There, in the dark, away from the other men, Ross confided to McIntosh that he believed that Richard and Fountain had been murdered for two reasons. First, these fugitives must have been promised their freedom if it was as Bryant said. The men had been freed from the stockade. So, that was the easy part. Second, Chief Ross believed that men of power within the State of Georgia, wanted to sow discord between the Cherokee and Creek. If a conflict could be manufactured, the President was more likely to send in troops.

"They already have most of our land. You sincerely think they want all of it?" asked McIntosh.

"Joseph, it's not just the land. It is what it represents. This is about power," Ross said, he pivoted to return to the glow of the fire. He kicked soil on the flames. "Men, it's time to ride." More soil was thrown on the smokey embers, and the fire slowly disappeared beneath the scattered earth.

They rode until midnight before stopping for the night.

Sergeant Montgomery had gathered three men from the small brigade under his command.

Before leaving he wrote a note explaining his absence and left it for Commander Rogers.

Throughout the late afternoon and into the evening, his pace was steady, but he did not intend to ride into the darkness of night.

He understood from the men who had found Richard Lester, and also from the two bodies he had retrieved, that the men were indeed Creek.

The guards at the stockade had confirmed that four men had been released. Based upon that information, the sergeant thought he knew where to head, and who he was looking for.

The Sergeant had decided to take the trail that followed the Chattahoochee River south known as The River Road. This terrain was easier to cover, provided a constant source of water, and he believed he could arrive in Coweta after a few long days of riding. Most likely before Ross and McIntosh. Moreover, the Indian Agent at Coweta might be of assistance.

The sergeant was puzzled over the record of the men released.

The fact that there was no indication of who had pardoned the men was not troubling. Few people on the frontier could read. What was troubling was the fact that the warden did not know, or at least would not reveal who had ordered the men released; and the sergeant had no authority to press the matter further without some proof of conspiracy.

The travel south towards Coweta was easy. The trail was far enough from the river that it was mostly dry. And, in that there had been no rain for several days, this had helped further dry the trail. When the trail was wet, there were portions of the trail that were impassable, forcing the travelers up and away from the river on higher, roughly blazed ground that was further from the river.

The men were making good time, but because the route followed along the Chattahoochee River, it was not a straight line. This meandering would add to the distance the sergeant and his men had to cover.

The first night, after covering probably 15 miles during the late afternoon and early evening, they camped on a low bluff over the river. The first day had primarily taken them west and south. In the coming days, the trail would gradually head more deliberately south, as did the river.

His men were all farmers or sons of farmers. None of them were true soldiers, but rather they were part of the Georgia Militia. Their training had been limited to attending irregularly scheduled "Muster Days," which, since the frontier was in a relative state of peace, had largely become social gatherings for the community.

Sergeant Montgomery reported to a Captain, who took his military duties less seriously than he did his responsibilities around elections and tax collections.

He knew all the men in his detail, and for the most part liked all of them. They traveled light. They shot true, and he had no doubt that if a confrontation arose, they would be steadfast.

The day had been hot, but now, a light breeze out of the west was cooling both the men and their horses. The sergeant looked up and thought for a moment… it would rain.

Bryant had not slept. And given the tossing and turning he heard from the bedding next to his, he was pretty sure that Paul had not slept either. He saw the sky turn gradient shades of red, then white as the sun cleared the horizon. He thought of the old adage – "Red sky in the morning, Sailors Warning." Yes, it would rain today.

He listened as the forest awoke with the sounds from birds and insects growing in intensity. Paul was awake too, sitting with his back to a tree.

Bryant threw off the blanket and stood stiffly.

"Paul, I would ask, 'how are you?' but I think we are both in a sorry state this morning. You lost a father. I lost a brother."

Paul blinked. He looked at his uncle. "My father saved me. An arrow went past my head. He put me on the faster, stronger horse, and he saved me."

Bryant looked at the boy. His nephew had quickly stopped crying the day before and had not shed a tear since. Bryant wondered if that was good.

"Paul, your father was a remarkable man. In that moment, he did exactly what any father would do. He would not want you to dwell on it."

A silence followed.

"We need to pack our things. I need to go collect your father's remains and then we will leave." Bryant had hired a man to construct a pine box for the journey back to Covington.

"Where is Banner? We cannot leave without him!" Paul stated, standing quickly at the realization.

"That horse is injured. He ran through a forest for you yesterday."

"Yes. He did. And I am not leaving him here. Where is he?" Paul was insistent.

"We left him over at the livery stable as collateral for the horse you are riding. Frankly, it was an exchange."

"I will meet you at the livery then. You collect father. Can you meet me there?"

Bryant looked at the boy and agreed to meet him at the livery.

Paul thought he knew where the livery stable was. It was still early and there were very few people awake this early. Fortunately, there was only one livery stable in Standing Peachtree, and it had a sign.

Paul walked up to the man who was busy watering horses and distributing hay to the various stalls. He turned as the boy walked in.

"Hi, I wanted to return your horse and get mine back," Paul said.

"Your horse is the chestnut that ran through the woods yesterday?" he asked. "You're not planning on riding him today, are you?"

"Yessir, I am. I need to take my father home. And that horse was his horse."

The man knew of Richard Lester's death. Everyone in Standing Peachtree knew.

"Follow me." The man turned and Paul followed him into the barn.

The man opened the gate to the last stall. Banner was lying down. Paul had never seen the horse lay down. He had seen the horse roll in the dust or mud, which was a violent thing to see, but he had never seen him like this.

The man stepped aside.

Paul walked in and knelt by the horse. He placed his hand on the horse's soft nose and rubbed it for a moment. Banner had always liked it when his father rubbed his nose. When he said "Banner. Oh, Banner." The horse lifted his head, sat up and then staggered to stand. Paul stood up and stepped back as the horse struggled to his feet.

"I removed a lot of thorns, burrs and even a large stick that was lodged in his chest," the man said pointing to a deep wound. "It will heal. But I would take it easy on him for the next few days. Can you tell me what happened?"

"My father was here on business, and I traveled with him to keep him company. We had left to head home and some men attacked us yesterday. I really don't know why," Paul said firmly. "When my father realized what was happening, he put me on his horse, this horse, and told me to ride back here."

The livery stable owner stepped forward and put one hand on Paul's shoulder and the other on Banner. He softly rubbed the horse's neck. "When a man goes through something like that with a horse, the man and the horse are bonded for life." The man looked at Paul, and back at the horse. "Whatever your relationship was before, I am telling you, it will be different from this day on." The stable was quiet.

Paul held the rope bridle in his hands and looked into the horse's eyes. At that moment, he believed it. He would do anything for Banner. He already knew Banner would do anything for him.

"Where are you headed?" the man asked as he backed out of the barn.

"Covington," replied Paul, not leaving the horse's side, rubbing it as he walked down the side of the horse, around the back and up the other side.

"That is a long way. You need to slow walk him home. Understand?"

"I will." Paul said.

With the man's help, Paul moved the saddle from the horse they had borrowed back to Banner. Banner protested slightly. Paul turned to the man and said, "I only have my lucky half crest. My uncle is coming and will pay you whatever we owe."

At that moment, Uncle Bryant appeared in the distance leading three horses: his horse, Danny, and the pack horse. Behind Danny was a small sled that held a pine box and the body of Richard Lester.

"You keep that lucky half cent. You returned my horse. Your account is settled."

Paul, taking the reins, led the horse from the stall and out of the barn. There, he mounted Banner. The horse stomped his hooves lightly. It was hard to tell if the motion was a protest or the horse simply moving to make sure it could. Looking at his uncle and the pine box that held his father he said, "I would like to have Danny's lead line." Bryant untied the line from the horn of his saddle and handed it to Paul. Paul tied the line off on the horn of his own saddle and swung his leg over the lead.

With Paul leading Danny and the sled that held his father, he followed his uncle who led the pack horse with their meager provisions for the trip home. They began the long, slow trip to Covington.

It had not rained, but the day was cloudy and there was a halo around the rising sun as Sergeant Montgomery roused his men. From the embers of the fire from the night before, a fire was quickly roused. A pot was pulled from the pack horse and as it heated, coffee was thrown into the steaming water.

A second man had taken out a brown skillet and quickly heated bacon. The half-cooked bacon was placed on a hardtack biscuit. This combined with the coffee would be their breakfast.

The men quickly gathered their blankets, rolled them, and tied them to their saddles. The two pots that had barely cooled were stowed in the large canvas-cloth pouches that were fixed to the pack horse.

As the men mounted their horses, Montgomery turned to them and said, "Have any of you been to Coweta before?" Only one man replied that he had. "So, for two of you, you have never been on this trail and not really dealt with the Lower Creek Indians…" It was a question. Not a statement.

Again, only one man spoke, and it was the same man, "My family and I have traded livestock for pelts."

"I see." The sergeant thought for a moment. "Do you know those people well? Could they be of assistance to us?"

"It is entirely possible. The dealings were fair, and we have continued to deal with the same families for several years."

As the men mounted their horses, a light rain began to fall. From the appearance of the clouds approaching from the west, the rain would intensify and linger.

◦◦◦

John Ross and Joseph McIntosh shared growing concerns. The entire morning as they traveled south, no one had reported seeing two men with four horses.

It was mid-morning and clouds were approaching when Ross paused the pursuit.

"I fear the men we are trying to find have turned off this road, and frankly, it makes sense to me that they would do that," he stated firmly.

The men drifted further to the side of the dirt road as two wagons approached.

Joseph thought for a moment raising his eyes to the sky, "Well, if they turned off and we hope to find their tracks, it is going to get much harder after this rain falls. The rain is sure to wash away most of the signs of their passing. And the truth is, there is so much traffic on this road, we really cannot track anyone."

As the wagons passed, McIntosh, almost out of habit asked, "By any chance did you see two men traveling east on this road? We believe they were both riding horses and probably both had a horse tethered in lead."

The man in the first wagon replied he had not seen two men. The second replied, "No, but about two hours ago we did pass one man. He was on horseback, and he also had another horse that was blanketed with no rider. I thought that odd."

Ross looked at McIntosh and asked. "Do you think they would have split up?"

"I would have stayed together, but then, if I did not know the man well, yes, I might have gone a separate way. After all, we have been looking for two men, this does give them a slight advantage in that we have been looking for and providing people with the wrong description."

"Yes, I guess it does." McIntosh replied, "Frankly, if we split up, we don't know what trail we are looking for, much less who we are looking for. I think we should stay together. Ride as swiftly as we can for Covington. From there, we can take the road south to Milledgeville. It would not be a bad idea to report the murder ourselves and that we are in pursuit of the men who did it.

Ross nodded in agreement, so they rode on in pursuit of the two fugitives while the rain was pursuing them.

Bryant and Paul had made their way along the Piedmont ridge as the rain started to fall. The pace was slow, as it should have been. Neither wanted to topple the pine box and what it carried, and Banner was in no shape to make the trip with any speed.

Bryant turned and looked at his nephew. He had not spoken since they had started the journey. He stared at the tree-covered trail before them. Bryant thought that he was doing remarkably well for a boy of 11 who had literally survived a waking nightmare. Bryant thought the boy was well-composed.

"Paul. Do we need to stop?" Without waiting for a reply, "We should think about stopping soon and stretching our legs, water the horses, and let Banner have a healing rest for the journey."

Paul nodded his approval and understanding but did not speak.

Using his fingers against the sun and the horizon, Bryant surmised that another hour had passed before they stopped for a brief break. With the clouds and the rain, it was more difficult to tell, but he could see the faint outline of the sun behind the clouds. Guessing each finger that the sun moved in the sky from the horizon was about 15 minutes, and all four of his fingers were an hour, it was time to rest.

As they went about the ritual of removing saddles, blankets, and tethering their horses, Paul stopped and looked at his uncle.

"I am trying to make sense of this." he finally spoke. "First Uncle Fountain dies. And now my father." His voice trailed off. "The two incidents seem separate, but they can't be. They just can't."

Bryant turned looking at his nephew. "I don't disagree. But I am curious, what makes you say that?"

Paul turned and paced behind the horses who were now peacefully looking for edible ground cover on the forest floor. "There just aren't that many murders. I know it happens, but it does not happen like this. Two brothers killed just weeks apart?"

There was only one other person in the woods with Paul. The pines and dogwood trees remained silent witnesses. The question was posed to him. And he was the only one who could possibly, without torture or duress, shed light on the murders. The truth was, Bryant was trying not to think about the mess he had gotten himself and his family into.

"It is hard to make sense of," Bryant said as he pulled jerky out of one of the large pouches that the pack horse had been carrying. Handing an ample piece to Paul along with an apple, he sat down with his back to a tree. Paul did the same. "The frontier is a violent place, Paul."

"I know, Uncle Bryant," he interrupted, "but don't you think the death of Uncle Fountain and my father could be connected?"

Bryant looked at the ground between his legs and thought of how to respond. He simply could not tell the boy all that he knew.

Paul continued. "Uncle Bryant. I know something. My father told me I should not repeat it. I heard it two nights ago. The minister from the mission, Reverend Trott, had told my father." He paused.

Bryant looked at Paul. The boy was struggling with something. "Well, if your father told you not to repeat it, you should definitely keep it to yourself until you absolutely believe with all your heart that you need to share it." That statement had just spilled out. But the truth was, Bryant desperately wanted to know what the boy and his dead father knew.

"The thing is," now it was the boy's turn to stare at the ground between his feet and legs, "my father actually said that people had been killed over things like this."

A cloudy breeze was blowing on the Piedmont ridge as the sun tried to heat the spine of the ridge that the trail followed.

Both Bryant and Paul turned towards the forest. There was a change in the sound of the woods. The birds had stopped chirping. The trees swayed and groaned. The sound of leaves rustled. Rain, heavy rain was approaching.

The rain would cool the horses if it lasted. If it was just a brief shower, the humidity would be stifling.

"Paul. If Reverend Trott said something to your father in confidence, you should hold it as that. At the same time, if you think it might help us understand why you and your father were attacked, and possibly even link your father's death to Fountain's, you should probably tell me, your mother, or your grandfather. We can then help you decide whether it should be repeated outside the family."

Bryant could tell that the boy was thinking, but he did not think the boy was ready to share what he knew. At least not yet.

Both stood and began the process of saddling their horses. Paul lightly checked the wound in Banner's chest. It had not reopened. But they would need to continue the trip at an easy pace.

Just as they were ready to mount, Paul looked at his uncle and said, "There is a rumor that gold has been found in the mountains of North Georgia on Cherokee land."

There it was. He had almost blurted the secret. The quiet of the forest had been shattered. He had just repeated what his father had told him not to repeat, but he had done so with a man he knew his father loved and trusted. Paul felt relief. But as he said the words, a look came across his uncle's face that he had never seen on anyone's face.

"Uncle Bryant, what is it?" Paul asked.

Bryant stood before his nephew, fully clothed, but everything about the situation made him feel naked and totally exposed. In this instance, he felt vulnerable, not knowing what to reveal or how to reveal it. He had been so naïve.

"I need to think." Bryant stood still. Was he paralyzed by uncertainty, confusion, or betrayal? Was it him who had been betrayed or had he betrayed his brothers?

The rain began to fall even harder.

Everything around Bryant felt relief. Paul for having told the secret that he had held. The boy had carried so many burdens for the last day. He felt better having loosened, at least in part, the weight of all that he carried. The clouds felt relief for having let loose the moisture that they carried. The plants and trees for the welcomed relief from the dry, warm day. The horses… everything and everyone seemed renewed. Everyone except Bryant.

Paul blinked as the rain matting his hair ran down his forehead and into his eyes. He turned to Danny and the pine box that was tied to the sled. He looked up. He had given way just as the clouds had. He closed his eyes as his head tilted back and the cool rain washed him clean. He took a few long breaths and then opened his eyes. Paul knelt and checked the rope that held his father's coffin in place. "Do you think my father is secure? Do you think this will hold in the rain?"

Bryant approached, knelt opposite his nephew checking the ropes on the other side of the sled. Paul looked at his uncle. The rain was covering the man. If possible, the rain drops were larger than before and it dripped heavily from the brim of the hat that Bryant wore. Mixed with the rain, Paul was certain he saw tears.

Talof, "The Bear," continued east towards Covington. He was not sure where or when his path would cross with the boy. He could take his time. Deep down, he knew the boy had to die. He was certain the boy could identify him because he knew he could do the same.

By the end of the day, Talof thought, he would be close to Covington. He was unsure as to how he would find the Lester boy. But Talof was a man of contradictions. While it was true that he could be impulsive, at the same time, when needed, he could be patient. Hunting had taught him this, and in many ways, as primordial as it sounds, this was a hunt.

By mid-afternoon rain had come. He could still smell the stench of the prison in his nostrils and wondered if the smell would ever leave him. He silently hoped the rain would wash the smell away. Some smells can haunt a person. The smell of battle was one. The smell of prison, that was a second, he thought to himself. The clothes the commander had given him were too small for his frame. He had cut off the sleeves and left the shirt unbuttoned – in the heat, the fresh air felt good on his skin and the new shirt seemed to work well as a light vest. He had made a slight slit in pants in the legs in several places so that his large legs could fit. His waist had fit easily, and he was certain this was only due to the weight he had lost while imprisoned. At best, his appearance was odd and tattered, but he was clean. Despite all this, his appearance was much improved, and his old clothes – he had discarded those in the fire the night before.

Talof had passed a sign and a trail that headed north. While he could not read the sign, it had pointed to Decatur and east toward Covington. Traffic on the road during the day had been steady. But now, as the day came to an end, traffic was reduced as people either got to where they were going or began to camp for the night along the road.

He had ample provisions, as he had barely eaten what had been provided and he now had provisions for two.

Talof pulled his horses off the road and into the woods. While the clouds had covered the sun in the early morning, the rain had only just started. Making a fire would be more difficult, but not impossible. He dismounted and led the horses through the woods. About two hundred paces off the road, he came to a small clearing that had obviously been used as a campsite before.

He tethered the two horses to two separate trees and removed their blankets, placing each over two nearby branches to air. But, in the rain, neither would dry. Next, he gathered a handful of pine straw taking care to remove any sticks and twigs. Holding the straw firmly in his hand, he lightly brushed down both horses.

Once this was completed, Talof stepped deeper into the woods gathering wood for a small fire. Traveling even further into the woods he came upon a thicker canopy of mature trees. Here, the wood would be drier and more inclined to burn.

He gathered some wood and returned to the small clearing to build the fire.

Taking a large post, he whittled one end into a point with his knife. He was careful to save the dry wood shavings. He pounded the pointed end into the ground and then forced the hole wider by violently pushing the post in several directions. This would be where he built his fire. Talof then took a less substantial branch and made to two additional holes that both began about a foot from the edge of the larger hole. Pushing the branch, with difficulty towards the base of the first hole, eventually he saw the earth in the large hole move. He removed the branch and the dirt from the larger fire hole. He was pleased. The holes were connected. He placed a few smaller twigs and the dry wood shavings in the bottom of the hole.

Taking a rock from his pouch, he struck the rock several times with his knife. On the fourth strike, the shavings began to glow. He knelt, blowing gently on the shavings exciting a flame.

In short order, the flame grew, and the twigs began to burn. As the flames grew, he placed larger sticks and branches on the small fire. As the fire matured, he drew comfort from the air as it was drawn through the small air holes that fed the base of the fire. The fire would be his companion for the night. The sound of the air whistling through the smaller holes to the base of the fire, would speak to him.

Once completed, he settled down as night began to fall.

It was good to be free again, he thought. This was the first moment he really had to think. Since he had left the prison, he had been reacting with little thought to his actions.

He thought of his home, which he would probably never see again. He thought of his family – which had been killed at Horseshoe Bend. People called it a battle. It wasn't. Andrew Jackson had attacked a group of Indians, most of whom were women and children camped in a bend in the river. As Jackson's militia had closed in, people were left with few choices. Flee to the river, where many drowned, or fight. With three children, Talof lifted the smallest and youngest of the three into his arms, and ran for the water, followed closely by his wife and two children. His oldest son had survived the swim, only to be killed by Jackson's pursuing troops. His wife and daughter had not made it across. They had been bludgeoned in the water by members of Jackson's militia who had been waiting in boats at the water's edge. For most of the Indians encamped in the sharp bend in the Tallapoosa River, there had been no escape.

Both he and his son that he swam to safety had survived the battle. But his son had died of a fever the following winter.

It had been over 13 winters since they had died and the Red Stick rebellion with them. Their loss still haunted him.

He would head to Florida where he hoped he would be welcomed. He knew a few people there. Most of them had fought with him in the rebellion and fled to Florida afterwards. Why had he not followed them? He did not know.

Talof thought he might find peace among the Seminole.

'What good is freedom without peace?' he thought to himself.

His thoughts turned to his former traveling companion. He wondered where Harjo was. 'Surely our paths will cross again,' he thought to himself. He had liked the little, strong-willed man.

It was night when Chief Ross, Joseph McIntosh, and their men rode into Covington. All of them were wet and tired from the long day's ride.

The first tavern that they came to did not have any rooms left for the night. Fortunately, there was more than one tavern, and the second had three rooms available. Each had a bed that the men could share.

The men were able to stable their horses in stalls provided by the tavern. Once the horses were settled, watered, and fed, the men gathered at a table in a corner of the main room where a meal of warm rum, stew, and bread was provided. The men, obviously on a journey, did not share their purpose or destination, as they knew many of the people in the tavern, or at least some, would know the Lester family.

McIntosh spoke first. "Tomorrow, we will ride out early and take the Rogue Road to Milledgeville."

Chief Ross translated the comment to the three Cherokee men in the group to make sure everyone understood.

"How long should it take us to get to Milledgeville?" one of the men asked.

"Men have done it in a day, but given the distance we have just covered, we will not get there until mid-day on the second day."

The men nodded.

For the rest of the evening, the conversation turned towards home, their fields, horse races, and family.

Chief Ross said little.

He knew why the Lester men had been killed. At least he thought he knew, and he believed that neither Richard nor Fountain Lester had known about the discovery of gold in the mountains of the Cherokee. While he felt horrible for the Lesters' loss, he knew that this was just the beginning and his nation would bear the brunt of future events, however they unfolded.

The Cherokee would do something for the Lester family if it was in his power to do so.

He had been silent and staring at the pewter mug in his hand. When he looked up, Joseph McIntosh was looking at him squarely in the eyes. McIntosh raised his cup in Ross's direction, tilted his head back, and finished his drink. He then stood. "Men, I need to walk and then head to bed. If I don't walk a while, I will be stiff as an oak come sunrise."

"I will walk with you," Ross said, as he stood. Both men walked out into the damp night together. The rain had stopped. The clouds had cleared revealing a clear sky.

As night had fallen completely in Covington, the small town had become quiet and still.

The men walked through the muddy street together, dodging the deeper puddles. When they approached the edge of town, Joseph pointed out the small house that belonged to German and Catherine Lester. The house was completely dark. Both men, independently, wondered to themselves if the Lesters had already gone to bed.

Joseph pointed out the small one-room school that doubled as a church on Sundays.

In return, Ross remarked that all Methodist buildings "looked strangely alike." And, at that point, they did. They were all built out of the same materials, many of them by the same hands with the same vision.

Many of the genuine carpenters in the area got their start on the docks and shipyards of Charleston and Savannah. For this reason, most of the larger structures in the area resembled capsized ships. The rafters of a church were cut and assembled in the same way a craftsman would build the ribs and beams of a ship.

The men turned and walked in silence back down the street, retracing their steps towards the tavern and sleep.

German and Catherine had enjoyed the day with their daughter-in-law and grandchildren. The following morning, they planned to return to Covington early.

The morning had been busy as the men and boys continued the work towards clearing the new field. The list of tasks for the day had been shortened as the fields and garden had been watered earlier in the week, and with the day starting out gloomy, the family had decided not to water the fields of corn, beans, and squash, hoping the gathering clouds would do so for them.

As night fell, the family fell into its new, normal rhythm. Their grandmother, ever the teacher, had taken it upon herself to school all the children at various times. Alice and Betsy enjoyed the attention. Grandmother Catherine had begun to teach the girls early in the afternoon, before night fell. In the short time that their grandmother had spent with the girls, they had both learned many of their letters. Their grandmother beamed as she was certain that both girls would be reading on their own quickly.

Mary had noticed Lucy watching and listening to the lessons. Lucy was smart. That much was obvious. There was little doubt that she could pick up a great deal by listening to Catherine as she taught the two girls.

The boys appreciated the attention to a lesser degree, which, from any viewpoint was understandable, as a full day clearing the field was exhausting. All the same, they were obedient and accepted the instruction well.

Their grandfather had accepted the role of taking the boys down to the stream in the late afternoon. They would wash the sweat and dust from the work of the day, but more importantly, the cool stream water was refreshing.

Once that was completed, he would return with the boys and disappear in Richard and Mary's bedroom for a brief nap (when the grandparents visited and stayed overnight, Mary slept with the two girls in their small room).

The girls had suggested the previous night that they could sleep in the loft with the boys. A heated conversation had ensued where the boys had objected strenuously to the girls sleeping in the loft – the three boys believed doing so would somehow infringe on their world. Mary had disagreed. Besides, sleeping with both girls had left her exhausted. She enjoyed sleeping with them and believed the girls did too but they both tossed and turned restlessly throughout the night. The wakeful sleep had left her tired and light-headed…

… She missed her husband.

As the boys argued against the idea, Mary, in the end, had supported it.

Tonight, was the night. All four children would be sleeping in the loft together.

Before heading to bed, Grandfather German would read to the children. While disappointed that they were not excited by his recitations from the Bible, he was pleased that all the children seemed to demand that he read more from his well-worn copy of *Gulliver's Travels* with each passing night.

Despite being tired and ready for sleep, the dynamic of having Betsy and Alice in the loft changed everything.

For several minutes, the adults listened to the children as they whispered and giggled. Some of the discussion they heard, but much of it they could not discern. Gradually, the conversation became more boisterous, and Mary had partially climbed the ladder only to see all the children on Eugene's bed huddled together.

"Hey now. It is bedtime. You all need to get in your own beds. It is way past time for you all to be asleep and tomorrow will be a busy day."

With little protest, the boys settled into their beds, Alice onto Paul's bed, and Betsy onto the quilts they had laid on the floor of the loft.

Mary lingered for a moment longer, wished them all good night, and returned to the floor below.

"They are good children," Catherine said, "and you are a fine mother to all of them."

Mary smiled and returned to the table where she had been mending one of her dresses.

Harjo's journey along the Flint River had been better than he expected. The trail was less traveled than the road, and he had only seen a few people.

The rain had come and gone. He had slept well and was up early – the morning sky was still dark, only giving a hint of the day that was to come.

He wanted to get close to Fayetteville and the road that would take him east to Milledgeville.

Throughout the day, he maintained a steady pace, and as he approached the small town, traffic increased. He found three men traveling the same direction and he settled in behind them. Keeping about three horse lengths between himself and them, he believed it far enough away to not infringe on the men, but close enough to where he might be considered a part of their group.

When they arrived in Fayetteville, the men had stopped at one of the general stores, and Harjo had continued a substantial distance beyond. When he got outside of town, he rested for a few minutes and waited. When he saw the men emerge, he quickly mounted his horse so he would be in front of them should they follow in that direction.

Fortunately, the men were traveling north and east, towards Milledgeville.

As he had hoped, he continued at a slow pace and soon the group of men came alongside.

When they did, a brief conversation followed. Harjo learned that the men were traveling through Milledgeville and beyond to Augusta. They had come to Fayetteville to pick up items for a relative who lived in the small frontier town and needed those things taken to Augusta. Harjo knew the journey, he had been arrested near Augusta, and the other men did not, so, he offered to journey with them for a short while, at least to Milledgeville.

The men graciously accepted his offer. Since the journey would take the men through a small section of the Lower Creek Indian Nation, having a guide who was also a member of that nation was not a bad idea.

Harjo hoped that in traveling with the men, by the time they reached Milledgeville they would have some familiarity and be viewed as "traveling companions" by others. He hoped this ruse would help him avoid capture.

For Bryant and Paul, the journey from Standing Peachtree to Covington was slow and arduous.

While this was totally unintended on Bryant's part, it was good for Banner, as he seemed to be getting stronger by the hour and day.

When they left Standing Peachtree, Bryant had thought that they could complete the journey to Covington in three days. Now he estimated the trip would take longer.

They had stopped often to rest horses and adjust the ropes that held Richard's coffin in place. Each time they crossed a stream, they had stopped and completed the crossing by hand – not wanting to drench the coffin's contents. If the stream was both narrow and shallow, Paul would lead the horse across while Bryant lifted the sled holding his brother's coffin and the bracing that held it in place while crossing the stream. However, if the streams were deeper and broader, the two Lesters would wait for someone to come along and help. This was often needed as the rain from the day before had replenished the streams and creeks which would normally be reduced to a trickle during the hot, dry months of summer.

Fortunately, help was never far away on such a busy road, and aid of this type was never declined, as it was obvious to anyone that Paul and Bryant were trying to return a body to family or loved ones.

As the second day came to a close, the Lesters found a quiet place to rest for the night, well off the road and close to water for both them and the horses.

Dinner would go largely unchanged until they reached Covington. It would consist of salted meat or fish, apples, and cheese.

Sleep on the second night came easier to Paul than it did his uncle. The guilt Bryant felt was becoming more acute. In addition, if it were true that gold had been discovered in North Georgia, his recruitment by Gilmer and Mitchell had been a pretense for something much larger. It was not just about the health of the nation. The desire to sow discord between the settlers and the Indians was motivated by greed.

Regardless of the motivating factors, the result would be the same: the Cherokee were going to be forced from the state. Gradually, Bryant was being overcome by shame for his involvement in the subterfuge.

There was no way he could ever tell his father of his involvement. While forgiveness was something his father preached, he was certain neither his father nor his mother would ever be able to forgive him.

He looked at his sleeping nephew and thought to himself, 'Perhaps I will be able to tell Paul one day. One day.'

PART VI

Map of Milledgeville — Circa 1830

Joseph McIntosh and Chief Ross had risen early in the morning along with the men they led.

The travel up to the Rogue Road that would take them south to Milledgeville was quick.

They had long given up asking about two men, each leading a horse, and had resorted to asking if the travelers they passed had seen a man or men leading a riderless horse.

The trail had gone cold.

By mid-day, McIntosh and Ross had encouraged several of the Cherokee to return north. They could wait for Chief Ross in either Covington or Standing Peachtree. One Cherokee would travel with the chief to Milledgeville, where a report would be filed concerning the murder of Richard Lester. Both McIntosh and Ross believed that since the death seemed to indicate the involvement of Indians, the news would be better received if they delivered it, and did so together.

From Milledgeville, McIntosh would continue to his home with his Creek brethren.

It was early evening when the men pulled into Milledgeville.

While the terrain had not been hard, the men had covered a lot of ground. Everyone was tired.

The new state capital was situated immediately west of the Oconee River. While just over 25 years old, the town was orderly. The capital contained a number of clapboard homes, and several inns, most of which also contained a tavern. There were law offices and frontier bordellos as well. Given the population, the town supported a wide range of blacksmiths, merchants, and even a bookseller.

As the capital became established, wealth had flowed into the town and prosperity spilled outward. Elegant homes, financed in part by the boom in cotton which floated down the river to Darien and from there shipped to the cotton mills of England, were becoming more numerous.

From the street, travelers could often hear heated interactions between lawyers and their clients as well as politicians from various factions. Many of the lines that separated the men of Milledgeville had been drawn two decades earlier when William Crawford (who had run for President) had faced off against Elijah Clarke for the soul of the state. The divisions were deep and often lead to duels in the street.

The town was lively, and even though their numbers had shrunk greatly, a few of the men in McIntosh's party had great difficulty finding lodging for the night. Chief Ross and his fellow Cherokee slept in one inn, The Planters. The three Creek Indians traveling with McIntosh found lodging in a second inn, the Farmers Hotel, which was directly across the street from the State House Square. McIntosh went to his father's house, which was further west of the town's center, where his visit was a surprise, but welcome.

Ross had said he would meet McIntosh the next morning on the steps of the capital and from there they would inquire who to speak to concerning the attack and death of Richard Lester.

As the sun rose the next day, Ross and his companion arose and headed to the State House Square, just two blocks away. When the chief saw Joseph emerge from a street several blocks away, he sent his Cherokee friend to get their horses and gather a few provisions for their return home, instructing him to meet him back in front of their hotel.

The two leaders exchanged early morning greetings and headed into the large doors of the State House building. They were quickly directed out of the capital to a building a short distance away where the state's sheriff's office was located.

The sheriff's office was positioned near the jail and next to the courthouse. Behind the jail was the state penitentiary, which had been completed a decade earlier. With its establishment, the frontier stockades near each fort would be gradually decommissioned.

The sheriff's office had been established in 1732 and, while enforcing the law on the frontier was difficult, it was the sheriff who was given this challenging task. While monumental, the state's sheriff did have county sheriffs that reported to him, and, depending upon the county, that sheriff might have a marshal or two at their beck and call.

As Chief Ross and Joseph McIntosh entered the small building, they were met by a Marshal who was leaving. The marshal related that the sheriff should be arriving shortly, and that the two men should wait for him.

A long hour passed before the sheriff arrived.

"I am Chief Ross, of the Cherokee nation, and this is Joseph McIntosh of the Creek nation."

The sheriff nodded to the men and offered his hand, shaking them both ardently. Addressing Joseph, "I believe I know your father."

"That would make sense. He moved here a few years ago and built a home off Jefferson Street near the stream to the west."

"I know the home well," said the sheriff. "My family and I live nearby. It is a beautiful home."

"He is proud of it," replied Joseph. "My father and my family have done well. There are rumors that he is thinking about expanding the ironworks, really it is just a large blacksmith shop, to include whitesmith operations. We have a man that seems to have talent in that area."

"That is nice to hear. The wood mill and ironworks are both well respected and they have benefited from the growth here in Milledgeville." There was a moment before the sheriff continued. "Chief Ross, you have come a long way and I cannot recall the last time two important men from both the Creek and Cherokee nations came to see me. In fact, this might be a first for me. What can I do for the two of you?"

McIntosh deferred to Ross on the matter at hand, "We need to report a murder."

"Oh. I see." The sheriff's face turned grim. "Was this a white settler or an Indian?"

Ross answered, "It was a white settler, but we fear the evidence might point to the crime having been committed by Indians."

At this, the sheriff sat down and pointed to chairs in the small room. "What evidence was there?"

"Arrows. The man was shot with arrows," McIntosh replied. "And we did find two men wounded at the scene who were in fact Indian, and we believe there were two additional men involved in the attack."

The sheriff had a curious look on his face. "So, it seems four Indians were responsible for the murder. Who was killed?"

"Richard Lester. His brother Fountain was murdered in a separate incident several weeks ago," McIntosh stated. "I believe Bryant Lester brought his father here to speak with you about that as well."

"Yes, they were here weeks ago. Unfortunately, there were no witnesses, and there was no one that the family knew with a motive. So, we really are at a dead end… This is a horrible thing. Two sons and a wife." The sheriff thought for a moment. "Was there a witness to this killing?"

Chief Ross straightened and said, "There was, but we are not at liberty to tell you who that was at this time." He paused and his eyes locked for a moment with Joseph's.

The sheriff stiffened in his chair. "Well, withholding evidence will not be viewed kindly by me or anyone else."

"And it should not be," replied the chief. "But at this point a family is under siege, and frankly, so are we." At that he stood. "You can travel to Covington and meet with Richard Lester's father and wife. They will know everything we know. What I can tell you is: neither Joseph McIntosh nor I had anything to do with this. What you need to understand is, the four men who murdered Richard Lester were in state custody and released just one day before the murder. Since that time, we, Joseph McIntosh and I, have been in pursuit of the two remaining killers. We believe they are headed south on horses supplied to them by the State of Georgia."

The sheriff, who had not taken a single note, stiffened and suddenly began writing. He was now on the defensive. "How do you know the horses were supplied by the state?"

"Because Bryant Lester, Richard's older brother, sold the horses to the state and delivered them to Fort Peachtree. He saw two men riding south — each with a horse in tow. They were the four horses he had delivered just days earlier." McIntosh was still seated as he had spoken, but he moved to stand. "I believe Sergeant Montgomery, from Fort Peachtree, can confirm everything we have told you."

"We wanted you to have information so that you could begin your search for the men, but you also need to know, we believe the State of Georgia may be complicit in this murder." The two men had said what they needed to say, they turned to leave.

Ross reached for the door but paused and turned before leaving. "And sheriff. Our two nations are resolved to find these men. Yes, they are Indian, but we believe there is more going on here. Men who were friendly to the Creek and the Cherokee, men from the same family, have been murdered." The sheriff registered the certainty in Ross's voice as he spoke. "We are also determined to protect the Lester family. Let it be known that friends of the Cherokee and Creek have nothing to fear." The chief had spoken with an authority that Joseph could not, but by Joseph's stance, the sheriff understood that these two men were allied.

There was an awkward, tense moment before the sheriff finally spoke. "Can I ask where the body is?"

"Bryant, Richard's brother, is bringing the body back to Covington. I would imagine he will get there today or tomorrow," was Joseph's terse response.

"I will need to get there before they bury him," the sheriff thought aloud.

"You should hurry," Ross said as he stepped through the opened the door.

The two men stood for a moment in front of the jail. Looking down the street, both men noticed the increased activity on Wilkinson Street, and Chief Ross could see his man standing in front of their hotel with the other men in their cohort.

The two men walked in silence for several paces. Chief Ross stopped for a moment. Taking hold of McIntosh's arm, he halted their progress. "I cannot tell you now, but I think I know what is behind this." Looking back toward the jail, and then towards the hotel, he stepped back. "Joseph, we must keep our nations together. We both know, or at least are fairly certain that the men who killed Richard Lester were Red Sticks." Joseph nodded as the chief continued, "I am of the conviction that powerful men are behind this murder, and they are not Creek."

"You will stand with us?" asked Joseph.

"About that, let there be no doubt. Our treaty must hold." Chief Joseph held out his hand and the two men shook hands in the dusty Georgia morning sun.

They returned in silence to the men standing in front of the hotel.

Joseph spoke in Creek to his men and Chief Ross spoke in Cherokee with the man who had retrieved their horses.

"What should we do now?" asked Chief Ross.

Joseph thought for a moment, looking back towards the jail and the State House.

"I think my men and I should head south towards Coweta." He replied. "We can stop at my home, get fresh horses if needed, and a nice meal before we head west and south." He stopped turning to Chief Ross. "I don't believe there is reason for you to travel further. I thank you for going with me to the Sheriff. The fact that we both were there should send a powerful message to him."

"That was my hope," Chief Ross said.

Joseph turned to his men, "I need to retrieve my horse from my father's house. If you men gather your things and horses, I will meet you back here in a few minutes." The men turned to leave.

"Chief Ross, thank you again. Safe travels on your return trip."

The two men shook hands again. Ross and his man mounted their horses and rode north.

The Creek Indians were now left to pursue the nameless men who had killed Richard Lester. The names of the men were still only known to Sergeant Montgomery.

Talof had found the spot he needed. It was relatively close to the road to Covington. It was a short distance from where he had camped, and he was pleased that his camp would be concealed from the road.

From this hiding place, Talof could watch the steady flow of people traveling into Covington.

He closed his eyes and enjoyed the respite, stirring slightly when he heard the sound of horses, wagon wheels, or people walking.

It was late morning when he saw a man leading a pack horse pass by the thicket where he laid in wait. He was followed closely by a boy on horseback leading a second horse that pulled a sled. On the sled was a pine box that

Talof was certain held the body of the man they had killed. There was no doubt, this was the boy who could identify Talof.

Looking further down the trail toward Covington, he could see men approaching.

"Patience," He thought to himself. He must be patient. Now was not the time.

As the two travelers continued into Covington, he saw them progress through town. He would wait a few minutes and follow.

His thought shifted. Soon, his home village would be celebrating harvest. How he longed to be somewhere familiar. The celebration was called "Puskita." The village would take a generous quantity of the emerging green corn and sacrifice it to ensure an ample harvest.

The white settlers referred to the celebration as the "Busk," or Green Corn Celebration. In truth, it was much more.

The entire village would gather for several days. The first day involved fasting and, surprisingly, this was one of Talof's favorite days of the year. As he sat there by himself, he realized that no one really knew that about him. Because of his size, people just assumed certain things of him. And, while some of it was true, most of those around him would be surprised to know that he really liked solitude. He liked the quiet. And he also enjoyed the fast that preceded the Puskita.

His wife had known. She was the only one who had known that about him.

In total, the ceremony lasted four days, with the fast ending at sunset on the third day. That night, the stomp dance would be held, lasting well into the early morning. It was a joyous time for the entire village as this was also when young boys, about 13 years of age, became men.

The fond memories faded, replaced by the thoughts that his own children never celebrated their thirteenth Puskita and never would.

Talof blinked and his thoughts returned to the present.

He could see the far edge of town. He squinted slightly and could see the boy leading his horse to a stop. Both he and the older man had dismounted from their horses and seemed to be stopping. They had stopped in front of a small two-story home on the far edge of Covington.

The large man stepped further back into the forest. He could still see the house, but he was now less visible to anyone on the road. He sat down and leaned back against the relatively smooth bark of the large poplar tree nearest him. He looked up at the late afternoon sky. While he liked being alone, he did not like the loneliness.

Another aspect of the Puskita was atonement. It was customary for members of the clan to come to terms with anyone with whom they had a quarrel. This settling of disputes was taken seriously by most people, and it did seem to keep peace within the community. For this reason, when arguments arose, it was very rare for an Indian to bring forward an event or dispute from years gone by, as those, from the community's point of view, should have been settled and held invalid in terms of any current claim against another member of the clan or community.

The Bear sat in silence. In that he had been imprisoned, no one in his clan should have a grievance against him. It was nice to be free of guilt towards those of your family and community.

German and Catherine had left their son's homestead before the sun had topped the trees. They wanted to be home before mid-day so that they could tend their garden and he could put the finishing touches on his Sunday sermon for the following day.

As Mary was certain her husband would return that afternoon or the following day, she implored her in-laws not to return, but promised to send Simm or Boston to town if her husband was delayed further.

The two had traveled largely in silence.

Catherine had enjoyed her time with her grandchildren. She was warmed by the fact that both Alice and Eugene had settled in with their cousins so quickly. She thought of the lessons she had taught, and the lessons she hoped to teach. The children were so bright.

German was lost in thought himself. He had hoped to write his sermon during his stay, but there had been no time. He pushed through verse after verse in his head, searching for a source of inspiration.

After much thought, he settled on John 14. Yes, that would do. It would do for him, his wife, his family, and the church.

"But the advocate, the Holy Spirit, whom the Father will send in my name, will teach you all things and will remind you of everything I have said to you. Peace I leave you; my peace I give you. I do not give to you as the world gives. Do not let your hearts be troubled and do not be afraid."

"Yes." He thought to himself. Yes, that will do.

It was mid-morning when they arrived at their home.

Catherine busied herself unloading the small wagon while German un-hitched the horse.

She had the last small loads in her hand when she saw Bryant and her grandson. She thought, "How wonderful," and disappeared quickly into the house. A moment later she emerged quickly as she realized – she had not seen Richard and was curious why Bryant was riding with his nephew.

Her husband joined her, putting his arm under his wife's.

Their smiles retired swiftly when they saw the box being led by their grandson.

German and Catherine helped each other steady themselves as they stepped back towards their home and sat on the front step. Catherine buried her head in her husband's shoulder and began to cry.

The uncle and his nephew stopped their horses in front of the house. Paul remained on Banner. Bryant slipped down and walked steadily towards his parents.

He embraced them both.

The three wept.

⌒

The ride to Joseph McIntosh's home had been longer than anyone expected. They had arrived late in the afternoon.

His wife, Talease, had initially greeted the men warmly. However, this turned to concern when he related that Richard Lester and his son had been attacked and that Richard had died.

While she did not know the Lester family, she had met Fountain several times. She saw the concern in her husband's face and felt his anguish.

"These men are hungry and dirty," Joseph said turning towards the men milling about just outside the cabin. "Do you think we have enough food on hand to feed them?"

Talease hugged her husband and looked up into his face, brushing matted hair away from his eyes. "We do. We certainly do. And you!" she stood back and looked at him, then stepped forward, "If you plan on sharing my bed, you will need to bathe."

A smile crossed his face, and he exited the cabin. "Men, if you expect to eat, we will need to get cleaned up. Follow me. Let's take care of the horses and then go for a swim." The men disappeared around the corner of the cabin towards the barn.

Talease called to one of the house slaves and asked for her to prepare three hens for dinner.

By the time the sun had set, the horses had been watered and fed, the men washed, and the meal prepared.

As dusk turned to night, the men found places to sleep: two in the loft of the barn, and two on the floor of the cabin.

Joseph did not have to search for his place to sleep as it was found in the warm, welcoming arms of his wife.

Talof had followed behind Paul and Bryant a short distance.

By the time he pulled into town, a small group of people had started to gather at the far edge of town. It seemed everyone was heading in that direction.

He dismounted his horse and walked into one of the general stores. As he passed a man who was walking out, Talof asked, "Where is everyone going?"

"One of German Lester's sons was killed," the man replied as he passed. The only thing he noted was his height.

Talof stood in the doorway for a moment, then turned back towards his horse where he busied himself adjusting the horse's tack.

Unfortunately, the crowd did not seem to dissipate. If anything, the gathering was growing.

He mounted his horse and passed the house. He did not see the boy. But he knew he was there as his horse was still tied to the post in front of the house.

Once out of town, he turned off the road quickly and disappeared into the woods. He again dismounted from his horse and led both animals deeper into the cover offered by the forest. He found a place in the woods that was dominated by a tall oak. Because of the large tree, little else grew underneath. Talof thought the area would suit him and his horses well for the night.

He tethered the horses to two smaller trees. Satisfied that they were secured, he walked back toward the road, keeping his distance from the road, he came to a place where he could see both the road and what he thought was the boy's house.

He could see the people gathered in front of the house and thought back to the brief conversation in the general store. This was not the boy's house. This was German Lester's house. 'Certainly a relative,' thought Talof.

From this vantage point, Talof hoped he would be able to see any activity to and from the house. Although, as darkness fell, it would be difficult to see exactly who was coming and going.

As night descended, the gathering in front of the Lester home began to disperse. In ones and twos, people returned into the small town. A few people had ridden out of town passing Talof's hide.

He dared not light a fire. Tonight, he would wait and watch. There would be very little to eat tonight.

Several men led the horse that carried Richard Lester's coffin to the front of a building just east of the town and a short distance from the home. Talof believed the building was religious because there was a tall cross mounted on the roof above the main door. There, the men untied the box and carefully lifted it, placing it in the building.

After a brief discussion, the men went separate directions, with one of the men returning to the Lester home.

A short time passed before two people emerged from the home. A lady and a man walked slowly towards the building. They walked inside, closing the door as they entered. A moment later, Talof could see the glow of candlelight from the windows on either side of the door.

Minutes passed. An hour passed. Then, a third person emerged from the house. Short in stature, a boy. Talof thought 'it must be Richard Lester's son. It had to be.' In the dim light, he could not be certain.

The boy knocked on the door. After a brief moment, he entered and closed the door.

Again, minutes passed.

Talof was tempted to walk from his hiding place in the woods to make sure it was the boy with whom his eyes had locked.

Just when he resolved himself to do just that – standing to leave the protection of the forest, the door had opened. Talof took a half step back into the woods knowing his shape would be less visible. The boy walked into the frame of the door and stood for a moment. Talof could see more clearly as the boy stood washed in the light coming from the church. It was indeed the boy he was looking for.

He took a few steps into the tall grass between him and the road. The light in the church was now extinguished and the man and the woman emerged from the church. German Lester walked forward and placed one hand on Paul's shoulder and the other on his wife's. The three walked slowly towards the house and disappeared once again inside.

Talof sat down and waited.

A slow, but steady stream of people was coming to the home. Mostly, there were couples, but a few were solitary. Some came empty handed, others carried items. Some of the people lingered for a long time, while others simply knocked on the door and the articles they carried in their hands were given to whoever opened the door.

This went on well into the night. Finally, the flow of people into and out of the home subsided.

It had been quite some time since sunset when a door opened, and two men stepped outside in front of the house. Talof could hear the voices of the men, but he could not make out the words. The men spoke for a short while before returning into the house.

Again. Talof thought he needed to wait. Tonight would not be the night. He would remain patient.

Initially, German's wife had been inconsolable. German himself had found it difficult to contain his emotions as well.

As night had fallen, his wife had asked German to walk her to the church to be with her son and German had done so. There, they had sat in silence for a long time. They prayed. They cried. Both together.

Catherine's heart was clearly broken. The woman wept, overcome by grief. She felt an ache in her heart she had never felt. There was a weight on her chest and at times, she found it hard to breath. She thought back to the day of his birth and the days that had followed. She had nursed all her children. The combination of the deaths of two boys in close succession was too much. She longed to hold them as children again. With all her heart, she wanted to start over. Not because of anything she wanted to do different-ly – both boys had turned into good fathers and husbands. In her soul, she wanted a different outcome. She wanted to relive the last 60 days. She wanted her boys back.

German was filled with grief as well. While his wife's turned to sorrow, German's turned to anger. He wanted answers.

As he sat in the church that he had built with his own hands he wondered if he would ever find answers.

Probably not, he thought.

He thought about Providence. He thought about free will. He wondered how the two could exist together at the same time.

"This is a test of faith," German reasoned. "I must accept this as God's will."

Wait. No. That was not right. This was the result of men acting outside of God's will. He recalled the prayer that he knew so well and had said each Sunday when he and his congregation prayed for God's will to "be done on Earth, as it is done in heaven…" God's will is not done here, he thought. It is done in heaven. He pondered on the thought for a long while, realizing that it was a prayer, a hope that God's will would be done on Earth. It was not a certainty.

The door opened, and his grandson stood in the door. He stepped into the small church and closed the door as he entered.

He sat next to his grandmother, who put her arm around him as she stifled her tears.

After a long silence, Paul finally spoke, "He saved me." Paul said. "I would have died if he had not put me on Banner and sent me down the stream."

Silence returned to the large room.

It was Catherine who spoke first. "I am so glad he saved you, Paul. I am certain that is exactly what he wanted." At that moment she knew. Her husband knew as well. They knew because both would have given their lives to save their son too… either son.

It was as it should be. Their son had saved *his* son.

The three sat together for a long time together.

"Let's get back to Bryant," Catherine said as she rose to leave. She stooped, put her hand on the pine box for a long moment, and then led the way to the door.

They walked in silence back to the house.

When they entered, they found Bryant sitting alone staring into the fire.

A slow stream of people had brought food and other items. For such a small community, the outpouring was both surprising and humbling.

Finally, and thankfully, the visits had stopped.

Bryant said, "Tomorrow, I will go to Richard's and tell Mary."

German interjected that he thought they should all go.

The three adults were shocked when Paul spoke. "There is a lot to do here. I will go. I need to do this."

There was a resolve in his voice that was unmistakable and surprising.

Catherine looked at German and shook her head. "No. No. I have never known you to make that trip alone. That will not happen."

"Grandma Cat," he said, "It is time I did."

"I will go with you," Bryant said. "You are not going alone."

The adults nodded agreement.

Sergeant Montgomery was still at least a day's journey from Coweta. Armed with two names, he continued his steady march to Coweta. He thought that he and his men could reach the town and the Indian Agent the next day.

As they traveled along the river, the sergeant noted the size of the farms seemed to have increased. The last time he had made this trip, he did not recall so many large farms.

During that first day, Sergeant Montgomery had come to learn a few things about the men under his leadership. William Dodd was the man Montgomery found most like himself. He was industrious and loyal. Some men did not take their service in the Militia seriously. That was not the case with William. More importantly, William had knowledge of the Creek Indians that Montgomery did not. The sergeant would have to rely on that knowledge if they were going to find the fugitives.

As most of Montgomery's dealings had been with the Cherokee, he was most familiar with that nation. He could converse adequately in their language, but no Cherokee would have considered him fluent. When conversing, he bumbled through their language at best.

When it came to the Creek language, he initially thought there were similarities that he recognized. But he was wrong. The more he came to know about the Creek, the more he came to understand this. In fact, even the Cherokee called themselves "Tsalagi," which literally meant "people with another language."

Most of the farms were being worked by slaves, and because it was the middle of summer, the crops were maturing. It was easy to tell which crops were corn or cotton. He was certain that there were more cotton fields on this journey than the last.

Montgomery's plan was simple. They would take the names that they had been given to the Indian Agent and ask if there were people in the area who could identify them. They needed one person who could identify the men to travel with them as they searched for the fugitives.

If the Indian Agent could not help, they would see if William's trading contacts could. Montgomery wondered to himself if the Creek would be helpful at all to his efforts.

Neither German nor Catherine had slept. They both rose early in the morning.

Bryant heard his parents moving about downstairs and climbed out of bed, emerging from the room that he had once shared with his brothers. Catherine busied herself putting food out for breakfast as well as putting food away, so much had been brought by friends the day before.

German rose from the kitchen table and went to a small writing table in the corner where he put a few final thoughts on paper for his sermon. In the background, he heard the comforting rhythm of his wife as she busied herself in the next room.

German would be leaving soon to go over to the church. He needed time to compose himself and collect his own thoughts. He was certain that Catherine would follow in short succession.

Bryant rose, telling his mother he would go out and saddle horses for the ride to Richard's. He would also ask one of the family friends if they could take a message to his wife. Sara would want to come to Covington, and, as he had been delayed returning, she would have begun to worry.

When he arrived inside the barn, he was shocked to see that Banner was gone. He looked in the other stalls and noticed that the saddle that Paul had been using was gone, too. He frantically turned and ran towards the house. As he ran, he noticed a man riding past the house leading a horse. In the dim morning light, he saw the horses, but only in a cursory way. By the time he thought to look closer, the man was well into town. They seemed familiar. But the man was heading in the wrong direction. It was as though he was coming from Augusta and heading into Covington, possibly back to Fort Peachtree.

He bounded up the two steps that lead into his parents' home and looked one last time at the man and two horses as he rode through Covington.

"Father! Mother! Banner is gone. I think Paul has left. Please check his room"

His mother quickly rose and climbed the stairs. His father stood and turned as his wife came back down the steps. She shook her head and said, "He is gone."

Bryant, still standing on the front stoop as his shoes were dirty from his brief activity in the barn, was immediately distracted to see Chief Ross and his companion arrive.

"Good morning, Bryant," Ross said.

"It is a tough morning, sir." Bryant replied with his hand on the latch to his parents' front door.

"My apologies. It is. Are your parents here?" Ross inquired.

"Yes, they are," Bryant said distracted by the rider who had just passed.

"I would like to pay my respects."

"Certainly. But first. You see that man in the distance?" Bryant said pointing.

"I did not get a close look at the horses. I only got a glance. Those could be two of the horses I delivered to Fort Peachtree. The markings on one of the horses – I cannot be sure, but I think that maybe the man we are looking for."

Ross squinted. He looked at his companion and in Cherokee said, "See that man? Go see who he is and where he is headed. If he is Creek, don't confront him." At that moment, the man and the two horses had disappeared over the horizon.

The Cherokee kicked his horse and galloped quickly into the distance.

German emerged from the house heading over to the church. Ross dismounted his horse and Bryant walked with him as German slowed to meet the man.

"Father, this is Chief Ross. He knew Richard," Bryant said.

"I am sorry for your loss." Ross said sincerely. "Your son was a friend to both the Creek and the Cherokee."

"I did not know," German's response was halted, as he choked back his own grief.

"I am cancelling the services for today. I am going to put this note up on the door. We must find Paul."

"Is Paul missing?" Ross said.

"It seems he left earlier this morning on his horse. He wanted to go tell his mother about his father." Bryant said. "I am heading out just now to go catch him."

"Can I ride with you?" asked Ross.

"No, let us handle this as a family. It is kind of you to offer, but no thank you."

"I understand. I will need to go follow my man and find out what he learned about that traveler who just rode through." Ross mounted his horse, turning it back towards the road, and trotted quickly into the distance.

Bryant quickened his pace. He saddled his horse and led the horse to the front of the house and told his parents that he was heading to Richard's. They replied that they would be following just as quickly as German could harness his horse to their wagon.

In response, Bryant asked if his parents could send word to Sara. They said that they would.

Bryant turned quickly, climbed his mount, and turned his horse down the road through Covington.

A few short minutes into his ride, Bryant crested a hill and saw Chief Ross kneeling by the side of the road.

His friend had been stabbed. Bleeding, but not dead, the man had a deep gash in both his forehead and a defensive wound in his left arm. The wound on his forehead was long and shallow, but blood was everywhere. The wound on his arm was deep and would need to be stitched.

"We have found one of the men we are looking for," Chief Ross stated.

Bryant climbed on his horse, "I must catch up to my nephew. This man must be tracking him down."

Ross agreed. "I will bandage this man and send him back to Covington. I will follow."

Ross's friend replied, "Go now. Stay together. This man will not go quietly… I have had worse wounds and can make my way back to Covington."

Bryant was already turning his horse to pursue his nephew. He looked over his shoulder at the man and said, "Go to my mother and father's house. They will care for you. Ask someone to take you to Pastor Lester's home." Without waiting for an acknowledgement, Bryant kicked his horse and sped away.

Ross tied off the bandage on the man's arm. The flow of blood had been stemmed. He knew that the wound on the man's forehead was not serious. It looked worse than it was. Taking a cloth from his pocket, he handed it to his man and stood.

Mounting his horse, he looked down as the man struggled to his feet, steadying himself as he did so on a tree that edged the road. "I am sorry to leave you. I will come back to Covington, and I expect to find you well and resting."

"You will. Now hurry off," replied the Cherokee.

Paul had gotten out of bed. He had known he would leave early but had intended to leave before the sun had come up. It was late in the night before he had finally fallen asleep, and he was slightly upset with himself that he had slept through the first hint of dawn. He had slept in his clothes so that he could leave quickly. Hearing noises from the floor below, he had woken startled. He knew he would need to be quiet and quick.

Initially, the family had lived in a one-room cabin. That cabin had become the church and school room. The community had come together to help build the Lesters current three-bay home.

He would descend the stairs to the main floor and exit out the back door. Both the stairs and the front and back door were in the middle bay of the house. If he was careful and quiet, he believed he could leave without being seen by anyone already awake on the main floor, as the middle bay of the house was separated from the bays on either side by walls. He was confident that if both of his grandparents and uncle were up, they would be in the kitchen, which was also where the family ate.

The middle bay was essentially a wide hall that contained the stairs to the second floor and several bookcases. It was basically a wide hall that also served as a parlor when there was a large gathering. The third bay contained a more formal room where German studied and a bedroom where German and Catherine slept. During the summer, both the front door and the door out the back remained open most of the day, allowing a breeze to move through the house.

Paul knew he would need to be quiet as he walked out the back door and passed the doors to the kitchen and the bedroom.

Making his way down the steps, he could hear the voices of his grandparents as they interacted. It was only when he reached the bottom step that he could make out the conversation.

They were discussing his mother, him, and his family. He paused as he thought he heard his name mentioned.

He stepped onto the floor and heard the well-worn wooden floor complain from his presence… he paused. The cadence of their conversation had not changed.

In that moment, he decided he would not go out the back door. From the sound coming from the kitchen, he was certain that both of his grandparents were towards the back of the house in the cooking area of the large room. He thought it best to exit through the front door – which had yet to be opened for the day.

He stepped forward, lifted the latch, and opened the door cautiously stepping onto the front porch. He stepped through the barely opened door and into the morning air.

He turned, and carefully closed the door, lowering the latch as quietly as he could.

He stepped out onto the wild grasses in front of the house, crouched low to the ground and made his way quickly to the barn. Knowing better than to walk into the barn in his bare feet, he sat down and put on his shoes.

He quickly rose and walked into the barn. Banner was quietly standing in the second stall. His hind quarters were leaning against the wall of the stall as he stood peacefully on three legs. His back right hoof barely held any weight.

Paul removed the two ropes that were looped across the opening to the stall and acted as a gate. He let the loops drop to the floor. Banner, one ear forward, the other ear back, was walking slowly. Paul removed the rope bridle and replaced it with his leather bridle and bit. As the horse accepted the bit and moved it around, there was the normal accompanying munching sound while Banner positioned the bit where he preferred. Leading the horse into the breezeway of the barn, he quickly saddled the horse and led him out into the brightening sky.

He walked slowly into the road that was the main street of Covington. The small town was starting to wake – smoke could be seen lazily rising from most of the chimneys. One of the blacksmiths could be heard already banging with a hammer on some object that seemed to be unyielding.

He continued to walk Banner slowly through the town.

Once he had walked through most of the town, he stopped his horse and heaved himself up into the saddle. Placing his feet into both stirrups he encouraged Banner forward.

He had no real reason to be doing this by himself other than he felt that he needed to be the one to tell his mother. He did not want his uncle or grandfather to do it. He wanted to do it. He had been there. He had seen it happen. He was the one who had been saved. He believed he should be the one to tell his mother. But also, he just wanted to be home.

Aside from his horse, there was no one on the road. There were two horses already tethered to posts, but no one was heading towards him. He could see lanterns and candles lit in a few homes. He heard chickens protesting as a woman entered their coop to harvest eggs, presumably for the morning meal.

As he got to the edge of town, he thought how the turn to the trail that would take him home would come alongside quickly on his left. It was the first turn to the left once the confines of Covington had been escaped.

'There it is… there is the trail to my mother and family,' he thought to himself.

He laid the reins gently across Banner's neck and realized he did not need to do so. The horse would have taken the turn on his own, without any encouragement.

As he turned, he looked over his shoulder and saw a man at the far edge of town. A lone rider leading a second horse. He could not see that far in the dim light, and the long shadows of early morning made it difficult to see anything in detail at that distance. But he was sure the rider was not his uncle or grandfather.

From his hiding place in the thicket, Talof had seen the boy exit the house.

The boy was alone. This was his chance, he thought.

He rose to make his way across the field and thought better of it. He stood on the edge of the woods and waited as the boy had put on his shoes and darted into the barn.

A short time later, the boy emerged from the barn leading a horse.

The tall Indian waited a moment longer to see what direction he would head. When he saw that the boy was walking the horse quietly towards town, Talof had darted back to his own horses. He quickly placed both blankets on the backs of each horse and placed both saddle bags on the horse he did not intend to ride.

Before hopping on his horse, he slid the blanket back an inch or two to make sure the blanket lay quietly against the hair of his horse and with its grain so no sores would arise.

He untied the rope reins of both horses and led them quickly out to the road. He mounted his horse and encouraged him into a quicker, but quiet gait. As he rode past the Lester home, he noticed two men were standing in front of the house.

He rode past the Lester home and could see the boy on the far edge of town mount his own horse and begin to ride.

A short distance later, the boy had turned off the main road.

Talof slowed his horse to an easy walk. He assumed that at a slower pace, he would draw less attention, and this did seem to be so, although there really was no one to see him at this early hour.

Continuing to the top of a small rise, he began to wonder where the boy had turned. A few paces further and he saw the trail – he could tell by the width and wear that this road was less traveled. For that, he was pleased.

He could not see the boy in the distance. He would give it a few more moments before he quickened his pace.

At that moment he heard a horse approaching with some speed.

Talof maintained his slow casual pace, that of a man with no urgency.

The man approached quickly, slowing his horse as he approached.

"Excuse me sir, do you know if this is the road to Milledgeville?" inquired the man.

Talof had understood perfectly. He gave a quizzical look to the man and shrugged. The two road in silence for several steps.

Finally, Talof broke the silence and said, "I am Creek, and I am looking for a man who is interested in buying this horse," he said, raising the rope leading the second horse. "I am not sure, but I believe he lives down this road."

In perfect Creek, the man replied, "I see. What is the man's name, I may know him?"

"I would not want to say," replied Talof. "It really is business between him and me."

"I just thought I could help." Again, relative silence with the only sound coming from the waking woods that surrounded them, and the hooves of the three horses. Then the man said, "Actually, I am looking for a man. Come to think of it, I am looking for two men." The man paused, measuring Talof. "Both of them have spare horses… I am thinking you're one of them."

Talof had been resting his left hand across his lap with the lead for the second horse tied to his wrist. His right hand was holding the rope reins of his horse.

Quickly, Talof's left hand moved with surprising speed from its resting place on his horse, moving quickly up and towards the man next to him. As he was larger and longer, he did not need to leave his horse to strike the man.

The man reacted quickly, but not quick enough.

Talof struck the man's forehead squarely with the butt handle of his knife. There was a loud crack as the handle struck the man. He saw the initial shock in the man's face, and the futile lifting of his arm, raised in defense. He then saw the man's eyes flicker as he lost consciousness.

Talof turned to strike him a second time as he flailed out of his saddle, away from Talof and the horse he was on. As he fell, his right arm swung wildly above his head as though grasping for something imagined, and as it did so, Talof's knife cut a deep gash in the man's forearm.

The "Bear," seeing the man was no threat and that his body was quickly falling away from him, drew his knife back towards his body. He encouraged his horse forward on the trail a few paces. Looking down at the man, he considered for a moment that he should finish him. Kill him and drag his body into the woods.

His adversary sprawled in the dirt of the lightly traveled trail. His horse, startled by the commotion, had settled quickly, and was now turning. It toed the ground in front of him.

Talof, while he was formidable, was not in the habit of killing people. The truth was, while he had been in fights, and fought in wars, because of his size most people backed down from a confrontation with him. As he thought about his present circumstance, it was an uneasy realization that in the past few days he had attacked two people.

He really wanted to find peace.

It was also true that while he had been among the men who had attacked Richard Lester, he had not killed the man. No. He had not. His mistake, and it was one that now found him entangled, was that he had attacked the boy. Harjo had been right. He should never have attacked the boy.

Looking both directions, Talof kicked his horse and turned away from the Lester home. If this man had found him, there certainly could be others. The boy, he thought, could live another day.

He would wait. Again, patience.

He returned to the main road and turned west, heading away from Covington. He would watch the road for a while and see if anyone else was with the Cherokee that he had just attacked. If needed, he would camp at the site he had used just two nights before. "There will be a funeral. The white settlers always gathered to bury their dead." He thought to himself. "I will wait until after the funeral."

It was still early morning when Simm saw the boy ride into view. He thought it odd that the boy was traveling alone. Even though the sun was not yet high in the sky, both he and his father had begun to sweat.

As Paul approached, he slowed Banner down to a stop. The horse protested slightly, knowing that rest, water, and feed awaited a short distance away.

Boston and Simm stopped working and approached the wide dusty lane that led down to the boy's homestead.

Boston immediately noticed the scars and wounds that flanked Banner's light summer coat.

"Your horse looks a bit tore up," said Boston.

"Yes, he is," replied Paul. "Is my mother about?"

"She should be." Boston's voice trailed off as the three heard Mary's voice calling to her son down the hill. He felt a little slighted that the boy had not bothered to tell him how Banner had received his injuries.

Looking at Boston and Simm, Paul said, "It looks like the field is about cleared, and that stack of wood is something else."

"Yes, we should have the field cleared in another month or so. I am betting we will be pulling stumps out till the kingdom comes, though." Boston gave Simm a satisfying look of approval. "I really am not sure what your father is going to do with all the wood. It would be a shame for it to go to waste."

"Well," Paul said looking at the large piles lining the dirt lane as it approached his home, "someone else will have to decide that." With little encouragement, Banner continued down the slow descent to the house. The closer he got to the home, the quicker the horse moved. The gait that had been that of a weary and injured beast of burden became lively again.

Paul had directed the horse towards the house, but Banner turned toward the barn, stopping in front of the hitching post just left of the barn's entrance where just days before, Paul had whipped his father. Paul had initially protested, but the horse's will was stronger.

It was only now, now that he was here, that Paul realized he had no idea what to say to his mother.

He had so desperately wanted to be the one to tell her.

As he sat on hise horse, he realized he had no words.

His mother approached the horse and with joy in her voice said, "Welcome home! You have been missed. Where is your father? Why are you traveling alone?"

Her son's eyes had not left the space between Banner's ears. He released the reins and turned slightly to see the joy in his mother's face change to one of concern.

"Paul. What has happened? Where is your father?"

Paul placed his hand on the horn of the saddle and lifted his right leg out of the stirrup and over Banner. Holding onto the saddle he slid down the left side of the horse. He placed his head against the animal and began to cry.

"Oh, Paul. Paul." She knelt to the ground, clasping her hands in her lap, she doubled over. She began to rock slightly back and forth.

By now, James and Eugene had emerged from the barn, Alice, Betsy, and Lucy had come to Mary's side as well.

Lucy turned to Alice and Betsy and ordered, "Go fetch your brother some water from the well. James and Eugene, you two help me take care of Banner."

James protested, "But, but."

"No but's. You two help me. Come along," Lucy said, taking Banner's reins in hand and leading the two boys into the barn.

Paul knelt beside his mother and placed his hands on hers.

Mary continued to rock gently back and forth, and Paul continued to cry, although he had finally found his breath.

"Mother," the boy said, "we were attacked by men. Four Indians."

His mother stopped rocking. She gasped and placed both hands to her mouth, pressing the skin so tightly to her face that no sound or air could escape. The skin on her cheeks were pressed tightly, distorting her face and the color of her skin entirely.

Controlling his tears, he placed both hands on his mother's shoulders and looked her in the eyes. "Father is dead… he died there in Standing Peachtree." There. It was done. With that he placed both arms around his mother and embraced her tightly.

The sheriff had wasted little time.

He would send a Marshal to Covington that day to investigate the situation there and make inquiries. While he did not know the Lester family, he did not want this to become an issue for either him or the Governor. He thought it best to send a man there. If nothing else, doing so would bring some calm to a situation that was becoming a chronic problem.

The man he selected was Benjamin Brewton.

Benjamin was in his thirties. The man was well-liked and competent. The sheriff thought Benjamin a good choice because he was not from an area near Covington or Standing Peachtree. He hailed from south of Milledgeville in Tattnall County. Given his ambition, the sheriff thought the man would be more than suitable and that he would return to the capital with whatever information there was to gather.

By noon, Benjamin had sent word to his wife and family that he would be traveling to Covington, but that he did not anticipate being gone for more than a few days.

Benjamin had been married for several years. His brother had died, and he had married his widow after a short courtship. Some viewed the marriage as one of convenience. It was true, his wife was wealthy, but she was also attractive, and Benjamin had been drawn to the woman for many of the same reasons as his brother.

Benjamin had been instructed by the sheriff to ride with earnestness to Covington. If he arrived before the funeral, he was to see what evidence, if any, could be gathered from the body of the deceased. If the funeral had been conducted, he was to obtain statements from the family concerning the attack and the wounds. The sheriff specifically instructed the Marshal not to disturb the body if it had been buried.

"This is the turn to my brother's farm," Bryant said to Ross.

They had ridden at a steady gallop hoping to catch Paul, or even better, the man they believed they were chasing.

Bryant and Chief Ross began the descent down the path that led to the Lester farm and as they did so, they slowed their horses to a slow trot.

This was Ross's first glimpse of the farm, and he could see evidence of activity almost everywhere. A new field had been cleared and planted with corn on the left, a large pasture was on the right, and it seemed that they were expanding that pasture. In the distance, a small orchard with several trees that soon would have matured fruit.

As the house and barn came into view, Bryant saw the small gathering in front of the house.

As the group parted, Bryant was relieved to see Paul in a deep embrace with his mother.

Ross looked at Bryant and said, "Where is the man who attacked my friend? How did we miss him? Do you think he doubled back?"

"Maybe so," Bryant nodded agreement, although his gaze never wavered from the sight of Mary and Paul clinging together. His eyes fixed on the mother and son he said blandly, "He very well could be lurking about." He blinked and gained his senses. "We should be alert."

The two men came to a stop and Paul quickly stood, as did Paul's mother. Both of their faces were streaked by the tears they had shed.

Alice stood near her mother with her hands to her mouth and chin, her eyes flitting about, as she tried to grasp the gravity of events.

Behind her, Betsy stood with her arms by her side. She stood back for a moment, then, as Bryant swung his leg over the neck of his horse and slid to the earth below, she ran forward hugging his leg tightly.

She clung there for long time before Bryant reached down and picked her up. He gave Betsy a big hug in return and a kiss on her check before setting her down and walking towards his sister in-law.

Mary threw her arms around Bryant's neck and began to sob again.

Paul stood in silence, wiping his face as the other children stepped forward. Alice returned to holding Bryant's leg as she craned her neck to see her mother's face, which was still buried in Bryant's chest.

Boston stepped forward, taking the reins of Bryant's horse, and passing them off to Simm. He then turned to Chief Ross, "May I water and cool your horse?"

"Why, yes, but I will not be staying long," the chief replied as he swung down from his saddle.

Lucy stepped forward approaching slowly placing her hands on Alice's shoulders, "Child, come with me."

Reluctantly, Alice loosened her grip on her Uncle Bryant's leg. Placing her small hand in Lucy's, she turned heading toward the cabin, with Betsy coming forward and grasping her other hand.

"James. Would you mind taking Paul and Eugene down to the stream for a few minutes?" Mary agreed with Bryant and motioned as such with her head.

With Simm and Boston moving about in the barn, Bryant and Chief Ross were alone with Mary.

"Tell me. Tell me everything… What happened to my husband?"

"First, allow me to introduce you to Chief Ross of the Cherokee Nation."

Mary bowed her head slightly looking almost angrily at the man.

Chief Ross, unsettled by her gaze, stepped forward offering both hands, "I am sorry to be meeting you under such circumstances. I am truly sorry."

Mary tilted her head back and took a deep breath. She closed her eyes and wished for the sun to dry the tears from her cheeks.

Hearing Lucy and the girls stirring about in the kitchen, Mary led the men to the bench beside the front door where she sat down, while both men stood before her.

"Honestly, I don't know much. Paul knows more than I do and even though we traveled for over two days together to return to Covington, we did not discuss the attack in any detail."

"Attack? My son was attacked too?"

"Yes." Bryant replied, "Obviously, he was not seriously injured. He escaped the attack on Banner, and the horse bore the brunt of the attack."

"What we know, ma'am," Chief Ross interjected, "is that your husband and son left Standing Peachtree after he and Reverend Trott helped settle a dispute between my Cherokee brothers and the Creek Nation." He paused. "It appears that four Creek Indians were released from prison, and the next day, they attacked your husband and son shortly after they left our gathering."

"According to Paul," Bryant continued, "they had stopped by a stream to rest and were attacked. Richard put Paul on the faster of the horses they had and stood his ground long enough for Paul to make an escape."

The tears returned to Mary's eyes. Large tears. She put her hand to her face for a moment and shook her head and waived her hand in front of her face as if fighting off a swarm of bees.

"These people, were they just criminals? Why did they attack my men?" Mary asked.

"We don't know." Bryant replied, "But we do know the state wants there to be strife between the two tribes, and we believe the state wants there to be war."

Ross stepped forward, placing his hands on top of Mary's. "Mrs. Lester, there is more." He paused, turned, and looked at Bryant. "What I am about to tell you can go no further. Truly, it cannot." He stood and looked at Bryant. "Bryant, you must give me your word that what I am about to say goes no further. If it does, my people will pay a heavy price."

Mary stood, shaking her head. "What greater price must I pay to understand why my husband was killed?"

Ross stepped back. He looked down at his feet. He knew she was right. But he also knew that this was the beginning of the end.

Bryant stepped forward, taking Ross's elbow with his left hand, turned Ross slightly to face them both, "Tell us. What do you have to say?"

Ross looked at Mary and sighed, "We have discovered gold on our land. It is only a matter of time that the news gets out."

Mary shook her head, "Gold. This is about gold?" her voice trailed off. There was a certain worthlessness in the very way she said the word. It was as though she was referring to a pile of rusted metal.

Ross looked at Bryant's face and saw something completely different. There was an anger welling that he had seen in men before. Bryant turned his back and took two steps toward the barn, then turned back and began pacing. He removed the hat from his head with one hand and brushed his matted hair with the other.

When his nephew had said it, he thought it was just gossip. But now, the Cherokee Chief had confirmed it.

Again, Ross turned to face Mary. "The treaty your husband composed for us did not just settle a land dispute, it also negotiated a peace between the Creek and the Cherokee. A peace we will all need."

Bryant had stopped pacing and was staring at his feet. He stood there and shook his head. He took a deep breath.

"Well, I have more to add." He turned and faced the Chief. "We, I… well, we have been told to stop trading with the Indians. We have been instructed to not use your businesses either. And, where credit has been extended, I know business owners have been instructed to call in the credit and not extend any credit on future purchases to members of either nation."

"Who has asked this of you?" Mary stood and approached Bryant.

"Men. Men at the state," he replied. "Powerful men."

Shaking his head and looking at the ground before him, Chief Ross muttered, "They know. They already know."

Mary left Covington with Bryant and the children in the wagon leaving Boston, Lucy and Simm to care for the farm. Chief Ross left with them and returned to Covington to attend to his friend.

The following day, Ross collected his man, who had been recovering in one of the taverns and seemingly left for New Echota and North Georgia.

Arrangements were made to hold the funeral for Richard in two days.

Bryant sent word to his wife, Sara, that he would be home in a few days, and included details about Richard's death. He had no doubt that she would want to come to Covington and see Mary as well as the children. While Bryant's wife did not know Mary well, the two women liked each other immensely. And being older by a few years, Mary did confide in Sara a great deal as she viewed her as the older sister she never had.

That afternoon, Mary and Bryant returned with the children to the farm.

When they arrived at the farm, Mary said little to anyone. She gave brief instructions to Lucy and disappeared into the small room that she and her husband had shared.

Lucy busied herself giving orders to the children as to what she would need to prepare dinner.

Bryant unharnessed the team of horses from the wagon. Having watered both horses, he turned the horses loose into the pasture beyond the barn. He then took his horse, which had been tethered to the back of the wagon and walked him into a stall – he did not want his horse fighting with Banner over the stud rights among the small Lester herd.

Paul came into the barn with the other boys. They took the hawk from his perch and walked into the newly cleared field.

Bryant watched as the boys went through the motions of discussing who would fly the hawk, and who would hold the lure.

Boston and Simm were wrapping up their work in the same field for the day and walked towards the boys. They added a few choice words, and then continued down the lane that led to the house and the slave cabin.

Bryant stood as the two approached. In the brief time since Simm had been owned by the Lesters, he had grown and added muscle. Bryant thought to himself that the boy would end up being a solid addition to the farm, and if not, bring a handsome price to the Lester family if Mary decided to sell him to someone else.

"Done for the day?" Bryant asked.

"Yes, sir. I figured we might be needed down here to help Ms. Mary," Boston replied.

"I think you two should make yourselves scarce. Lucy has things under control, I can promise you that." Bryant stood, looked at the boys and then back at Simm, "I best check on my sister-in-law."

Simm and Boston walked past the house and headed toward the slave cabin.

In the field, the boys had decided that they would see if they could get the hawk to fly for a greater distance. To do this, they would need the blacksmith gloves from the barn.

Paul placed the hooded hawk on one of the logs in the piles of timber that clearing the new field had yielded. Leaving both James and Eugene in the field with the hooded hawk, Paul returned to the barn for the other glove.

As he walked out of the barn, he was startled to see a tall man emerge from the back corner of the barn – how had he missed him when he walked in?

Immediately he recognized the man. Moreover, he saw the healing wound he had inflicted with his own knife. From the look on the man's face, he knew Paul too.

He dashed back into the barn… "if only I could make it to the tool room…" he could arm himself with something.

Three steps into the barn, the Bear was upon him.

He pounced on the boy's back, driving the boy's chest and face into the dirt.

Paul could not scream or yell. He had no breath with which to create a noise – the weight of "The Bear" on his back had knocked all the air out of his lungs. He gasped.

Paul felt the man's large hands grasp his neck as he struggled to free himself.

At that moment, there was a loud "Pop." It was the unmistakable sound of a musket.

Talof lurched forward, releasing his grip from the boy's neck. He felt a sharp pain as the metal musket ball pierced his rib and left lung.

He rolled off Paul, and the boy scrambled to his feet. Turning to the door of the barn, he saw his mother standing in the doorway with a musket held firmly to her cheek. The smoke from the discharge still billowed about her head.

Bryant ran up behind her, he took the gun from her hands, and placed the butt of the musket on the dirt floor and leaned the barrel against the side of the barn.

The tall man laid on his back looking at the loft above him. Like any wounded man, he tried to make sense of it. How had it come to this?

Bryant stepped forward, taking a knife from the sheath in his belt, looked at Paul. "Take your mother back to the house."

Bryant knelt next to the tall Indian and asked, "Who are you and why did you do this?"

The man refocused his eyes now from the ceiling above to the man hovering over him.

"I did not kill Richard Lester." Talof paused and coughed. As he did, blood spittle gathered in the edges of his mouth and trailed down his left chin as he turned his head. "I did not want any of this."

The words hung in the air as a second man, much shorter and better dressed than the first, stepped into the breezeway of the barn from the door that opened into the pasture.

He raised his musket to his cheek and said, "I killed Richard Lester. And this man is coming with me."

Bryant stood and stepped away from The Bear.

"TALOF! Get up. You are not dying here. You are coming with me!"

Talof rolled onto his chest and raised himself to his knees. Slowly, he stood and stumbled toward Harjo exiting the barn. He staggered into the pasture beyond and stopped.

Harjo's gaze never left the Lesters and the sight on the end of his musket never left Bryant's chest. He continued to slowly back out of the barn into the pasture beyond, following the sound of Talof's feet.

Suddenly Talof stopped. He heard the unmistakable sound of an arrow leaving a bow and a hiss as the feathered shaft flew through the air. The arrow struck Talof in his chest. The large man stumbled back and fell to the earth beneath him.

Harjo turned. He saw three men coming toward him. He did not recognize any of them. Raising his gun, he pointed the musket at Mary and fired.

Bryant, stepping in front of her, spun and slammed into the wall of the barn as the force of the musket ball struck his shoulder. Bryant spun violently and fell to the ground.

Harjo ran, passing Bryant, the boy, and his mother into the yard in front of the cabin.

He ran past the cabin toward the cornfield. Surely this field would provide cover for him to make his escape.

"Five more quick paces will see me into the field…"

… Those were Harjo's last thoughts.

Boston and Simm had heard the commotion from inside the slave cabin.

He was hanging his clothes to air inside the cabin when he heard the unmistakable sound of gunfire.

Instinctively, Boston turned towards the door, grabbed the old family musket that Richard Lester had given to him, and walked to the door. "Simm. Stay here," he said as he left the small cabin.

Looking to his left, he saw Bryant Lester on the ground with Mary kneeling at his side.

A man was running across the front of the house. As Lucy emerged from its doorway, she pointed to a man running from Boston's left towards the maturing field of corn.

Without thinking, he raised the musket to his shoulder and pulled the trigger.

He watched as the man's skull shattered and he fell to the earth.

That night as he fell asleep, Boston would think back to how he had fought in the War of 1812 and the Battle of New Orleans. He also realized that he was wrong and that he would fight for someone else.

Chief Ross had never left Covington with his Cherokee companion. They stayed in the woods near Covington to allow his companion to recover from his wounds.

When German Lester realized the men were near town, he had offered their home to Chief Ross and his companion, and they had accepted.

Later that day, the marshal arrived and was directed to the Lester home. The marshal asked, "I understand there was an eyewitness to the attack."

"That is correct," Replied German Lester, "My grandson was a witness and was attacked as well."

"It would be helpful if I could ask him a few questions. Does he live close by?"

German replied, "Yes, not far. You could go there and back here in less than a day. Unfortunately, I cannot guide you there, as much as I would like to. Having said that, I am going there tomorrow afternoon if you can wait."

"Obviously, I would prefer to go now and return to Milledgeville as soon as I can."

Chief Ross stepped forward, "We can take you there, and I would be happy to do it."

"Thank you. When can you leave?" the marshal inquired anxiously.

"We can leave as soon as our horses are saddled. I know the way and it is not a difficult distance to cover on horseback. With any luck, you may make it back here before darkness falls entirely – after all, the days are long." Before he completed his sentence, Chief Ross was turning to go saddle his horse.

With little left to say, the three men rode through Covington at a steady trot.

Given the pace that they set, the three men said little as they traveled down the lonely trail that led south to the Lester farm.

As they topped the hill that descended to the farm, the shadows of the day were growing long. They slowed their three horses from the steady gallop they had been using to a slow trot, then to a walk.

"Is this their home?" asked the Marshal.

Before Chief Ross could answer, the three men heard a loud "pop."

The wounded Cherokee pointed to a tall man who was backing out of the barn, "That is the man that attacked me."

The men quickly dismounted their horses.

"Marshal, what would you have us do?" Chief Ross asked.

The marshal thought as he assessed the land and buildings before him and asked, "Are you two good shots?"

"He is the best marksman I have seen. I typically hit my target." Chief Ross' modest statement did not instill confidence in the marshal.

"There is a second man coming from the barn. Those must be the two men we have been looking for." Chief Ross turned. "I am going to use my bow."

The unusually tall man that was backing out of the barn was now fifty paces away.

"I need to get closer. Come with me." Without waiting for a reply, Chief Ross placed a hand on the middle of the three fence rails and ducked under the top rail. Staying low in the grass, they quickly closed the gap.

Thirty paces away, he stood up and took an arrow from the quiver at his feet. Drawing the bowstring he let the arrow fly.

The arrow flew true to its mark.

The large man never saw the arrow. He staggered and fell forward, and as he did so, the short man turned, running into the barn with his gun. The three men stood a ran towards the barn. They heard a second gun shot but could not see anything as the barn obscured their view.

All three men were now running towards the barn. They passed the large Indian and ran toward the barn.

The marshal was first to arrive.

He entered the breezeway of the barn. There, he found a woman bent over a man lying in the dirt.

Hearing another gunshot, he looked and saw that a slave had shot the shorter man as he tried to escape into a cornfield. Even from this distance, the marshal could tell that the wound was fatal.

"Thank you," the wounded man said as the woman knelt beside him.

"And you are?" the marshal asked.

"I am Bryant Lester. This is my sister-in-law, Mary. And that is her son, Paul."

Paul, still stunned, was standing close by. He had regained his breath but was still breathing hard.

"I am Ben Brewton. The Sheriff in Milledgeville sent me here. I am a State Marshal and I have come to ask you questions about Richard Lester's death. But, I think that can wait. We should take care of Bryant here."

"Thank you," Mary said as she stood. "I will get bandages and hot water." She turned and left the barn walking slowly to her home. She walked passing Lucy and the two girls.

Eugene and James ran down to the barn, leaving the hawk tethered and alone.

Chef Ross walked over and looked down at the fallen Bear. He placed his foot on the man's chest and pulled the arrow from Talof's body.

Later that night, the chief handed the arrow to Bryant saying, "This arrow didn't kill your brother, but it was meant to. It did kill one of his attackers. I think your family should have it."

Everyone grieves differently.

The Lester family was proof of this.

German Lester would be presiding as the minister for the second time in two months for the funeral of yet another dead son. He would grieve later. He did not know when or where, but he knew it would come. It would come at an unexpected moment when something captured his heart and reminded him of his boy. It would be this way for the rest of his life. It would be unexpected, and in that unguarded moment the depth of his emotions would be revealed.

His wife's emotions had become more frayed. Raw. German could not grasp it or relieve it in any way. If he could take it from her and wear the pain for her, he would. But he could not. Years later, Catherine confided to friends that she had "mourned the loss of Fountain, but she grieved for Richard." Some understood the difference. Those who could not, should be grateful.

She loved both boys equally. All parents say this, but Catherine believed it. At the same time, there was something about Richard that had touched her heart differently. Perhaps it was that he was the only child that had remained close by. This access had allowed both her and German to know him more deeply as a man, husband, and father. The other children had all moved further away and their visits were infrequent. Richard had remained. He was the dutiful son. He was the prodigal son's brother. The one who stayed and, in so far as he could, Richard did what he could to please both parents.

This had endeared him to Catherine.

While Catherine and German had raised their children to be independent, it had come as a shock when all of them, save Richard Henry, had moved further and further away.

After the unrest at the farm, it was difficult to leave the farm. But Mary knew that she must make the journey to Covington, and in truth, she did want the warmth and love that fellowship from a close community would bring to both her and her young family.

She, Bryant, and Chief Ross had loaded the children into the wagon and made the journey back to Covington leaving the Marshal, Boston, and Simm to bury Harjo and Talof. Mary had requested that she never be told where they were buried; and, if possible, that they "not be buried on our farm."

Chief Ross left "his man" to oversee the resolution of the situation but mainly wanting him to recover more fully.

Richard Henry's funeral was well-attended. Few could recall a funeral where so many had come from so far away. Bryant's family had made the trip, as had the Sims, who, because of the distance, had traveled through much of the night from their plantation to Covington to cover the greater distance.

When the hour for the funeral came, German stood, gathered himself and began.

"I must confess that I am struggling today with how to consign my son to God's earth. By His providence, I am still weakened by the events that required this same duty of me for my son Fountain less than two months ago." He paused, avoiding the eyes of those gathered about the grave. "Having said all of this, we gather today not to discuss me, my wife or even Mary and the grief we all share. But rather, today is about Richard Henry.

Knowing this. I am comforted. Because I know he found great comfort in Romans 8:38-39. If you would allow me, I would read this for all of us:

'For I am persuaded, that neither death, nor life, nor angels, nor principalities, nor powers, nor things present, nor things to come, nor height, nor depth nor any other creature, shall be able to separate us from the love of God, which is in Christ Jesus our Lord.'"

German paused again to gather his composure.

"And so, it is. Nothing can separate us from the love of Christ. And, if this is so, I find great comfort knowing that if Richard is not separated from Christ, and I am not either – we are never, ever, far from each other. But again, this takes the focus back to me. Please forgive me and indulge me one moment. Let us take it one step further.

This is the power of Christian fellowship for all of us. And I firmly believe that this can only be found spiritually."

The old man had been looking down at the Bible he held in his hands. He had not lifted his eyes, preferring not to see anyone's face.

German closed his Bible, shifted his feet taking a wider stance, as if he were bracing himself against a strong forceful breeze. He raised his eyes. Looking first at his wife… Their eyes met. He smiled gently and through moistened eyes absorbing lost love, the gentleness was returned.

He then looked at Mary, Paul and the rest of the grandchildren standing nearby before continuing.

"Richard's life was too short. Today, I, we all grieve for the things he did not finish and are left to the living to do." He thought for a moment. "My son was no saint, and I will not venerate him to that extent. But he was a good son. A faithful husband. And he enjoyed being a father. Like many of us, it was rare, but it did happen, when he was filled with the Holy Spirit... When he was... he was a joy to be around.

Let us all dedicate ourselves to that... let us strive to be filled... for when we are filled with His Spirit, through grace, there is no room for anything else... and I truly believe this is when God enjoys us most."

German closed his eyes. Took a deep breath and bent over taking a handful of earth in his hand. He approached the grave and halted as he looked into the reality that would be his son's resting place. He released the earth from his hand. He heard dirt landing on the pine box just a few feet below him.

He stepped back. He led the group in prayer, which neither he nor his fellowship would later recall.

After a few moments, he walked the four steps to his wife, took her elbow, and led her away.

Most of those gathered followed close behind. The Methodist fellowship along with the residents of Covington had prepared food for those who had traveled so far. It was expected that many of the people who had gathered would stay for some time that afternoon.

Mary lingered at the graveside for a longer time, her mother and father never leaving her side. There was little doubt that the elder Sims would seek to have her daughter return to his home, where he and his wife could better provide for her and her children, but this had not yet been shared with Mary. Finally, Mary, steeled by her parents, left the graveside to join the gathering of family, friends, and community.

Only Bryant and Richard Paul remained.

Bryant's left arm was in a sling. His left shoulder would take weeks to heal, and those closest to him would say that he never recovered from the gunshot wound he suffered during the confrontation in the barn just the day before.

Richard Paul stepped toward the grave and looked down at the pine box that held his father. "Uncle Bryant." He said, "I don't think we will ever know why my father died." He paused. "They did not rob us. We had little money. We had no possessions of real worth. The men who did this gained nothing. It simply does not make sense." Bryant could see the boy searching the depths of his brother's grave for an answer. "Was this done just for violence?"

Bryant stepped forward and placed his hand on his nephew's shoulder. He was quietly searching for what answer to give: Was this the moment for him to tell what he knew?

"Paul. Someday. Someday, maybe we will know why." That was all Bryant could bring himself to say.

Boston had thought he was the only one still awake.

Simm had gone to bed earlier. Normally, he slept in a small loft in the slave cabin that was barely large enough for the young man. But the heat in the rafters of the small cabin was so stifling, on most warm days, Simm slept on the floor. He had been followed closely by Lucy. She would be snoring before Boston even closed his eyes. Boston wished he could sleep that deeply.

He sat on a thick piece of a tree trunk that he had placed just outside the door to the cabin and used as a crude stool. Just days before, Simm and Boston had selected three trunk pieces of similar height and rolled them down from the field that they were clearing. Simm had suggested that the thicker portions would be good to sit on, and Boston had agreed.

Because the stumps were still wet and sticky from the bleeding sap, Boston had taken to dusting the tops with dirt before he sat down. For this reason, for this day, and the weeks that followed, the seat of his pants would be constantly dirty.

He looked over at the Lester home. The front door was still open, but only faint light shown through the door. It would not be long now. Mrs. Lester would come to the door, wave over to Boston, and then close the front door for the night.

The sounds of early night filled the woods and fields of the farm.

Suddenly, there was a distinct change in the sounds from the woods. There was a stirring in the cornfield and the edge of the wooded border. Boston could see birds that had settled down take flight from their night perches. Something had startled them.

Boston stood and reached into the cabin. He did not have to look. His eyes never left the field from where he had seen the disturbance. He reached deep into the slave cabin. There, his fingers wrapped around the barrel of the musket that leaned against the wall nearest the open door.

He drew the musket out of the door and stood.

Mary was in the house. The children had settled down for the night and quiet had descended on the farm. It was when the home was quiet, and Mary was left alone in her thoughts that sadness would overwhelm her. She had surprised herself at how strong she had been, and when tears came, for the sake of the children, she always tried to suppress them.

Earlier this very evening, she had been caught off guard when she had lit the courtship lamp. Alice had asked her mother to tell Betsy about the lamp. Reluctantly she had done so and finished the story with a calm and peace that even she had not expected. After all this was the lamp that in many ways had literally been a beacon during the courtship with her husband. While the lamp brought back fond memories, it now brought thoughts of death, loss, and loneliness. It was only when she wondered to herself "who will light the lamp when men come to call on these two girls?" that she began to cry. She had always thought that duty would fall to Richard, but she now realized it would be her responsibility.

The thought had simply caught her emotionally unprotected, and she had started to cry. It was only after a hug from Paul and Alice that she had been able to regain her composure.

Mary was exhausted. Following her husband's funeral, her father had passionately pleaded with her to return with him and her mother to their plantation. "It is where you belong. It is where I can provide for you and the children."

Mary appreciated the offer, but had declined, "Father, can we revisit this in the coming weeks or months? I really do not want to make such a momentous decision today or even this week."

He had promised that the offer would always be open and pledged his support regardless of her decision.

Mary loved her mother and father. It was comforting knowing that she could return home, but in the deep recesses of her mind, she wanted to stay on the farm that she and her husband had made their home.

She was inclined to stay, and, while she had reservations, she would become more confident by the day.

Following the retelling of the courtship story, the children had all gone to bed.

Mary had come to the door for one last visual inspection of the farm before closing the door for the night. Seeing Boston standing in front of the small slave cabin with the family's old musket, she was alarmed. She retreated quickly into the house and emerged a moment later with one of the rifles.

Mary walked a number of paces into the hard packed dirt in front of her home closer to where Boston stood.

Boston had changed his grip on the musket as he walked slowly towards where Mary stood, his eyes fixed on the nearest field.

Something was stirring, as they both could see the cornstalks rustling and birds take flight as the disturbance, whatever it was, approached the family home.

Boston raised his musket to his shoulder, as the first figure emerged from the corn forty paces away. His grip tightened on the stock and barrel as he took aim. Suddenly he felt Mary's hand on his shoulder.

"Boston. Don't shoot. We know them. That is Joseph McIntosh and Chief Ross."

The two men walked steadily towards Mary and Boston. They were followed by four men who stopped at the edge of the field, letting the two leaders approach the homestead separately.

"Mrs. Lester, it is good to see you. I am sorry that we startled you and Boston," McIntosh said in a friendly tone.

"It is late. And it has been a tense few days for us," she replied. "To what do we owe this visit?"

"On the contrary," Chief Ross responded. "Nothing is owed Rather it is due. And you are right to be alarmed. Frankly, we came as quickly as we could."

"What do you mean?" replied Mary.

"These four men are all from the Creek nation. They, or men in their stead, will be here each night until the next full moon. At that time, four Cherokee Indians will take their place," McIntosh said, acknowledging with his chin the men standing in the distance. "You do not need to feed them. They will have their own provisions."

"It is the intention of our two nations to guard your home and family until your boys are old enough to do so for you." The way Chief Ross had spoken, it was not a suggestion but a statement of fact.

"We know of no other way to express our sorrow over the death of your husband and his brother, and to also prove our innocence as well in their deaths. Both of our nations are firm in this."

Mary looked at the two men and beyond at the four men standing at the edge of the cornfield.

She took a deep breath and, as she exhaled, any reservation she had about remaining on her farm, the farm that she and Richard had lovingly carved out of the frontier, left her body. Mary looked at the first star as it emerged in the darkening night sky.

A peace descended over her and her farm that she had not known since her husband's death, and maybe even before then.

At that moment, she knew her family would survive.

EPILOGUE AND HISTORICAL NOTES

Every family has stories. Many of my favorite stories were bequeathed to my generation by our Great Uncles: Charlie and Billy Lester. Both men were professors at Emory University in Atlanta. Uncle Billy founded the Geology Department, and Uncle Charles, for whom Lester Hall is named, was a Chemistry Professor before he became Dean.

My grandfather, who I never knew as he died before I was born, and his brothers grew up in the Oxford / Covington area which is east of Atlanta.

Several times during the 1970's and 80's, my father took a tape recorder and placed it in front of the two men and asked them to tell him about growing up in Oxford. The stories were great – but more than that, it was the way they told them and the very words they used.

There was the daughter of a former family slave, Susannah, who lived on the farm and is buried in the family cemetery. I frankly do not know if she was the daughter of one of the family's slaves or not. I do know that both men loved her dearly and spoke of her more than they did of their own mother (whose name, as I sit here, I cannot recall).

One of the stories on these tapes is the genesis for this book. The places mentioned and the maps are as accurate as I can make them. The elements of this story that my family hold true include:

Richard Lester aided in settling a land dispute between the Creek and Cherokee. At their behest, he wrote down the settlement so there could be no misunderstanding.

On his way home, he was murdered. Appearances were that Indians had killed my ancestor. But our family and both Indian Nations maintained that white settlers had killed him as he crossed a stream. Their motive was to foster hostilities between the two Indian Nations.

Bryant Lester's treachery is fiction. The family has no knowledge of a fraternal betrayal and there is no animosity within the family. In that other historical people are named in the plot, it seemed appropriate to make at least one Lester complicit. Having said this, the efforts of the early leaders in the state of Georgia to undermine the sovereignty of both the Creek and the Cherokee is well-known and not disputed by historians.

Boston, Lucy, and Simm were slaves owned by my ancestors. I do not know where they came from or how long they were enslaved. Their names are included in a will.

The subsequent response of the two Indian Nations towards my ancestors following the death of Richard Lester has been re-told for four generations.

Time has obscured the facts around Richard Lester's murder. However, time has not obscured the motives of the then current Governor of the State of Georgia, the attitude of the Federal Indian Agent, and the subsequent treatment of the missionaries to the Cherokee.

In truth, I have taken great liberties to weave a fictional narrative around historical places and people.

Having said this, Lester family folklore is filled with interesting snippets:

The first Marshal of Atlanta, Georgia (1848), would be a relative of Richard Paul Lester – German M. Lester. At the time, the city had a population of about 2,500 people and this was also the year in which the first homicide is recorded. This is the same year that Atlanta held its first election for mayor. Records reveal that just over two hundred people voted.

Before him, there is a Lester (spelled Leicester), who was the sheriff of that city, and this explains my affinity for the Foxes, and my dismay over my eldest son's allegiance to the Spurs (See the Premiere League Soccer Table, hopefully the Foxes will not be relegated at this reading).

There is the "altercation" that occurred in our front yard during the 1960's when my father was the President of the Birmingham Football Officials Association (BFOA). He, at the encouragement of my Quaker mother and others, had integrated that organization because it did not make sense to have white officials officiating games with athletes, none of whom were white. Unfortunately, there are two things you don't mess with in Alabama – Football and Religion. After an important game in which a flag was correctly thrown by the black official against a team of white athletes, an angry group of men visited our home yelling for my father to come into the yard and address their grievances. That same night, they also burned a cross in the yard of the first black official, the man who had thrown the penalty flag – "Cap" Brown (a former basketball coach at Parker High School in Birmingham). Later in his life, my father confided that he had recognized several of the faces of the men in our front yard. Many of them he still considered friends and were fellow football officials. "They had come around."

There is the family plantation, south of Birmingham, "Mulberry." Much of it is gone. The large house was burned by Wilson's Raiders during the Civil War. As Wilson and his men approached the farm, the family matriarch handed her daughter a jar of petroleum jelly and told her not to resist. While only the foundation of the old house remains, some of the land is still in the hands of a distant cousin who boards horses on the land that has been in the family for over one hundred-fifty years. Fast forward to 2019 when I journeyed to Memphis on business. With time to spare before the flight, a business associate suggested that we go to the Lorraine Motel where Martin Luther King was shot and tour the Civil Rights Museum. The Motel has remained largely unchanged, and the museum is excellent. I cannot communicate the distress that street name has caused me. Some would call it irony. I must add the word – "damning." The motel is located at 450 Mulberry Street.

And this does not include the stories from my mother's side of the family – they trace their tree back to Cerdic the Norman and Alfred the Great.

This book, I believe, contains one of the more interesting of all these stories.

Again, the story was related to us by my Great Uncles, Charles Taylor and James G. (Billy) Lester. They were told the story by their grandfather, who, as a boy, survived the attack described in this book.

When I was about seven years old, I complained to my father that I really did not know any Lester men (both my Grandfather Lester and Uncle Rush had died). Stung by this, he took me to Atlanta on a business trip. While my father was in a continuing education class, Uncle Billy drove me down to the old homestead where he had grown up. We walked down to Dried Indian Creek, and he related to me that as a child, they "could find arrowheads all over the place. Coming out of the ground like turnips." I surmise that these early finds contributed to him entering the field of Geology.

After a short walk along the sleepy creek, we started to find arrowheads, just as he described. Many of them broken, but they were clearly not naturally formed. I picked up a few and returned home with them.

Georgia was the last of the thirteen original colonies to be established. Its founder, James Oglethorpe, was granted a royal land grant in 1732, and journeyed to North America in 1733. In giving Oglethorpe his grant, the British hoped to create a buffer between Spanish-held Florida and the British colony of South Carolina. While still in its formative stages of development as a stable colony, South Carolina was growing rapidly, and the crown was optimistic for its success.

These hopes were well founded. South Carolina's economic success is best understood with the knowledge that by 1860, Charleston would be the wealthiest city, on a per capita basis, in The United States.

By the late 1700's, Savannah, while only founded in 1733, was following the trajectory of Charleston, and its growth was punctuated in 1777 when the city was named the capital of the state. Growth was further spurred when in 1793, Eli Whitney invented the cotton gin, and by the turn of the new century, cotton was quickly becoming an important cash crop for Georgia and the entire South.

A land lottery was held to encourage settlers to Georgia. It was during the land lottery of 1805 that the farm, which Richard Lester would later purchase, had been first settled. The town of Covington was the center of commerce in close proximity to the Lester homestead.

The City of Covington was originally named Newtonsboro in 1822, but the name was quickly changed to Covington in honor of General Leonard Covington, a hero of the War of 1812.

If you have a desire to find a few of the historical locations mentioned in this book, I offer the following:

The Brick Store – One of the oldest if not the oldest surviving structures in Newton County. The store was built in 1821 and located along what was called the Rogue Road. The Rogue Road carried settlers from Savannah into Newton County and beyond. The Brick Store was constructed at an intersection with the road to Milledgeville. Milledgeville was the Georgia state capital from 1804 – 1868.

Cawita – A prominent Creek Indian Settlement located just south of present-day Columbus. The town was designated a "white" town (town of peace) by the Lower Creek Indians who inhabited this area. The Lower Creek Indians were called "Ani-Kawita" by the Cherokee.

Dry Indian Creek – It is still there and still known by this name. The story about how it got its name is thought to be accurate.

Etowah – Located south of present-day Cartersville, the area was important to the Cherokee Nation. The Methodist Mission near Etowah, Hightower, was located across the river. The mounds at Etowah are enticing and worthy of a visit off I-75.

Fort Daniel – Built by the 25th Regiment of the Georgia Militia in 1813. Named after Major General Allen Daniel.

Fort Peachtree – Built in 1814 by Rockingham Gilmer, when First Lt. Governor Mitchell sent Gilmer and a detachment of solders to build a fort at Standing Peachtree. Upon completion in July of 1814, the fort boasted a boat yard, five boats, two large block houses, six dwellings, and one store house. Some claim that the historical marker is improperly placed as the actual location was on the south side of Peachtree Creek.

New Echota – One of my favorite places in all of Georgia. A quiet afternoon at New Echota is a day well-lived. You will leave with a greater appreciation of the efforts that the Cherokee Nation had taken to try to assimilate. And you may find yourself staring at Jackson's face on our currency and wondering "why?"

Peachtree Creek – it is a sad and true legacy that this area still floods. The Indians were right not to permanently settle there.

Peachtree Road – May have initially been known as "Pitch Tree Road." The road connected Fort Peachtree and Fort Daniel.

Rev. James Jenkins Trott – was a missionary to the Cherokee. He married a Cherokee woman and served at the Methodist Missionary Station at the Cherokee Nation Capital in New Echota for many years. A segment of the Cherokee leadership believed that the best way to maintain their lifestyle and customs was to develop a large number of educated elite leaders. For this reason, missionaries from several denominations were granted access to their Nation. By 1830, the Methodists claimed to have converted over 1,000 to their religion. The letter in this book to Rev. Trott is entirely contrived. On May 29, 1831, Rev. Trott would be arrested by the Governor of Georgia. His crime was failure to obtain a permit to live and preach within the area of the Cherokee Nation. Something he had done for well over a decade.

Lastly, like many, I struggle with my family's association with the institution of slavery, much less write about it. I will no doubt be criticized about my treatment of this issue; and to be clear, this is not fiction to be trivialized. We have copies of wills from the 1800's that bequeath people – naming them (Boston, Lucy, and Simm are just three), invoking God's providence and at the same time treating people as chattel.

SOURCES

[1] "Cherokees and the Methodists, 1824 – 1834" by William G. McLoughlin

[2] Georgia Charter, June 9th, 1732

[3] The Third or 1820 Land Lottery of Georgia, by S. Emmett Lucas.

[4] Unconquerable: The Story of John Ross, Chief of the Cherokees by John M. Oskison.

[5] Creek Indian History: A Historical Narrative of the Genealogy, Traditions and Downfall of the Creek Indian Tribe (1788 – 1845) by George Stiggins.

[6] Georgia: A Brief History by Christopher C. Meyers and David Williams.

[7] A Dictionary of Creek/Muskogee, by Jack B Martin.

[8] The Slave Trade: The Story of the Atlantic Slave Trade (1440 – 1870) by Hugh Thomas.

[8] Narrative of the Life of Frederick Douglas, by Frederick Douglas

[9] "The Story of 'The Standing Peachtree'," by Eugen M. Mitchell. Atlanta Historical Bulletin 1, no.2, January 1928.

[10] "Standing Peachtree," Early Georgia 1, no.2 (Fall 1950), by Wilbur G. Kurtz.

[11] "A New Take on an Old Story: Fort Daniel, Fort Peachtree, and the Road that Connected Them," Gwinnett Historical Society Heritage 43, No.1 (Spring 2014), James D'Angelo.

CHARACTER SUMMARIES

Alice Lester – Richard and Mary Lester's only natural-born daughter.

Ben Brewton – Marshal, serving under the Sheriff of Georgia in Milledgeville.

Betsy Lester – Fountain Lester's daughter, raised by Richard and Mary Lester.

Boston – Slave originally owned by Fountain Lester. Upon Fountain's death Boston, his wife (Lucy) and Simm (son) become slaves owned by Richard Lester

Catherine (Reid) Lester – Richard Lester's Mother. German Lester's wife.

Chief John Ross (b. October 3, 1790; d. August 1, 1866) – Chief of the Cherokee from 1829 – 1866. Ross was the son of a Cherokee mother and Scottish father. Chief Ross was a successful businessman and considered one of the founders of Chattanooga, TN. Much of his initial wealth came from farming 160 acres of tobacco. In 1816, he founded Ross's landing, a ferry service. Upon the deaths of Pathkiller and John R. Hicks in 1827, Ross became chief. Ross was a part of the National Party. When the much smaller "Treaty Party" or "Ridge Party" agreed to and signed the New Echota Treaty (1835) which required the Cherokee to leave their lands by 1838, Chief Ross led a delegation to Washington to seek the treaty's invalidation. This effort was unsuccessful and led to the Trail of Tears. Following their removal, Ross worked to restore unity among the Cherokee. Years later, Ross died in Washington D.C. after falling ill while trying to negotiate concessions for the Cherokee Nation with then President Andrew Johnson.

Commander Buford Rogers – Fictional character.

David Brydie Mitchell (b. October 22, 1766; d. April 22, 1837) – Indian Agent to the Creek and 27th Governor of Georgia (elected in 1809). Mitchell was born in Scotland. Mitchell resigned as governor in 1817 to accept the position of Indian Agent to the Creek Nation, a position to which he was appointed by James Monroe. Prior to him, that position had been held by Benjamin Hawkins. In 1820, Mitchell was prosecuted for importing slaves illegally from Spanish Florida. Mitchell died on his plantation, Mount Nebo, which was located near Milledgeville.

Eugene Lester – Fountain Lester's son raised by Richard and Mary Lester.

George Rockingham Gilmer (b. April 17, 1790; d. November 16, 1859) – 34th Governor of Georgia serving from 1829-1831. Served as US Representative. As a young adult, served as Commander of Fort Peachtree. Served as first lieutenant in the Forty-third Infantry Regiment from 1813 – 1815 in the campaign against the Creek during the War of 1812. He practiced law as a profession. During his political career, there were two political factions in Georgia: the "Crawford Men" and the "Clarke Men." He favored Crawford. Gilmer served three terms in the Georgia House of Representatives (1818, 1819, 1824). He also served four terms in the US House of Representatives (although he was never formally seated for the term that was to begin in 1828). He initiated the prosecution of the missionaries to the Cherokee in 1831. The Cherokee sued the state of Georgia (Worcester v. Georgia), which struck down the Georgia statute imposing its laws on the autonomous Cherokee Nation. Backed by Georgia Militia and the Georgia Assembly, Gilmer dissolved the Cherokee government and annulled the laws and Constitution of the Cherokee Nation. During his second term as Governor of Georgia in 1837, Gilmer oversaw the removal of the Cherokee.

German Lester – Richard Lester's father. Married to Catherine Lester.

Children of German and Catherine Lester (Birth order):
Bryant – Married to Sara

Fountain – Married to JoAnne

Sarah

Robert

Nancy

Richard – Married to Mary

Barksdale

Harjo – Shorter Creek Indian – Fictional Character.

James Lester – Youngest son of Richard and Mary Lester.

Joseph McIntosh – Creek Indian. Fictional Character.

Lucy – Slave owned by Richard Lester. Boston's wife. Simm's mother.

Major Ridge – Died in 1839. He was a Cherokee leader. Served under Andrew Jackson in the Creek and Seminole wars. Along with Charles Hicks and James Vann, Major Ridge was considered a part of the last great Triumvirate of the Cherokee nation. He was of mixed race. Owned a large plantation in what is now Calhoun, GA. Was educated in Cornwall, CT.

Mary Minor Sims Lester – Richard's Wife.

Pathkiller – Died in January of 1927. He was a Cherokee warrior and Chief of the Cherokee nation.

Paul (Richard Paul) Lester – Oldest natural born son of Richard and Mary Lester. Richard will grow up, become an attorney, marry Mary Waddel, and lead a regiment during the Civil War.

Richard Henry Lester – Main Character. Reader of the Law and farmer residing in Covington Georgia. Son of German and Catherine Lester. Married to Mary Lester.

Sergeant James McConnell Montgomery – member of a large family. Served as area postmaster, owned a large farm, and operated a ferry near Standing Peachtree.

Simm – Slave owned by the Lesters. Parents are Boston and Lucy

Stockade Warden – Never named

Talease – Joseph McIntosh's wife. Fictional Character

Talof – "The Bear" – Taller Indian – Fictional Character

Reverend James Jenkins Trott – Methodist Missionary to the Cherokee. Married a Cherokee woman in 1828, Sallie Adair. He would be arrested by the state of Georgia on May 29, 1831, for preaching to the Cherokee without a permit and his unwillingness to sign an oath of loyalty to the state (which would have denied the Cherokee land rights in the state). Died on December 10, 1868.

The Sims – Mary's family. Mary's father was Issac Watts Sims and her mother was Susan Daniel Sims

William Hicks – Wealthy farmer and leader of the Cherokee Nation. Lived from 1769 to 1837.

William Pettus – Sarah Lester's husband.

William Millar – Blacksmith – Fictional Character.

ABOUT THE AUTHOR

Peter H. Lester, Sr.

Pete Lester and his wife reside in Baltimore, Maryland where they raised three children. Pete grew up in Mountain Brook, Alabama. He received a BA in Economics from Grove City College (PA) and an MBA from Emory University in Atlanta (GA). For over 25 years, Pete has been an Executive Benefit Consultant. During his career he has provided guidance to several Fortune 50 Companies whose brands are globally recognized. During his career, he taught Microeconomics for nine years at a college in Maryland. Prior to moving to Baltimore, he and his family lived in Atlanta for 13 years where he was a founding partner in a commercial real estate firm. In 1991, the Atlanta Board of Realtors named him the Top Commercial Realtor.

Pete competed in track and football in college until he tore his Achilles his junior year. For several years, he played keyboards in a jazz quintet and drums in a rock and roll cover band.

BOOK SUMMARY

In 1828, Richard and Mary's quiet life with their three children in rural Georgia is upended by the untimely death of his older brother and sister-in-law. When Joseph MacIntosh, a Creek Indian, seeks his help in settling a land dispute between the Creek and Cherokee nations, Richard sees an opportunity to assist in settling the dispute and uncover why his two relations died so tragically.

Once his brother's orphaned children and slaves are settled on the farm, Richard and his son, Paul, embark on a perilous journey. Accompanied by Joseph and the Creek Indian delegation, the expedition takes them into the center of disputes between the two Indian nations and the pressing claims of white settlers. The stakes are high, and for the powerful few it's not simply about expansion for the young nation. It is about much more.

Based on true events, this tale of family love and treacherous political intrigue sheds a bright light on life and turmoil along the early American frontier.